RAILHEAD

PHILIP REEVE

SWITCH
P R E S S
a capstone imprint

PART ONE
INTERSTELLAR EXPRESS

1

Listen . . .

He was running down Harmony when he heard it. Faint at first, but growing clearer, rising above the noises of the streets. Out in the dark, beyond the city, a siren voice was calling, lonely as the song of whales. It was the sound he had been waiting for. The Interstellar Express was thundering down the line from Golden Junction, and singing as it came.

He had an excuse to hurry now. He was not running away from a crime anymore, just running to catch a train. Just Zen Starling, a thin brown kid racing down Harmony Street with trouble in his eyes and stolen jewelry in the pocket of his coat, dancing his way through the random gaps that opened and closed in the crowds. The lines of lanterns strung between the old glass buildings lit his face as he looked back, looked back, checking for the drone that was hunting him.

*

Who'd have thought that the goldsmith would send a drone after him? Zen had come to believe that the merchants of the Ambersai Bazar didn't much mind being robbed, as long as you didn't steal too often from the same shop. Like maybe they felt a bit of pilfering was a price worth paying for a pitch in the biggest market on the eastern branch lines. For as long as anyone could remember, the Bazar had been a happy hunting ground for people like Zen who were young and daring and dishonest, the low heroes of this infinite city.

Ambersai was a big moon. The dirty yellow disc of its mother-world gazed down upon the busy streets like a watchful eye, but it never seemed to notice Zen when he filched food or bangles from the open-fronted shops. Sometimes the shopkeepers noticed, and chased him, bellowing threats and waving lathi sticks, but they mostly gave up after a street or two, and there were always crowds to hide in. The Bazar was busy day and night. Not just the cafés, bars, and pleasure shops, but the stalls of the craftsmen and metal dealers too. There was a whole district of them, selling stuff that the deep-space mining outfits brought in. Ambersai's local asteroid belt was as full of precious metals as an expensive necklace.

By coincidence, an expensive necklace was just what Zen had lifted that night. He could feel it in his pocket, swinging against his hip as he went down the greasy stairs toward the station and the approaching train.

He wasn't usually so ambitious. A couple of anklets or a nose ring was all he usually scooped up on his visits to Ambersai. But when he saw that necklace lying on the goldsmith's counter, it had seemed like too good a chance to miss. The goldsmith herself was busy talking to the customer who'd just been looking at it, trying to interest him in others, even more expensive. The guard she paid to watch her stuff was watching sportscasts or a threedie instead; he wore a headset and that glass-eyed look that people got when they were streaming video straight to their visual cortex.

Before Zen's brain knew what his fingers were planning, he had snatched the necklace and slipped it into his coat. Then he was turning away, trying to look casual as he melted back into the crowds.

He hadn't gone twenty paces when someone blocked his way. Zen had his head down, so all he saw of her at first were her clumpy boots and her red raincoat, the belt knotted around her waist. He raised his eyes and glimpsed the dim outline of her face in the shadow of the raincoat's hood. A girlish face, he guessed, but he had only that one glance, because the goldsmith had worked out by then that she'd been robbed, and her guard had woken up and skimmed back through the stall's security footage and seen Zen take the necklace. "Thief!" the goldsmith screamed, and the guard grabbed a lathi and came wading through the crowd toward Zen.

"Come with me!" said the girl.

Zen pushed past her. Her hand shot out and gripped his arm, surprisingly strong, almost pulling him off balance, but he twisted free. Behind him he could hear the lathi boy yelling and shoving shoppers aside. "Zen Starling!" yelled the girl in the red coat—only she couldn't really have said that, he must have misheard her, because how could she know his name? He ran on, losing himself in the crowds on Harmony Street.

He was just starting to think his luck had held when he heard the flutter-thud of rotors, and looked back to see the drone behind him, hovering like a May bug over the heads of the crowd. It was sleek and serious and military-looking. Neon reflections slithered over its carapace and its laser eyes glowed red. Zen had a nasty feeling that those pods on its underside held weaponry. At the very least, it would be able to flash his image and location to the local data raft when it found him, and that would bring cops or the goldsmith's thugs down on him.

So he chameleoned his old smartfiber duffel coat from blue to black and pushed on through the crowds, listening out for the sweet sound of trainsong.

*

Ambersai Station: grand and high-fronted like a great theater, with the K-bahn logo hanging over its entrance in letters of blue fire. Booming loudspeaker voices reciting litanies of stations. Moths and Monk bugs swarming under the lamps outside; beggars and street kids too, and buskers, and vendors selling fruit and chai and noodles, and rickshaw captains squabbling as they touted for fares. Through the din and chatter came the sound of the train.

Zen went through the entrance barriers and ran out onto the platform. The Express was just pulling in. First the huge loco, a Helden Hammerhead, its long hull sheathed in shining red-gold scales. Then a line of lit windows and a pair of Station Angels flickering along the carriage sides like stray rainbows. Some tourists standing next to Zen pointed at them and snapped pictures that wouldn't come out. Zen kept his place in the scrum of other K-bahn travelers, itching to look behind him, but knowing that he mustn't because, if the drone was there, it would be watching for just that: a face turned back, a look of guilt.

The doors slid open. He shoved past disembarking passengers into a carriage. It smelled of something sweet, as if the train had come from some world where it was springtime. Zen found a window seat and sat there looking at his feet, at the ceramic floor, at the patterns on the worn seat coverings, anywhere but out of the window, which was where he most wanted to look. His fellow passengers were commuters and a few Motorik couriers with their android brains stuffed full of information for businesses farther down the line. In the seats opposite Zen lounged a couple of rich kids: railheads from K'mbussi or Galaghast, pretty as threedie stars, dozing with their arms around each other. Zen thought about taking their bags with him when he got off, but his luck was glitchy tonight and he decided not to risk it.

The train began to move, so smoothly that he barely noticed. Then the lights of Ambersai Station were falling behind, the throb of the engines was rising, the backbeat of the wheels quickening. Zen risked a glance at the window. At first it was hard to make out anything in the confusion of carriage reflections and the city lights sliding by outside. Then he saw the drone again. It was keeping pace with the train, shards of light sliding from its rotor blades as it burred along at window height, aiming a whole spider-cluster of eyes and cameras and who-knew-what at him.

The train rushed into a tunnel, and he could see nothing anymore except his own skinny reflection, wide cheekbones fluttering with the movement of the carriage, eyes big and empty as the eyes on moths' wings.

The train accelerated. The noise rising, rising, until, with a soundless bang—a kind of *un-bang*—it tore through the K-gate, and everything got reassuringly weird. For a timeless moment Zen was outside of the universe. There was a sense of falling, although there was no longer any down to fall to.

Something that was not quite light blazed in through the blank windows . . .

Then another un-bang, and the train was sliding out of another ordinary tunnel, slowing toward another everyday station. It was bright daytime on this world, and the gravity was lower. Zen relaxed into his seat, grinning. He was imagining that drone turning away in defeat from the empty tunnel on Ambersai, a thousand light years away.

The K in K-gate stands for KH, which stands for "Kwisatz Haderech," which means "the shortening of the way" in one of the languages of Old Earth. Only the Guardians know how it works. You step aboard a train, and the train goes through a K-gate, and you step off on another planet, where the sun that was shining on you a moment ago is now just one of those tiny stars in the sky. It might take ten thousand years to travel that far by spaceship, but a K-train makes the jump in seconds. You can't walk through those gates, or drive through in a car. Rockets and bullets and lasers and radio waves can't make that crossing. Only trains can ride the K-bahn: the old, wise trains of the Empire, barracuda-beautiful, dreaming their dreams of speed and distance as they race from world to world.

Nowadays most people rode from one star-system to another as carelessly as if they were traveling between the districts of a single city. But Zen was one of those who still sensed the magic of it. That night, like all nights, he kept his face to the window, watching the worlds go by.

Un-bang. Tarakat: chimneys belching vapor and some big moons hanging. (The train sped through without stopping.) *Un-bang.* Summer's Lease: white streets above a bay; the kind of place people like Zen could only dream of living. *Un-bang.* Tusk: giant gas planets tilting their rings like the brims of summer hats across a turquoise sky. There was a big market in Tusk. Maybe next time he'd go there rather than risk showing his face in Ambersai too soon. Or maybe he should just keep off the K-bahn altogether for a while; there were plenty of things to steal at home in Cleave.

But he knew he wouldn't. His sister, Myka, said he was just a railhead, said he needed the K-bahn like a drug. Zen guessed she was right. He didn't make these journeys up and down the line simply to steal things, he made them because he loved the changing views, the roaring blackness of the tunnels, and the flicker of the gates. And best of all he loved the trains, the great locomotives, each one different, some stern, some friendly, but all driven by the same deep joy that he felt at riding the rails.

Those locos didn't care what loads they pulled. Shining carriages or battered freight cars, it was all the same to them. They didn't usually take much interest in their passengers, either, although they were romantics at heart, and you often heard about them helping fugitive lovers, or good-looking thieves. And now and then a murderer might board a train, or a banker absconding with other people's savings, and the loco would whistle up the authorities at its next stop, or just set its own maintenance spiders on the creep . . .

Zen was thinking about that as the Interstellar Express tore through one last gate and the long darkness of a tunnel gave way to a cavernous rail yard. Stacked freight containers like a windowless city. Chilly reflections in ceramic tiles, the name of the station sliding past the windows. The gentle voice of the train announcing, "Cleave. End of the line. Cleave. All change." Stepping out onto the platform, he noticed a couple of maintenance spiders scuttling along the carriage roofs. It made him wonder if the drone had pinged his details to the train before it left Ambersai. Maybe it was going to turn him in. Maybe he was not good-looking or romantic enough. Maybe the train felt sorry for the goldsmith he had robbed. As he went along the platform he imagined those many-legged robots jumping down on him. Pulling him apart with their mechanical pincers, or just holding on to him till the local law arrived.

They did neither. He was just letting his fears run away with him like Ma did. *I ought to watch that,* he thought. He knew where too much imagining could lead you. The spiders went about their work, checking couplings, repairing scratches in the train's paintwork, while Zen walked through the barriers and out of the station amid a little crowd of other passengers, a herd of roll-along suitcases scurrying behind them, nobody looking exactly delighted to be getting off at Cleave.

*

Zen's hometown was a sheer-sided ditch of a place. Cleave's houses and factories were packed like shelved crates up each wall of a mile-deep canyon on a one-gate world called Angkat whose surface was scoured by constant storms. Space was scarce, so the buildings huddled into every available scrap of terracing, and clung to cliff faces, and crowded on the bridges that stretched across the gulf between the canyon walls—a gulf that was filled with sagging cables, dangling neon signage, smog, dirty rain, and the fluttering rotors of air-taxis, ferries, and corporate transports. Between the steep-stacked buildings, a thousand waterfalls went foaming down to join the river far below, adding their own roar to the various dins from the industrial zone. The local name for Cleave was Thunder City.

Zen had been just ten standard years old when he came there with Ma and Myka. Before that they had lived on Santheraki, before that Qalat, and before that he couldn't even remember; so many worlds; a blur of cheap rooms and changing skies. They tended to leave places in a hurry, always running from the people Ma said were following them. But by the time they got to Cleave, Myka and Zen were starting to understand that the people were just bad dreams leaking out of Ma's imagination, like the "thought waves" that she saw coming off walls and windows sometimes. So there they had stayed, managing Ma as best as they could. Myka had found a job for herself in the factories. Zen had been drawn to easier ways of making money.

Well, not *that* easy. The chase in the Ambersai Bazar had shaken him. As he came out of the station he could still feel the weight of that stolen necklace dragging his coat down on one side. It felt like bad luck. Wanting rid of it, he walked through the neon puddles and the white noise of the falls to the street where Uncle Bugs kept shop.

He did not notice the drone that followed him, training its cameras on him through the rain and the spray and the crowds.

*

Uncle Bugs wasn't really anybody's uncle. He wasn't even technically a "he." He was a Hive Monk, a colony of big brown beetles clinging to a roughly human-shaped armature, which they'd made for themselves out of sticks and string and chicken bones.

There must be millions of them, thought Zen, as he stood in the dim little office behind the shop, holding up the necklace. A rustling sound came from under Uncle Bugs's grimy burlap robe. In the shadows of the hood there was a paper wasp's nest of a face, like a chapati with three holes poked in it—two eyes and a ragged mouth, with shiny bug bodies crawling and seething in the dark behind. The voice that came out of the mouth hole was made by a thousand saw-toothed limbs rubbing together.

"That is a nice piece, Zen. Better than the usual junks you bring me." Long black antennae wavered at Zen through the holes in the mask. Most Hive Monks spent their time riding the K-bahn on endless, mysterious pilgrimages. It was odd to find one running a shop, but Uncle Bugs was good at it; he could haggle as well as any human. "Two hundred," he buzzed.

That was at least a hundred less than Zen had hoped for, but he was tired, and he didn't like that necklace anymore. So he put it on Uncle Bugs's greasy counter, and a crude, insect-covered, coat-hanger-sculpture hand reached out from beneath the burlap robes and took it.

He came out of the shop counting the wad of notes, each with its smiling video portrait of the Emperor. Then he headed for home, feeling like he always did at the end of a job—like he'd flown free for a while and now he was going back into his cage.

He didn't think to look back. He did not see the drone descend out of the neon fog onto the roof of Uncle Bugs's shop. There was a flare of light, a quick clattering sound from inside the shop, and the drone reappeared. It hovered outside until a girl in a red raincoat arrived. She looked up at it. The drone angled its rotors and took off after Zen, with the girl following on foot.

3

The Starlings were living that year on Bridge Street, a low-rent district built on one of Cleave's spindly suspension bridges. The houses there were all bio-buildings, grown from modified baobab DNA. They huddled on the bridge like dejected elephants planning to fly off to warmer climes. Most had gone to seed, sprouting random balconies and bulbous little pointless extensions. Zen's family rented the top floor of one of them: a few shapeless rooms that opened unexpectedly off a winding corridor. They lived there like three beetles in an oak gall. Their front door was a chunk of plastic packing crate, stenciled with the logo of a Khoorsandi rail-freight outfit.

Zen pushed the plastic door open and went in. Dim yellow light on fading carpets and cancerous-looking walls. There had been a time when his sister, Myka, had tried to keep the place nice. She'd cleaned daily, and tried out holowallpapers that made the living room look like a beach on Summer's

Lease or a meadow in the Crystal Mountains, if you ignored the downstairs neighbors' amped-up bhangra booming through the floor. But none of it made much difference to Ma, who was as scared of beaches or meadows as she was of blank walls. When Myka started working extra shifts and hadn't time to do housework anymore, Zen couldn't be bothered to take over. Dishes heaped up in the sink, dead flies dotted the windowsills, and the wallpaper had shut down long ago.

Ma looked up at him with scared eyes as he let himself in. Her fine, graying hair made crazy pencil scribbles against the light from the window behind her. She said, "You're back! I didn't think you'd ever come back; I thought something had happened to you . . ."

"That's what you always think, Ma. That's what you say when I go to the food store for five minutes."

(*And one day it will be true*, he thought. One day soon he'd find the courage and the money to leave this place for good, take the Interstellar Express all the way to Golden Junction, and keep going . . .)

"I was sure they'd caught you," his mother grumbled. "Those people . . ."

Myka came through from her small room, still wearing the gray overalls and grumpy scowl that she wore every day to her job in the factory district. She didn't look too pleased to see her little brother.

"Where have you been?"

"Here and there."

"Riding the trains?"

"Those trains are part of it," Ma interrupted. "And the Guardians. The Guardians see everything."

"With everything that's going on in all the worlds, the

Guardians are hardly going to bother watching you and me and Zen," said Myka wearily.

She was nothing like him, this sister of his. Or half sister, maybe—Ma had never told them who their fathers were, and they'd not asked. Myka was big, taller than Zen, broad across the hips and shoulders, with darker skin, and a cloud of black hair, which spat angry lightning when she tugged a comb through it. She knew what Zen did on his jaunts through the K-gates, and she didn't approve, but she never turned away Uncle Bugs's money. Without it, they couldn't afford to live anywhere half as nice as Bridge Street.

"She's been bad," Myka said, deciding to talk about Ma rather than Zen and his thieving ways. "She was in a real state when I came home . . ."

"They've found us again," said Ma. "They listen to us. Through the walls."

"It's all right, Ma," said Myka softly. She wasn't a soft sort of person usually—she was usually angry at everyone—Zen, her coworkers, the company she worked for, the corporate families, the Emperor, even the Guardians themselves. She had taken part in the anti-Moto riots, and sometimes Zen found her frowning over illegal pamphlets, dreaming of rebellion. But with their mother, she always kept her temper.

"It's not all right!" Ma whimpered. "They're watching us! We're going to have to leave this place . . ."

"No one is watching us, Ma." Myka gently laid a hand on Ma's shoulder, but Ma, with a hiss of irritation, slapped it away.

Zen didn't know where Myka got her patience from. Perhaps it was because she was older than him, and remembered Ma in times when Ma's imagination was still under control, before the men started hunting her, the walls started listening. Myka just pitied her. Zen pitied her too, but mostly he felt angry. Angry at the way his whole life had been shaped by her delusions. At how many years she'd had him believing in her made-up conspiracies.

"They're outside now!" she whimpered. "Spying on us!"

He crossed to the window, peered out through the misted cellulose. "Ma," he said, "there's nobody—"

And then he stopped.

He was looking down onto the bridge, at the narrow roadway that ran between the two lines of bio-buildings. It was crowded with pedestrians: day-shift workers like his sister trudging back from the factory district, night-shift workers tramping in the opposite direction to go on duty. Rickshaws and maglev cars pushed through the river of wet rain capes, hats, and umbrellas. And on the far side of the street, the girl in the red coat stood motionless, staring straight at him.

*

Just before a train went through a K-gate there was a moment of quiet, so short that only railheads caught it, as the wheels moved from the normal K-bahn track to the strange, ancient, frictionless rails that ran through the gate itself. That was what it felt like to Zen when he recognized the girl: a heartbeat's silence, and then he was in a new world.

"Nobody there," he said, trying to keep the fear out of his voice. He took a step back from the window, although he didn't really think the girl would be able to see him. He kept watching her. How had she followed him here? She must have been on the same train as him out of Ambersai. But she couldn't have been; he had not seen her get off at Cleave. It couldn't be the same girl . . .

And then she raised her face and seemed to look straight

at him, and although he still couldn't make out her features through the rain and the shadow of her hood, he felt sure that it was her.

"Come with me!" she had said.

She had known his name.

So what was she? Police? An assassin? *The goldsmith must have sent her,* Zen thought. That didn't make much sense. It was only a necklace that he'd stolen, and once it went through the K-gate the insurance would have covered the loss. But it was the only explanation he could think of. The Ambersai goldsmiths must be hiring killers now, to hunt down anyone who robbed them.

The girl crossed the street toward his building.

Myka was asking Ma about the evening meal. When Ma was bad she always believed that they couldn't afford food, and that the water and power would run out at any moment. She didn't want to eat and she didn't want anyone else to eat either. Myka was being patient still, asking her if she could manage a little green curry. Zen wondered how he could warn Myka about the watcher without Ma overhearing and getting even more scared.

Through the smeared cellulose of the window he saw a shape slide past. If it wasn't the drone that had pestered him at Ambersai, it was another exactly like it.

He dropped to the floor. Ma screamed. At the same moment there came a knock on the apartment's plastic door, and a voice calling, "Zen Starling!"

Zen scrambled on hands and knees across the room and into his own narrow bedroom, shaking his head at Myka when she glanced at him. He stood in the shadows, as still as he could, like a kid playing hide-and-seek. He could hear Ma whimpering, then the sound of the front door opening. "He's not here," Myka was saying, and, "Can't you see you're frightening her?"

The girl saying something, too softly to hear, then Myka
again, angrier. "He's not here! Go away! We don't like *your type*
in Cleave."

Zen looked around his room. The unmade bed and strewn
clothes. Stuff from when he was a kid: his model trains, and the
brooch he'd stolen from a stall at McQue Junction when he was
seven. The brooch had been an impulse theft, followed by six
weeks of guilt and worry. By the end of that time he'd learned
something that he'd lived by ever since: it was possible to take
people's stuff without getting caught.

But he'd been wrong, it seemed. Retribution had arrived at
last. He heard the drone go clattering past outside, circling the
building. Myka was telling their visitor again that Zen wasn't
there. Ma was shouting too, words Zen couldn't catch, angry
and afraid.

There was a window above his bed, smeared and thickened
like all the apartment's windows, but big enough to squeeze
out through, if you were desperate. It hadn't been designed to
open, but it turned out that it did if you hit it hard enough. It
flopped out of its frame and dangled by a few strands of plant
fiber. Quickly, before the drone made another circuit, Zen threw
himself at the wet square of night outside, squeezed shoulders
and hips through, tumbled down the side of the roof. The tiles
were modified leaves, thick and leathery, overlapping like the
leaves of artichokes. He grabbed a fat cable, swung from it,
dropped to a lower roof, jumped across the narrow gap to a
neighboring building. From there it was easy enough to reach
one of the original supports of the bridge and climb down it,
glancing up for the drone as he went, not seeing it. Falling into
the microfiber mesh that was stretched under the bridge to catch
garbage and would-be suicides, he scrambled on hands and knees

through the dark under the roadbed, through the slices of light that came down through gratings, fighting his way past bundled greasy cables and the trailing roots of the houses. Below him buzzed air-jitneys and fat delivery drones. Below them, at the bottom of an abyss of lighted windows, Cleave River took out its temper on the rocks.

He reached the canyon wall that way, went sideways along some of the thick sewage pipes that clung to it, then down to the level below, using the neon ideograms outside a restaurant as a ladder. Waiters shrieked at him, but waiters were the least of his worries. What were they going to do? Flap him to death with their napkins? He scanned the busy air behind him for a glimpse of the drone, found none, and sprinted toward Uncle Bugs's shop.

Uncle Bugs wasn't the sort of person you'd usually turn to for help. But Zen had been thinking while he swung about on that mesh under the bridge. He reckoned his only hope was to buy the necklace back, return it to Ambersai, and make a full and groveling apology.

The shop was shuttered when he reached it. "Uncle Bugs?" he said, loud but not too loud, and knocked at the peeling door.

Which swung open, giving him a view into the cluttered shop, and a bad feeling.

He went inside. The back room was full of rain and the window-light-flutter of a passing train, both of which were coming in through a large hole in the roof. Uncle Bugs was still there, and yet he wasn't. On the floor lay his burlap robe, his paper mask, and a few pathetic twigs and wires that had been part of his stick-man scaffolding. The robe, the floor, the walls, the furniture were covered with insects. A lot of them were dead: crushed or scorched. The rest scuttled around waving their feelers, or buzzed heavily through the air, which still held the burnt metal smell of recent gunfire. Monk bugs only became intelligent when enough of them clustered together to form a Hive Monk: scatter them, and they were just mindless insects again.

That was bad enough, but as Zen stood there staring, he noticed something worse.

The necklace that he had stolen was still on the counter.

So it wasn't about that necklace at all. There was something else going on, and he had no idea what it could be.

4

On his way back out he helped himself to a rain cape and a hat from the rack of secondhand clothes near the door. The cape was too small for him and came down barely past his waist, but the hat fit. He pulled the wide brim down to shade his face as he walked quickly back to busier streets, trying to hide in the crowds. He reasoned that the girl and her drone would be following him, told himself he was leading her away from Bridge Street, drawing the danger away from Ma and Myka.

Truth was, he just wanted to be safely out of Cleave. He would hop on an outbound train, change at Chiba to the Spiral Line, change again onto the O Link at Kishinchand, be halfway across the galaxy before his pursuers knew he'd left town . . .

But how was he going to do that? The girl might have friends. That drone she had sent after him in Ambersai might be buzzing the streets. She would be watching the station.

He needed a plan. He stopped for a while in a damp, fern-grown cleft in the canyon wall where holo-images of the

Guardians billowed like tethered ghosts above a row of data shrines. People kept stepping out of the crowds on the street to stand in front of this shrine or that, uploading electronic prayers. Human beings had always dreamed up gods to guide and guard them, and the Guardians were the last, best gods they had ever invented. Artificial intelligences, created on Old Earth, as immortal and all-knowing as the gods in old stories. It was the Guardians who had opened the K-gates, and helped the corporate families lay out the rails and stations of the Great Network. In olden days they had downloaded themselves into cloned bodies and walked among humans. Now they mostly kept themselves to themselves; beings of pure information, spread across the data rafts of every world, busy with thoughts too huge and strange for human brains to hold. Zen was pretty sure they wouldn't be interested in his troubles.

He decided to call on human help instead. He stole a disposable headset from a vendor's cart and found a quiet spot among the shrines. The headset was just a cheap plastic one, but it did the job. One terminal fitted snugly behind his ear, transmitting sound through the bones of his skull. The other pressed against his temple, streaming images straight to the visual centers of his brain. As he opened a connection into Cleave's data raft, a storm of gaudy ads was superimposed over his view of the wet street. He blinked them away and found a messaging site.

He wanted to call Myka, but it was too risky; the girl in red was certain to be watching for messages. So who else could he turn to?

Zen didn't have friends. He'd left a few behind when he moved from Santheraki, and never bothered making new ones. The trouble with friends was, sooner or later he'd have to tell them about Ma's troubles and his life on Bridge Street, and those were sadnesses that he preferred to hold close and secret. It fitted the image he had of himself, too—the lone thief, all stray-cat-cool, walking solitary down some midnight street. Oh, he'd talk and joke sometimes with the kids who met up at the Spatterpattern Club, but he couldn't trust any of them to help him out of trouble this deep.

That just left Flex. Flex was Myka's friend, really, but maybe she would help him for Myka's sake. Flex had just the skills he needed.

With quick movements of his eyes he typed her contact details on a virtual keyboard, which folded away into the corner of his field of vision when he was finished. He blinked on the "Audio Only" tag. The "connecting" icon flashed for ages.

At last Flex's voice said, "Hey?"

"It's Myka's brother," said Zen, afraid to say his name in case anyone was watching for him on Cleave's communication nets. "I need help."

"What sort of help?"

"I need to get on a train, but I can't go through the station."

"Okay." Flex didn't seem to need any explanation. "Meet me here."

Coordinates pinged into Zen's headset. Battery Bridge. He thanked her, took off the headset, dropped it down a storm drain as he hurried on.

*

All the way to the bridge he kept wondering if the drone had intercepted his messages, but Flex was the only person waiting for him when he got there. A short, stocky figure, rain hat shining like a wet toadstool. Under the hat was another, with trailing earflaps, and under that a kludged-together headset with a big viewing lens that hid Flex's right eye.

Zen had never really been sure if Flex was a boy or a girl, but he mostly chose to think of her as "her." Her plain brown face and shapeless clothes gave no clues, but there was a gruff gentleness about her that reminded him of Myka. She lived rough somewhere in the Stacks, but sometimes the factories called her in to paint their vehicles and the murals over their gates. That was how Myka had met her.

The rest of the time, Flex was a tagger, one of those feral artists who liked sneaking into the rail yards to paint their designs on waiting freight containers, passenger carriages, even on the locos themselves. The trains' maintenance spiders would usually clean the graffiti off before the paint was dry, but if the work was good enough, some locos let it stay, and wore it with pride as they went on their way through the K-gates. Flex's stuff was more than good enough. Zen didn't know much about art, but when he looked at the things Flex painted he could tell that she loved the trains. She never rode the K-bahn herself, but her quick, bright paintings did. Her leaping animals and strange dancing figures were seen by people in all the stations of the Network, mobile murals traveling the galaxy on the flanks of the grateful trains.

More importantly for Zen, the long game of cat and mouse she'd played with the trackside security systems meant that she knew of ways to get to the trains that didn't involve passing through the station.

"Where are you going?" she asked.

"Anywhere," Zen said. "Away."

Flex grunted. "Myka always said you'd end up in bad trouble."

"I live for trouble," said Zen. "Anyway, you paint trains. Does Myka ever lecture you about that?"

"That's different. And I'm not her little brother."

"Will you help me?" Zen asked.

Flex nodded. " 'Course. Myka saved my life once. I owe her."

They climbed a stepped alleyway that led up beside the plummeting foam of a waterfall. The rumble of passing freight trains came down at them from above. Zen wondered what his sister had done to save Flex's life, and why she'd never mentioned it. But the industrial districts were dangerous, everyone knew that. People were probably saving each other's lives down there all the time . . .

Halfway up the staircase, Flex stopped. She must have sent a signal from her headset, because a rusty hatch cover slid open in the alley wall. She ushered Zen through it and came after him, switching on a flashlight as the hatch slid shut behind them.

"Used to be a power station round here," she said. "It served some old rail line that got closed down. This is one of the access passages. It comes out in the freight yards behind Cleave Station."

It was only a short way, but the passage was narrow and airless. Dark side-passages opened off it, full of the fury of the cascade being squeezed through the sluiceways under the K-bahn. At its end, rungs stuck out of the wall of a vertical shaft, and at the top of the shaft another hatch opened. Zen popped up like a gopher in a dead, weed-grown space between two gleaming K-bahn tracks. The brightly lit platforms were about a half mile away, tucked under the overhang of the canyon wall. The part of the line where Zen had emerged was in darkness, except for a fading Station Angel, hovering like an outsized will-o'-the-wisp in the wake of some train, which had just come through the gate.

"What are you waiting for?" asked Flex, down in the shaft behind him.

"There's a Station Angel . . ."

"Angels won't hurt you."

"I know that," said Zen. They were still eerie, though, and he was glad to see that this one was fading—Angels did not last for long this far from a gate. He scrambled out of the hatch and stood for a moment, staring toward the platforms, because he had never seen a K-bahn station from that vantage point before. Then Flex climbed out behind him and they set off across the tracks toward a line of parked freight cars in a siding. Zen was almost starting to enjoy himself now. Somewhere down the line he'd tell this tale in bars or coffee shops to lesser thieves. "They had drones out after me, but I just snuck onto the K-bahn and jumped on an outbound train . . ."

The waiting cars were ore hoppers, blazoned with the crossed keys logo of the Prell family and a lot of graffiti by artists who weren't as good as Flex. Zen saw her give the tags a quick look and wrinkle her nose at the poor workmanship.

"Do I climb in to one of these?" he asked.

Flex shook her head. "Wait here till a passenger train comes in, jump it, ride into the station, then slip inside when the doors open."

"Won't the train notice?"

"It will, but it probably won't care. I know the locos that come through here. Most of them are all right. The worst that will happen is it'll send a maintenance spider to look you over. Tell it you're a friend of mine."

"Train coming," Zen said. He could hear a flutter of engine sound, growing louder.

Flex looked up. The light from the station fell across her hard little face. "That's not a train," she said.

She was right. The rails weren't thrumming the way they did when a train approached. Whatever was coming was coming through the air.

"Drone!" Zen said, and at the same moment its searchlights came sweeping across the tracks. Flex vanished, giving him one warning look, then darting into a nook of darkness behind the freight cars. Zen turned to follow, but the light caught him. He saw his shadow pasted over the tags and logos on the side of the nearest car, as crisp as if Flex had sprayed it there in black paint.

He looked back. The drone hung in the air a few feet away. It must have seen him follow Flex into the passage, worked out where they'd emerge, flown up here to wait. Its battery of cameras and instruments was trained on Zen, relaying his image back to the girl in red or whoever else was controlling it.

"All right!" he shouted. "What do you want?"

Sparks flew from the drone's carapace. It spun in the air. Zen heard cracking noises, sharp dings. He looked left and right. People were running and shouting. Spurts of light flashed on gray raincoats. He thought at first these were the drone's handlers coming to pick him up, then realized that they were shooting at it. The drone tried to steady itself, but something heavy hit it and it flipped over and crashed down on the tracks. There was a blue flash; shards of debris zipping past like bats. Hands caught hold of Zen; flashlights shone in his face. The gray-coats were shouting at him, but the crack of the exploding drone had deafened him. They started to shove him toward the station along a ceramic footpath that ran between the tracks.

The train that had just arrived in Cleave was no ordinary

passenger train. It had, for a start, no carriages, only a long, double-ended locomotive, black, still steaming from its passage through the K-gate. The gaggle of trainspotters on the platform end were going wild, and well they might, thought Zen. On any other night he would have been there with them, fighting for a proper look. Because it was like something from the threedies, this train. A massive, brutal machine, horned and armored like a dinosaur, its hull barnacled with gun turrets and missile pods and stenciled with the logo of the Network Empire.

What was a wartrain doing in Cleave?

The bulk of the black loco hid Zen from the sightseers on the platform as he was hustled along between the tracks, then bundled up steps and through an open door. He was angry, confused, and secretly a little scared, but the railhead in him still felt excited to be boarding such a train.

Inside there was a white cabin, with screens on the walls where an ordinary carriage would have windows. Most of the screens were on standby, displaying the imperial logo, a zigzag lightning flash sparking across two parallel lines. *So these guys must be from Railforce*, thought Zen. "Bluebodies," people called them, because of the blue graphene-composite armor they wore in combat. Only, Railforce didn't usually bother much about what went on out on the branch lines, unless there was a rebellion or something. They certainly weren't in the business of hunting down small-time thieves.

"Name?" someone asked him.

"Zen Starling."

A man stood watching him, bald head gleaming in the light from the screens like a well-worn ebony newel. He had a black splinter of a face, sharp-featured and sour, with a thin scar that twisted one side of his mouth down. You didn't see scars much—the meanest backstreet body shop could fix up a scar for you. When people kept them, it usually meant they were trouble.

"What do you want with me?" shouted Zen. "I haven't done anything wrong. I was just—"

"It would be a bad idea to waste my time," said the Railforce man. "Where is Raven?"

Zen blinked. "Is this about the necklace? That girl—is she one of your people?"

"This is not about a necklace," the man said. "Where is Raven?"

Zen said defiantly, "I don't know what you're talking about."

The man looked past him again. "Maybe he's not made contact yet. Did you learn anything from the drone?"

"Fried," said one of the others. "Sorry, Captain Malik. It self-destructed before we could get anything out of it."

Captain Malik gave a cold smile. "Raven hides his tracks well."

"Who's Raven?" Zen asked.

The screens behind Malik filled with pictures of a man's face. A white face that was all angles. White faces were rare on the Network, where most people came in various shades of brown. Zen would have remembered a face like that.

"I don't know who that is," he said.

"Well he knows who you are," said Malik. "His Motorik contacted you tonight in Ambersai."

Photos from the Ambersai now, grainy blue images scraped from security footage. They showed Zen moving between the stalls, and behind him, in the crowd, the girl in the red raincoat. It looked as if she had been following him for several minutes before she tried to intercept him at the goldsmith's stall. That made Zen uneasy, because his instincts usually told him when he was being watched or followed, and he'd sensed nothing. So she'd only been a Moto? For some reason, he felt disappointed.

"I didn't *talk* to her. She got in my way, that's all."

"She helped you escape with that necklace."

"She didn't help. She tried to stop me. Isn't she with you?"

"No," said Malik. "We tried to track her, but she vanished. So we tracked you, instead, and followed you here to Cleave. What does Raven want with you, Zen Starling?"

Zen shrugged. He didn't know. Nobody had ever taken much interest in him before tonight. "I told you, I don't know any Raven."

"We'll see," said Malik. "My data diver's searching your records." He glanced at a man who sat beside him, eyes hidden by an elaborate headset. "Mr. Nikopol?"

The man smiled; a small, neat man, proud of his work. Divers were a special caste, not afraid to log out of the safe, fire-walled data rafts and surf the tides of information in the deep Datasea. You could find anything down there, as long as you were clever enough to deal with the things that lived there. "Zen has a sister who works in the refineries," he said. "Mother with mental health problems. Father not recorded. Station of birth not recorded. Current address not recorded. Before they lived in this dump the Starlings lived in Santheraki, which is also a dump. Before that—"

Malik held up a hand for quiet. "I don't get it, Zen. You're no different from a million other sneak-thieves up and down this line. Why is Raven interested in a punk like you?"

Zen started to say that he didn't know. Then his anger got the better of him. "You've got no right to drag me in here! If it's Raven and his Moto you're after, why aren't you out looking for them? She's here, in Cleave! Her drone shot Uncle Bugs!"

"Impossible," said Nikopol. "There's been no train from Ambersai since the one the kid came in on, and she wasn't on that."

Malik didn't look as if he thought it was impossible. He looked as if he thought it was interesting.

"Where?" he asked. "Where did you see her?"

Zen started to say, "She was at my apartment," but stopped. He didn't want these Bluebodies barging in on Ma and Myka with their questions and their drones. Ma would think all her nightmares had become real.

Malik grew tired of waiting for an answer. He said to a woman, "Faisa, stow him in the back. Dose him. I'll question him again when the drugs kick in."

He meant Truth drugs. Zen had heard of them. One shot was enough to make you spill everything. He struggled, but Faisa and her comrades were strong. They wrestled him past Malik, down a narrow corridor, into a blue cupboard of a cabin with a shelf for a bed. He struggled some more. He could feel the train stirring, engines coming on. There was a tiny, dirty window in the cabin wall and through that he saw the pillars of the station canopy idling past, and the flicker of headset flashes as trainspotters took final snapshots of the mystery train.

"Where are we going?" he shouted.

One of Malik's men said, "Back up the line. No point staying. Raven won't show his face here now."

The woman called Faisa was opening a plastic box. The train gathered speed and the window went black; they were in a tunnel, heading for Cleave's K-gate. Faisa fitted a tube of some clear fluid into an injector. "This will help you to concentrate on finding the answers Captain Malik needs."

The lights went out. The sound of the engines stopped too. The train was slowing. It couldn't be deliberate, because trains were supposed to speed up on the approach to a K-gate. The man holding Zen said, "Oh great Guardians!"

"What's happening?" asked Faisa.

Zen didn't know, but he knew an opportunity when he saw one. He lashed out with his feet at the black shapes in the blackness around him. One boot crunched into a body. There was a curse. Strong hands turned and twisted him. The man the hands belonged to shouted, "Dose him!" his mouth close to Zen's face, breath smelling of Ambersai beer. There was more scuffling, the cobra hiss of the injector, a scream.

"Not *me!*"

"Sorry! Sorry!"

"Where is he?"

A tangle of bodies, hands. Someone falling. Zen writhed in darkness past the others, groping for the doorway, finding it, stumbling out into the corridor as emergency lighting came on, dim and red. He heaved the door shut before his captors realized he was not among them anymore. There was smoke in the air. The train's engines whined and hiccupped, as if they were trying and trying to come back on line and something was stopping them. The door that led back into Malik's control cabin was opening and closing with exasperated hissing sounds. Looking through it, Zen saw the screens flaring with static. By their pale light, Malik was wrestling with Nikopol, who thrashed in his seat, blood bubbling from his nostrils. Malik sensed Zen standing there. He looked up, but before he could say anything the door gave one last hiss and shut tight, locking itself.

Zen turned the other way. At the far end of the corridor was a hatchway marked with fire exit symbols. He hurried toward it, hoping that wasn't locked too.

It wasn't. Just as his hand reached for the lever, the hatch opened.

"Zen Starling?"

The girl in the red coat was standing on the tracks. She had thrown back the hood of her coat and he could see that Malik had been right, she wasn't a real girl at all, just a Motorik—a wire dolly—an android.

She tilted her head to one side and smiled at him.

"Well, this is exciting!" she said. "I hope you're not going to run away again. There's no need. I'm on your side. My name is Nova."

While Zen was still trying to work out if she was a hallucination, she reached through the hatch, took his hand, and pulled him out of Malik's train into the chill darkness of the tunnel.

He snatched his hand free and stood in the middle of the tracks, looking back at the stricken train. It hulked there, lifeless under the tunnel's faint lights. Its engines wheezed and whined and died, wheezed and whined and died. Sometimes it rocked slightly, as if people were running about inside.

"Come on!" said Nova. "We mustn't keep the *Fox* waiting!"

"What fox?"

"Raven's train. The *Thought Fox*. Come on."

She did not act like a Motorik. No bow, no preset smile, just a quick grin as she turned away from him and headed off along the tunnel, a silhouette against the blue darkness. Zen went after her. Never trust a Moto, Myka would have told him, but he didn't see he had much choice. It was either go with her or climb back aboard the train, and the wire dolly seemed friendlier than Malik.

"If you'd just come with me in the Ambersai you could have saved yourself no end of trouble," she said.

"Your drone shot Uncle Bugs."

She glanced back at him. "I'm sorry about that. It was the *Thought Fox*'s drone, and the *Thought Fox* gets . . . carried away sometimes. But that Hive Monk isn't dead. He's just scattered about a bit. He'll pull himself back together."

"What about Myka and Ma?" he said. "Are they all right?"

"Oh yes!" She stopped and looked at him. "I wouldn't let the *Fox* hurt them. I'm pretty sure your sister would have liked to hurt me, though. Is she always that angry?"

"Myka doesn't like Motorik."

"She called me a putala," said Nova. "I thought she was very rude."

That meant something like "mannequin" in one of the Old Earth languages. Zen grinned, imagining how his sister would have spat the word.

Meanwhile, Nova had turned toward the tunnel wall. Zen could not tell what she was doing, but there was the sound of a door opening, then a rush of stale air against his face. He followed the Motorik into a narrow passage with ceramic floors and walls. Lights came on in the low roof as the door shushed shut behind them. The Motorik looked back at him with what he supposed was meant to be an encouraging smile. She had a cheap, generic face he'd seen on others of her kind: the eyes too big and too wide apart, the mouth too long. But there were patterns of freckles on her cheeks and across her small, straight nose. Whoever heard of a Moto with freckles?

They walked on. The floor sloped down, the tunnel turned. The walls weren't simply water-stained ceramic anymore, they were covered with thousands of glazed tiles, like slabs of clear toffee. The place reminded Zen of something, and a moment later they stepped out into a big, shadowy hall, and he knew why.

It was a K-bahn station.

He turned around, trying to work out which part of Cleave Station this was, and why it was so quiet. And slowly he realized that it was not part of Cleave Station at all. The high vaulted roof where shadows nested, the broken clock and shuttered shopfronts, the wide concourse, deep in dust and droppings, where rows of empty chairs faced a departure board decked with cobwebs . . . It was unmistakably a station, but it was not Cleave Station. It was another, hidden deep in the canyon's cliffs. Its name was stenciled in huge letters on the walls: CLEAVE-B.

"That's impossible." His voice echoed around the subterranean hall and sent small, unseen creatures scurrying for cover among the drifts of litter in the corners. "Cleave is on a one-gate world. There's only one line in."

"There is nowadays," agreed the strange Motorik. "There used to be two."

"I've never heard of a Cleave-B. It's not on the Network map . . ."

"Not anymore. The line from here runs to a K-gate under the Sawtooth Mountains. But that K-gate just links to Tusk, and you can get to Tusk much quicker from the main Cleave station. This place was shut down fifty years ago."

That felt right. Fifty years of dust and debris under Zen's boot soles. Fifty years of seeping water staining the tiles, drizzling scabs and stalactites down the frontages of cafés and waiting rooms. The fading ads on the walls for drinks and threedies that he'd never heard of. Everything stamped with a corporate logo he didn't recognize: Sirius Trans-Galactic. Old stuff. Antique. Valuable. Collectors paid good money for railway memorabilia.

But Zen knew that was too small a way to think about this place. A whole lost station! Surely he could find better ways to profit from it than just stripping out the fixtures to sell at Ambersai Bazar . . .

He followed Nova through an archway, onto a platform. There were other platforms beyond it, rails shining in the shadows between them. This place had been busy once. Zen wondered how he'd never heard of it, but memories were short in Cleave; people blew through on short-term contracts, earning what they could and moving on. They didn't hang about to discuss local history. Flex had said something about an abandoned line, he remembered. Maybe she had been down here. But Flex didn't talk much to anyone.

Across a footbridge, past screens that would once have told the times and destinations of the trains. Dry leaves crunching underfoot. Lights turning on, weedy and power-starved but doing their best as they sensed Zen and Nova's movements. Below the bridge, Zen saw trains. An old Foss loco, and a couple of others that he couldn't make out. Dead trains in a dead station . . .

No, not all dead. Light came from one, spilling through the gaps in the blinds on the carriage windows, and through shark-gill vents along the loco's side. Zen heard the faint waiting purr of it as Nova led him down the stairs to the platform. The loco was a streamlined slice of darkness, splashed with mysterious numerals and letters, stitched with rivets, exhaust ports, the housings of powerful drive-wheels. A huge engine idled like a heartbeat deep inside it.

Behind it were three carriages: double-deckers, massive and elaborate, but old; the type of rolling stock that Zen had only seen in historical threedies.

"*Fox?*" said Nova. Her voice echoed up and down the platform. "We have an extra passenger."

The train just sat there, but a maintenance spider scrambled out of a hatch on its hull and trained its cameras on Zen. One of the carriage doors slid open, and the wind it made sent more of those small dry leaves whispering and scratching along the platform. Zen was too lost in railhead awe at the strange train to wonder where leaves had come from, down there.

"This is the *Thought Fox*," said Nova. She patted the big loco's hull with one hand, steering Zen toward the first carriage with the other. He touched the loco too. His fingertips ran lightly over old ceramic, ridged and plated like a tortoise shell.

"It's a beauty!"

The loco made a noise. Just coolant shifting, deep in its engine compartment, but it sounded like a warning growl. Zen took his hand away, and peeked inside the first carriage. He saw luxury and lamplight, like something in an ad. No rows of seats, no luggage racks. This was—what was the word?—a *state car*. The sort high-ranking members of the corporate families rode around in: a sumptuous interstellar living room on wheels. It looked old: dusty mirrors, tarnished gilt, the leather of the deep seats cracked and faded. Shabby, but shabby in an expensive way; antique shop shabby, not the everyday worthless shabbiness that Zen was used to.

And sitting in the middle of it, smiling at him, was the man from Malik's photos. Same hollow face, same old black suit, same long hands and level gaze. The lights of the carriage shining on his pale hair. He was so white and motionless that he still looked like a photo, like someone frozen in the glare of a camera flash.

"Welcome, Zen," he said. "I'd hoped to gather you in at Ambersai. I didn't want Yanvar Malik to find his way to your mother and sister. But don't worry, he won't trouble them.

Railforce won't let him pursue his obsession any further now that he has cost them a train."

"What's his obsession?" asked Zen.

"I am." Raven steepled his fingers under his chin and smiled. Nova stepped into the carriage and looked back, smiling too, holding out her hand to welcome Zen aboard.

Some street-bred instinct told Zen to turn and run. He ignored it carefully. Instincts weren't always right. Raven had defeated Malik. He had taken out that wartrain. He was powerful. Whatever he had going on down here, with this hidden station and this secret train, Zen wanted a piece of it.

He did not take Nova's hand—he didn't like the touch of her, that synthetic flesh that felt so nearly like the real thing. But he stepped aboard, and the *Thought Fox* closed its doors behind him.

The carriage had been grown from livewood, with silvery bioluminescent lamps set into knots in the curved roof. It was like being inside an enormous hollow nut. Music came from hidden speakers. Waves of harmony, low voices singing words Zen didn't know. Old music on an old train. Nova went away, into another carriage or another compartment. She gave Zen the creeps, but he felt sorry she'd gone; Raven was creepier.

Now Raven rose from his chair. He was long and thin, and he looked wrong somehow, like something carved in cold white stone by a sculptor who didn't quite understand human bodies. He snapped his fingers and a holographic map appeared in the air in front of him.

"You know what this is, Zen?"

"Of course I do," said Zen. It was the same rail map that you saw in every K-bahn station, lines intersecting and branching to form a 3-D mass like glowing coral. "It's the Network."

Raven smiled. "When I was a boy, we called it 'Kilopylae.'

That means 'the thousand gates' in one of the languages of Old Earth. That was the ancient name for it, the Guardians' name. It seems to have fallen out of fashion now."

"Because it's not true," said Zen. "There aren't a thousand K-gates. There are nine hundred and sixty-four." Everyone knew that. Maybe the Guardians had planned to open a thousand gates, but it had turned out that there were only so many holes they could tear in the fabric of space-time before it came apart like an old dishcloth. They had stopped after nine hundred and sixty-four gates, saying that to make another would upset some symmetry and destabilize the whole Network.

"Yes," said Raven. "Nine hundred and sixty-four gates. And thirty of those are out of use, because the corporate families decided it isn't economical to keep those stations open anymore . . ."

He enlarged part of the map with a twitch of his thin hand, and among the branching, multicolored lines Zen saw one that he did not recognize. A rose-red line, which began at Sirius and went zigzagging through the center of the Network to a far-off station called Desdemor.

"You've heard of the Dog Star Line?" said Raven. "No? I'm not surprised. It was busy once, but the industrial planets it linked were mined out and all the important worlds it served can be reached more easily now by other lines. The corporate family who ran it went bankrupt, and it was closed down long ago. The rails are still here, though. Fuel, too, at some of the old depots. Enough to keep the *Thought Fox* running."

"So what's this got to do with me?" asked Zen. He didn't like Raven lecturing him like he was a kid in school. "Why are the Bluebodies after you? Are you a thief too?"

Raven grinned. "I prefer to think of myself as a freedom fighter."

"You sent that girl after me. That Moto."

Raven smiled calmly. *Not a man to trust,* thought Zen. *Nor a man to offend.*

"So what do you want with me?" he asked.

"I'll tell you on the way."

"The way where?" Zen said, and sat down without meaning to, jolted off his feet as the *Thought Fox* began to move.

7

"Hey!" he shouted as the *Thought Fox* carried him away through forgotten tunnels. "Where are you taking me?"

"Away from Cleave," Raven said calmly. "Railforce will be furious about what we did to their wartrain. If you stay in Cleave, you'll get the blame. You'll be much better off with me."

That was easy to believe. The seat that Zen had landed in was livewood, and so comfortable that it felt as if it had been grown especially for him. He sat there watching while Raven moved around, untroubled by the train's movements, opening seamless hatches in the walls, fetching out glasses, bottles. Tunnels rushed by outside the windows, vanishing sometimes to give a glimpse of dimly lit caverns, abandoned freight yards. The music soared dreamily.

"Is this *your* train?" Zen asked.

"*Thought Fox* is the last of the C12 Zodiaks," Raven said.

"Wow!" Zen had heard of those. Some of the fastest, most

beautiful locos ever to come out of the Albayek family's engine shops on Luna Verde. "I didn't think there were any left . . ."

"I found the *Fox* abandoned on a siding. A derelict, left behind when the line was closed." Raven poured a whisky for himself, a glass of purple juice for Zen. "Poor *Fox*. I helped it to repair. Now it consents to carry me to where I want to go."

"Its drone shot Uncle Bugs."

"Yes. Unfortunate. I'm afraid the *Fox* has anger management issues; something of an appetite for destruction. Don't you, *Fox*?"

The *Thought Fox* said nothing, but Zen sensed that it was listening. "I suppose nobody really *owns* a train," he said.

"Exactly." Raven came back to the table and set the drinks down, then paused as the *Thought Fox* slammed through a K-gate. The carriage shimmered for a moment in the weird non-light, then they were hurtling across plains of blue-gray mud. Zen leaned forward, eager to see what world this lost line had brought him to. Mountains showed in the distance, and the skeleton shapes of dead buildings.

"Tashgar," said Raven.

"What?"

"This place. It's called Tashgar. A former industrial world, much like Cleave, stripped out centuries ago. Most of the stations on the Dog Star Line are like this. It still runs through living places, too—Ambersai and Cleave, as you know, and Sundarban, and a few others, but the Dog Star stations are buried deep on those worlds."

They entered another tunnel, another gate. Roared through another dead station.

"Why were you looking for me?" Zen asked.

"You're of use to me," said Raven.

"What sort of use?"

"I need a thief. You're going to steal something for me."

Zen liked the sound of that. So Raven *was* a thief like him. And with access to this secret K-bahn, they could go anywhere, steal anything, get away clean. But he didn't want to sound too eager, so he just said, "Okay," like he was thinking it over.

"Don't worry," said Raven, as Zen had hoped he would. "I pay well. I'll make you rich. Once the job's done you can have a new life. Anything you need. Fine house, new name. Treatment for your mother. They could fix what's wrong with her easily enough, you know, if she wasn't living in a rathole like Cleave. Yes, I could arrange that. And all you have to do is one small job."

That sounded too good to be true. Zen sensed he was being played. Either the reward wouldn't be as big as promised, or the job would turn out to be bigger. But, as when he first decided to follow Nova, he didn't see he had much choice. And whatever the downsides were, to work for a man like this would be a step up out of his old life, wouldn't it?

"Okay," he said again.

Raven grinned, as if that sealed the bargain, and the *Thought Fox* passed through another gate into another world, and then another. And although he was on edge, high on the railhead thrill of riding the old line and excited by this new turn his luck was taking, Zen started to feel sleepy. He couldn't remember how many hours it had been since he rode the K-bahn out of Ambersai, thinking his adventures were at an end. He was starting to get seriously train-lagged.

He rested his head against the sculpted chair back and watched the view go by as the *Thought Fox* rushed on through those strange, enormous landscapes. Nighttime on a world in some nebula where the sky was a peacock's tail of huge stars blazing. Dawn over seas of methane under a shattered moon.

Un-bang. Un-bang. Un-bang. The music and the soft, familiar motion of the swaying carriage easing him into sleep.

*

When he awoke, the train had stopped. Greenish-golden daylight slanted into the carriage. The door was open. Raven had gone, but Zen could hear a sound like the slow breathing of some huge, sleepy animal.

He jumped up from his seat, and almost hit the ceiling. The gravity here was less than he was used to. The empty glass that he had just knocked from the armrest of his seat fell so slowly that he had time to catch it before it reached the floor.

The breathing was the distant sound of waves on a shore.

He stepped off the train into a big old station. The green-gold light came down through a glass roof. He walked along the platform and through open barriers onto the station concourse. Raven was there. He stood between the pillars, where the shafts of light came and went. He was doing—what? Exercises of some sort, Zen thought at first. Balancing on one foot and then the other, jerking like a marionette, twisting his spindly black-clad body into shapes Zen wouldn't have thought were possible.

And then the light shafts coming through the canopy faded, and as the concourse filled with shadow again, he saw that Raven was not alone. Two Station Angels flickered there, many-limbed wisps of light that knotted and writhed.

Station Angels were a sort of harmless energy that flickered sometimes in the wake of trains. They might *look* a bit like the ghosts of gigantic praying mantises, but everyone knew that was just the way human brains interpreted some sort of interference that got dragged through into the normal universe when a K-gate opened. But these Angels, rather than just wandering and fading as an Angel should, seemed to be echoing Raven's movements somehow, as if all three of them were dancing to the same music.

There wasn't any music, though. There was only the wind moaning, and the light tracking across dusty platforms, and Zen's heart going thud, thud, thud, as a fear he didn't understand rose up in him.

A cool hand closed around his wrist. Nova drew him backward into the shelter of a derelict food stall.

"You mustn't disturb him," she said, turning the volume of her voice down so low that he could barely hear it. "He is busy. He is talking to the Angels."

Zen looked at her. "You can't talk to Station Angels! That's like talking to marsh gas, or rainbows. They're not alive."

"Who says so?"

"Everybody. Experts. They've done tests."

"Oh," said Nova. "Well, I'm not alive either, not in your way. But Raven talks to me."

Zen watched the dancers. "It's a trick, isn't it? It's just magnetism or static electricity or something . . ."

And then the Angels weren't there anymore. Zen thought for a moment it was another change in the light that had hidden them, but they had simply gone.

Raven stood for a moment smoothing his hair. He squared his shoulders, straightened his jacket. Then he walked along the platform and went back aboard the *Thought Fox*. A moment later Zen heard the K-train's engines powering up.

"He's leaving!" he said. "He's leaving me here!" He started to run back toward the train, but Nova caught his arm again.

"It's all right. It's part of the plan."

"What plan?"

"Raven's plan. He told me to take you to the hotel, but I didn't want to wake you. We're to wait here for him."

"What is this place?"

"The city of Desdemor, on the water-moon Tristesse."

The end of the line. The far end of the Network from Zen's home.

"Is this world abandoned too?" he asked.

"There are some people at the hotel," said Nova, "but they're only Motorik."

He was surprised how scornful she sounded. "You do know that you're a Motorik too?"

She wrinkled her nose. "I am nothing like them. They're just puppets of their programming. I do as I like."

The *Thought Fox*'s engines rumbled, pushing the train backward out of the station, accelerating toward the tunnel mouth behind it, where the K-gate waited.

"Where's Raven going?" asked Zen.

Nova shrugged, looking as if she had personally invented shrugging and hadn't quite sorted out the fine details yet.

"Who is he?"

"He is just Raven," she said.

"Why does he want me? Why did he choose me?"

"I can't imagine," she said, looking him up and down. "Maybe it's the name. Starling and Raven. They're both the names of birds, from Old Earth. That's the sort of thing he thinks is funny."

"Desdemor!" announced a loud voice. "Jewel of the western branch lines!" But it was only a big advertising screen, woken by the movement as Zen and Nova emerged from the station entrance. The buildings of the city soared high and slender and abandoned, and empty bridges spanned its calm canals. The screen flashed images of crowded beaches and laughing children across a deserted piazza, welcoming tourists who would never arrive. Overhead shots showed Desdemor to be an island, but Zen had guessed that already; he could not see the ocean yet, but he could hear the boom and rush of it, and smell it in the clean air.

He looked up. Big clouds were sweeping overhead. The greenish-golden light, which shone between them, was not sunlight. It came from the immense gas planet that filled half the sky.

"It must have been lovely here in the old days," said Nova. "So full of people! Raven is the only one who comes here now."

"But why?" Zen asked, following her across the piazza. His voice echoed from the glass walls of towering buildings. "Why come here, I mean? Raven must be rich. Rich people live in nice houses. They have friends, and families, and nice stuff. They don't dance with Station Angels. They don't live in ruined beach resorts with only wire dollies for company. No offence."

"None taken," said Nova.

They walked beside a canal, following it down to the beach. The tide was in. Spray burst high into the air and fell back slowly in the frail gravity. Storms had stripped the shutters from the little shops behind the promenade. Buckets and spades lay half-buried in the drifts of sand inside, like treasures in desert tombs. Far out at sea, where big waves broke over reefs the color of bone, Zen saw a skein of ungainly looking birds flying, black against the face of the gas giant.

"That planet is called Hammurabi," said Nova. "Tristesse is one of its moons. And those birds aren't birds, they're sky-rays. Genetically engineered, based on the big manta rays that used to live in the oceans on Old Earth, you know?"

"Oh, right . . ." (Zen didn't know, but he wasn't going to let her see that.)

"They roost on the offshore reefs. People used to go out in boats, with special guns, to hunt them. And the ocean is called the Sea of Sadness—isn't that pretty? Like something in a song."

Another wave burst, towering over them, collapsing across the promenade like a drunken fountain. Zen stepped back, but Nova just stood there, raising her face to the falling spray.

"Is this all right for you?" he shouted, over the snore of the withdrawing wave. "All this water?"

She only laughed, shaking her wet hair. "Think it'll short-circuit me? I'm not a toaster, Zen! I have skin. Look! It's water-proof, and it covers me all over."

"It's not real skin," he said.

"No," she said. "It's better. I'm a very advanced model."

"Did Raven make you?" he asked.

"He *started* me, if that's what you mean."

"So that makes him, like . . . your *father* or something?"

She was silent for a while. They moved back, out of reach of the spray. She said, "It was in the storm season. In one of the old ballrooms at the hotel. He's done it up as a workshop. A laboratory. One minute I wasn't anything, and the next I was me. I was lying on a metal table and there was rain on the windows.

"He said I was an experiment. Which does nothing for a person's self-esteem, I can tell you. He said he was trying to build a Motorik that thought it was a human being. Only it didn't work, because I knew what I was at once. I lay there in the rain-light and watched menus opening in my brain. I could feel all my subroutines coming online. Raven just puttered about watching me, with the shadows of the rain on the windows running down his face, and the lightning flashing from his eyes. I saw an old movie once about a mad scientist, and he looked exactly like Raven did that day. Which makes me his monster, I suppose. That's not very good for my self-esteem either."

"Did Raven program you to be this way?"

"To be what way?"

"Well . . ."

"Nobody programmed me, Zen Starling. I program myself. Raven gave me passwords. He showed me how to open my own menus and rewrite my code."

"Is that why you have freckles?"

"Yes! It took ages to get the pigmentation just right. Do you like them?"

"Not much."

"Motorik are meant to look perfect," she said, as if she hadn't heard him. "Like dolls. That's why *stupid* people call us 'wire dollies,' I suppose. But I don't want to look perfect. It's so boring. I'm working on giving myself some pimples next. I wish I could make myself fat. Why don't you like the freckles?"

Zen felt embarrassed now. He wished he hadn't called her a wire dolly. He hadn't meant to hurt her feelings. He hadn't even realized Motorik *had* feelings. He said, "They make you look like you're trying to be human."

"I *am* human," she said. "I have a processor for a brain instead of a lump of meat, and my body is made of different substances, but I have feelings and dreams and things, like humans do."

"What do you dream about?"

"That's my business."

*

They walked back toward the K-bahn. The station was on the ground floor of a building called the Terminal Hotel, a soaring glass wing whose thousand windows all reflected the storms and rings of Hammurabi. There seemed to be people in the lobby, but when Nova led him inside, Zen saw that they were just more Motorik. One came to meet the new arrivals, bowing. She was gendered female, with a long, wise face, a blue dress, silver hair in a neat chignon.

"Mr. Starling? I am Carlota, the manager. Mr. Raven told us to expect you."

"Is this where he lives?" Zen asked.

"When he has nowhere better to be," said Nova. "He got the old place up and running again, woke up all these wire dollies to keep it working."

"Mr. Raven is a regular guest here at the Terminal," said Carlota. (If she was offended at being called a wire dolly, she did not let it show.)

"You'd better keep an eye on Mr. Starling, Carlota," said Nova. "He's a thief. Count the spoons. Keep the safe locked."

Carlota's smile was patient and preprogrammed. "Come, sir," she said. "I'll show you to your room."

At the heart of the Great Network lay Grand Central. All the main lines of the galaxy met there, which meant that whichever corporate family controlled Grand Central controlled the whole Network. For the past few generations that had been the Noons. Portraits of the Noon Emperors and Empresses beamed down from holoscreens, and the smiling golden sun of Noon flapped on bright banners above a garden city, which covered half the planet, the buildings spread wide apart, diamondglass towers and golden station canopies rising from a sea of trees. The imperial palace, the senate, the K-bahn Timetable Authority, all the dull, complicated departments that kept the Great Network running had their headquarters on Grand Central. The Guardians themselves kept data centers here: deep-buried vaults of computer substrate from which those wise old AIs could keep watch over human affairs. The Imperial College of Data Divers was always standing by to pass on their advice and instructions to the Emperor, although the Guardians seemed content these days to let Mahalaxmi XXIII rule without their instructions and advice. The Network ran itself happily enough in these peaceful times.

On Grand Central there were always silvery trains snaking from one K-gate to another across the long viaducts, and the sky was forever busy with drones and air-taxis. At morning and evening these were joined by green parakeets, which rose from the treetops to fly in raucous, swirling flocks between the towers. The buildings used magnetic fields to warn the flocks away, and the birds flowed around them like water around the prows of huge ships.

The shadows of their wings fell upon Captain Malik, who stood at a window high in the Railforce tower, looking out over the parks and lakes and malls of the galactic capital. The peace and luxury of the place unsettled him. He belonged on colder, rougher, dirtier worlds, and he was angry at being ordered back to Grand Central.

"Yanvar!"

He turned from the window as Rail Marshal Delius came into the room. A tall woman, taller than him, very dark skinned, her white hair combed and lacquered into a high arch like the crest of an ancient warrior. Her face was a warrior's, too: stern and handsome, but lovely when she smiled, which she did when she saw Malik. He let her hug him. A row of medals was pinned across her tunic. They reminded him of the coins that he and Rail Marshal Delius used to leave on the K-bahn rails when they were kids together in the rail yards on Lakshmi's Lament. They'd creep out to the lines and lay the coins on them like offerings, then hide and wait for a K-train to come by . . .

Lyssa Delius was one of the very few people Malik thought of as a friend. They had joined Railforce together, and fought side by side against the Empire's enemies all over the Network. But he doubted her friendship could help him much now. A wrecked wartrain was a serious business. He had whiled away his journey from Cleave by trying to calculate how many millions the armored loco must have cost. The Empire would be looking for someone to blame, and Lyssa did not have the imagination to blame Raven. Like the rest of Railforce Command, she did not even believe that Raven existed.

"I'm glad you're all right," she told him. "I'm sorry to have to drag you here, but this is a serious business . . ."

"It was a trainkiller," said Malik. "It cut straight through our firewalls, killed my data diver . . ."

"I read your report." Delius sat down on a gray sofa and patted the cushion beside her, inviting him to sit down too. Malik stayed standing. She said, "Our technicians went through what was left of your train's systems. They found no trace of any virus."

"If he can design a virus like that," said Malik, "he can design it to leave no trace."

"Mmm," said the Rail Marshal, with a half smile, but he knew that she didn't believe him. He noticed that she'd had her scar fixed the half-moon scar on her forehead from that firefight on Bandarpet. *A pity*, he thought. *Old soldiers should wear their scars with pride.*

"You were supposed to be on a routine patrol of the trans-Chiba branch lines—" she started to say.

"I was. I was in Ambersai when I detected Raven's Motorik, trailing a kid in the Bazar."

"Yes . . ." Lyssa Delius was embarrassed. Her smile looked like pain. "Yanvar, this theory of yours, that Raven is still at large—"

"It's more than a theory."

The Rail Marshal sighed. "Our data divers have spoken to the Guardians. They know nothing of Raven."

"They told you that?"

"Not in so many words—you know how they are—but if he was still out there, they would tell us."

"Raven knows how to evade them," said Malik. "They think that because he does not operate in the Datasea anymore, he is no danger. But he is."

"Oh, Yanvar," said the Rail Marshal gently. "If you would report in more often, go to the right parties, meet people, you would probably be *General* Malik by now. Railforce needs good people like you, here on Grand Central. But you're always out on the branch lines, chasing this . . . this . . . *ghost*. Raven is dead. We killed him, Yanvar. Twenty years ago."

"Raven is no ghost. He's planning something. He made contact with this kid from Cleave, a small-time thief named Zen Starling. I brought the boy aboard the train for questioning. That's when the trainkiller hit."

"And where is this boy now?"

"He escaped," said Malik.

"You have searched Cleave?"

"He's not in Cleave."

"Then how did he leave? Bearing in mind that your train was blocking the tunnel that leads to Cleave's only K-gate?"

"There is a second K-gate there. Cleave-B, on the old Dog Star Line. That's how Raven moves. That's where he hides."

"And do you have any actual—"

"There is no *evidence*, Lyssa. But I know it's true. If you give me another train, and let me take it onto the Dog Star Line . . ."

She looked away, sighing. When they were kids she would wait in the shadows with Malik, simmering with giggles, until the K-train passed. Then they would scurry back to the rails and find the coins they'd balanced there transformed: crushed thin as leaves by the weight of the wheels, and scoured to a high shine. Some similar change had come over Lyssa Delius in the forty years since then. She was no longer the girl he had grown up with. They were not alike anymore, he realized. Age and ambition had smoothed the hard edges off her; she was happy here in this civilized city, playing politicians' games. But Malik was made of hard edges: a violent, vengeful man. He wanted to hurt people, and he needed a war to let him do it. He needed a train.

"Let me hunt Raven down."

Lyssa Delius looked at him, and he knew what she would say before she said it. "I'm sorry, Yanvar. No more ghost hunting. Your team has already been reassigned. If it wasn't for me—if I hadn't put in a good word for you—you would be facing serious punishment. As it is, you will take six months' leave, and report for psychological evaluation."

She stopped in surprise as a sudden clattering sound filled the room like gunfire. Malik looked behind him. One of those wheeling flocks of parakeets had mistaken the window of the Rail Marshal's office for empty sky and flown straight into the diamondglass.

"Our magnetic field must be on the blink again," said Lyssa Delius. "You see, Yanvar? That's the trouble with peacetime. The Emperor keeps cutting our funding. We can't even afford bird repellers, let alone to keep you out there, wrecking K-trains, following this *hunch* . . ."

Malik went to the window. Dead birds were tumbling toward the treetops, leaving the glass smeared with blood and feathers. He took the Railforce badge from the breast of his jacket and set it carefully on the sill.

"I'll find Raven on my own," he said.

Lyssa Delius called his name as he walked to the elevator. He did not look back.

10

That night, Zen was woken by the wind howling around the glass blade of the Terminal Hotel. The suite Carlota had put him in was roughly the size of Cleave. His bed was about as big as the apartment on Bridge Street. He lay in it and listened to the wind, and the boom of the surf, and the hooting of the rays. He found a headset in the drawer of the bedside table, ripped open the plastic bag it came in, and clipped it on, but the local data raft was empty.

Not only was Desdemor not on the Network anymore, it wasn't even connected to the Datasea. Zen had never imagined that anywhere could feel so lonely.

When dawn came the sky was full of broken, hurrying clouds and the canals shone like wet lead. Zen went down to breakfast. Nova was alone in the hotel's huge restaurant, trying to decide which corner of a triangle of toast to put into her mouth first. A holomovie hung in front of her like a curtain of light: something so old that it wasn't even in color, let alone 3-D, and all the actors were white. Their strange voices filled the big room with words Zen couldn't understand. A man was saying, "The problemshathreeliddlpeeple doanamowndooahilluhbeansh in thish crazy world . . ."

"I like old movies," Nova said.

"Can't you just stream them straight into your brain?"

"Yes, but they're better this way. This one was made on Earth, thousands and thousands of years ago, before the Guardians opened the K-gates and brought us to the stars."

The Guardians brought us to the stars, not you, robo-girl, thought Zen. He said, "Since when do Motorik eat toast?"

"I can process organic material to supplement my power supply," said Nova, as if she were quoting from her own instruction manual. She nibbled the toast carefully so that the crumbs did not fall on her clothes. "It's a special modification. Raven says he likes company when he's eating, and not the sort of company that just sits and watches." She looked away from him suddenly, as if she'd heard something. All Zen could hear was the rain on the windows, the booming sea—but Motorik ears were sharper than human ones.

"The K-gate just opened," she said. "Raven is back."

"Where has he been?"

"I don't know. He goes to lots of places."

"Why? What does he do there?"

She shrugged, eyes on her movie. "I don't know."

Raven came into the breakfast room a few minutes later. He made no attempt to explain where he had been, or why, just said, "So are you settling in, Zen? Nova looking after you? I thought it would be nice for you two kids to spend a bit of time together. I worry about Nova, you know. She tells me not to, but I do. She needs someone her own age to talk to."

Nova blushed.

"Is that why you brought me here?" asked Zen. "I thought there was something you wanted me to steal."

Raven frowned a little, as if hurt that his guest did not want to make small talk. "Well, yes . . ."

"So what is it?"

"Oh, only a little box. About so big." Raven held up his hand, thumb and forefinger spread three inches apart.

"What's in this box?"

"Nobody knows."

"Okay," Zen said. "Where is it?"

"In a private museum on the Noon train."

Zen looked at him to see if he was joking.

He wasn't joking.

"So you think I can get onto the Noon train and just start stealing stuff?"

"I think you're the only person I could send to steal it, Zen." Raven smiled, and left Zen to think about that while he ordered breakfast from the Motorik waiters.

*

Zen had never seen the Noon train, but he had heard of it. Everybody had. When the senate was not in session on Grand Central, Mahalaxmi XXIII, Emperor of the Great Network, Chief Executive of the Noon family, traveled constantly from world to world, making sure that all the people of the Network had a chance to see him. He made these journeys aboard his private train: three miles long, pulled by twin engines and Guardians knew how many auxiliary power cars.

"Only two types of people can board that train," said Raven. "Members of the imperial family, and trusted guests. It takes a long time to win the Emperor's trust, and I want the box now. So if I'm going to get hold of it, I need a Noon family member on my side. Trouble is, those Noons tend to stick together. They're too rich to bribe, too clever to trick, too dangerous to blackmail."

Zen still didn't understand. "So how can I help you?"

"Your mother never told you who she is?" asked Raven. "Who you are?"

"No. She doesn't talk about things like that."

Raven thought for a moment. "Back in '65, young Mora Noon, from the Golden Junction branch of the Noon family, was married to one of the sons of the Lee Consortium. It was a big deal, in every sense. A grand wedding at the Noon Summer Palace on Far Cinnabar. Nine days of celebrations. Of course, once she was married, Mora was expected to produce a child. But someone as rich and important as Mora Noon doesn't have time to be pregnant. So the family geneticists implanted the fetus in a surrogate mother. A poor relation called Latika Ketai, the illegitimate daughter of some Noon or other, who worked on their country estates."

Zen's mother's name was Latika. She'd sung old Cinnabari folksongs to him when he was little. He started to see where Raven's story was headed.

Raven spread his hands. "Something went wrong," he said. "I guess she got fond of you. Decided that, after all the trouble she'd gone to giving birth to you, you should be hers to keep. So she ran. Skipped out with you, got to a K-bahn station, vanished into the Network. She must have kept traveling for weeks, changing lines whenever she could. The Noons sent people after her of course. Noon DNA is valuable; the corporate families guard their bloodlines jealously. But somewhere along the way

Latika managed to convince them you were both dead, and they stopped looking for you. It took me a long time to pick up your trail myself."

Zen wasn't sure what he was feeling. It was hard to imagine Ma ever having been together enough to slip out of a Noon family facility with a Noon family baby. It was hard to imagine her ever loving him enough to try. He supposed he should feel grateful that she had wanted him that badly, but he was too busy wondering how he could use this new knowledge. He was a Noon. By rights he should be living in a palace somewhere, heir to a great trading house. He was a Noon! He was related to the Emperor himself!

And he understood now where Ma's fears had come from. The Noons had given up hunting for her, but she had never stopped running.

"How do I know this is true?" he asked.

"We'll run a blood test if you like," said Raven. "You'll find you have Noon DNA. Which brings us back to this job I want you to do for me."

He took a little device from his pocket and set it on the table. A Baxendine holoprojector, its wooden casing shaped like a big, smooth bean. It hung a picture of a young man in the air above the table.

Zen stared at the image for a couple of seconds before he realized that it was not an image of himself. He had never had a haircut that expensively accidental-looking. He had never worn a Kendo Berberian smart-vinyl jacket, or grinned at a camera in those gardens of coral above that sapphire lake. No, this was someone else. This was some rich kid who looked like him.

"His name is Tallis Noon," said Raven. "You see the family resemblance?"

"There is a seventy-six percent similarity," said Nova.

Zen nodded, feeling wary. He could guess where this was going.

"Actually there are about thirty members of the Noon family who look pretty much like you," said Raven. "That's what you get for wandering about with their genes. I've chosen Tallis here because he's from an outlying branch, very minor, based at Golden Junction."

More pictures of the Noon kid flipped up. Zen hated him already, with his fine clothes and his cheerful smile. Who wouldn't be cheerful, living the life he lived? You could see he'd never done an honest day's work. (Nor had Zen, of course. But he thought he could imagine what an honest day's work must feel like, and he was pretty sure Tallis Noon couldn't.)

Raven said, "Tallis finished university a standard year ago. He should be taking his place in the family business by now, but he's a dreamer. Prefers poems and paintings to profit margins. He thinks he'd like to travel a bit before he settles. He's another railhead, in fact. You two have so much in common!"

Zen thought of the kids who had sat across from him on that train out of Ambersai. The Network was full of rich kids, aimlessly shuttling from one world to another in search of something their families' money couldn't seem to buy.

"It wouldn't surprise anyone if Tallis were to board the Noon train," Raven went on. "It's his family's most famous asset, and as far as I can tell he's never ridden it."

"But they'll know I'm not him!" Zen said. "I might look a bit like him, but I don't talk like him, I don't know anything about his life, his family . . ."

"I'll brief you. Posing as Tallis will get you through security.

Once you're on the train, you go straight for the box. It's in the carriage that houses the family art collection. It won't seem strange if you want to look around the collection."

"It's art, then? This box? We're art thieves?"

Raven grinned. "A step up from your old line of work, isn't it?"

The holo changed, showing an image of the thing Zen was supposed to steal. It was a small, dull, metal cube.

"It's called the Pyxis," said Raven. "Don't let the fancy name intimidate you. It just means 'box' in one of those Old Earth languages, Roman or Spanish or Klingon . . ."

"Ancient Geek, I think," said Nova.

"Is it valuable?" asked Zen. (It didn't *look* valuable.)

"It's unique," said Raven. "That makes it very valuable indeed."

He made the picture change again. Now they were looking at a map of the Network. A red dot marked the current position of the Noon train, way out on the Silver River Line.

"A few days from now, the *Thought Fox* will take us to Surt. From there you can catch a regular train to Adeli, where the Noon train will be pausing for a day or two. You can board it there. It will be traveling to Jangala, the Spindlebridge, and Sundarban. On the way, you'll snitch the Pyxis. I'll be waiting at Sundarban to whisk you away down the Dog Star Line again. And then you'll be rich, Zen."

"But I can't do it," Zen said. He flapped his hands at the holo, which detected the movement and changed to a video image of the Noon train like a river of grand buildings, pouring across a viaduct above some shining delta. "Look at it!" he said. "You think I can just walk on there and find my way off again with this box? There will be surveillance, security—"

"Nova will take care of that," said Raven.

"Nova's coming?"

"Of course. You'll be working closely together. A young man of Tallis Noon's status doesn't travel alone. You'll have your Motorik secretary with you." He handed Zen a stylish little headset of brass and ivory. "Nova can keep in touch via that, feed you any information you need. Now we just need to make you look the part. Get changed, for a start. You'll find clothes in the wardrobes in your suite. A young man of Tallis Noon's breeding wouldn't be seen dead in that junk you're wearing . . ."

*

Up in his room, Zen put on some of the new clothes and stood in front of the mirror. There were half a dozen outfits. He had chosen foil jeans, red ankle boots, a mirrorcloth windcheater. He stood up straight and pretended he was a young Noon. His hair did not look as if a Golden Junction stylist had cut it, but then Tallis Noon was supposed to have been riding the rails for a while. Zen knew where he'd been, too: the headset that Raven had given him came preloaded with Tallis's travel documents and his photos of the sights he'd seen—all faked or stolen by Raven, Zen presumed.

For the first time he started to think that the plan might work. It was daunting, the scale of it. Frightening. But nothing a Thunder City kid couldn't handle. Just one job, Raven had said, but Zen guessed that this was more like a test. If he could get away with the Pyxis, there would be other jobs. A chance to travel the galaxy, meet interesting people, and nick their stuff. With Raven's help, he could stop being a little thief, and become one of the greats.

And even if it didn't work out—even if the Noons saw

through his disguise and arrested him—well, at least he could say he had ridden the Noon train. At least he would get to see Jangala, and cross the Spindlebridge . . .

He fingered the foil of his new jeans. Too clean, he thought. He'd wear this stuff around Desdemor a bit, get some dust and scuff marks on it. If his clothes were in character, maybe the rest of him would follow.

11

When he lived on Santheraki, Zen had dreamed for a while of being an actor. He was still a kid then, still half believing the old lie that you could be whatever you wanted to be if you just wanted it badly enough. Ma had managed to outrun her fears for a little while, Myka had a good job by Myka's standards, and Zen went to acting lessons at a shabby little theater just down the street from the apartment they were renting. The teacher, Ashwin Bhose, was threadbare and down on his luck, but he'd been famous in his time. The corridors of the theater were walled with posters and holos of his performances.

The other students were from wealthier homes than Zen's. They took part meekly in the exercises Bhose set them, pretending to be trees, or trains, or breezes. It made Zen feel embarrassed, that stuff. He'd never wanted to be a tree or a breeze. He just wanted to dress up and pretend for a while that he was somebody important, or at least somebody else, anybody but Zen Starling, with his raggedy life and frightened mom.

When he was being himself, he never knew what to say. He stammered shyly, or stayed silent. Out on a stage, he thought, it would all be different. Words would pour out of him. He'd have whole conversations learned by heart.

Ashwin Bhose must have seen something in him. After a few months Myka's hours got docked and she couldn't pay Zen's fees, but Bhose kept him as a student anyway. He said Zen was good at watching. "You see the little details," he told him once. "The small habits that tell us so much about people's characters. But it's not just about watching. You have to understand what goes on in other people's heads. The feelings that underlie their movements and expressions. That secret inner weather."

Zen didn't really know what the old actor meant. He'd never been much good at understanding other people. He still wasn't. Maybe if they'd stayed on Santheraki, Bhose could have taught him. But Ma's fears caught up with her, and then Myka's factory went over to Motorik labor and she lost her job. The Starlings packed their lives into their plastic suitcases and took wing again, leaving Santheraki in the pink of a winter dawn, refinery flare-off shimmering in the mudflats, a long silver train taking them through the K-gates to Cleave.

*

Zen had not thought much about his old dreams since then, except to stop and wonder sometimes at what a fool he must have been to have had them, and to feel guilty about never saying goodbye to Ashwin Bhose. But there in Desdemor, as he got ready for this job of Raven's, the memories of those acting lessons came back. He started to enjoy himself. Partly it was the space and the quiet and the clean air of the place, all treats for a kid from Thunder City. But mostly it was the old thrill of dressing up and turning into someone new.

*

He spent each day in Desdemor preparing for the role of Tallis Noon. At dinner time he usually ate with Raven, and Raven made him stay in character, asking him what sights he'd seen on his way to meet the Noon train, what route he'd taken. Sometimes Raven took off in the *Thought Fox* on his mysterious travels, and then the Motorik were Zen's dinner companions— Nova, Carlota, and the hotel's physician, a dignified old Moto called Dr. Vibhat. They weren't much help with Zen's rehearsals. Nova was the only one who noticed when he made mistakes, and she seldom bothered to correct him. When Raven was there it was tougher, and Zen rose to the challenge, enjoying the game.

"And how are things at home, Tallis? How is your aunt Kalinda?"

"Still breeding those pterodactyls of hers. She found the genetic template in the deep archives. Uncle Bhasri says he's glad she has a hobby, but they're ruining the hanging gardens."

"Not bad, Zen. But you should work on your accent."

Zen worked on his accent. He worked on his look, too. He had a haircut from the hotel barber, and got Dr. Vibhat to alter his earlobes, which had been slightly larger than Tallis Noon's. He wore his new clothes every day, and even slept in them sometimes to crumple the newness out of them. He slung them on the floor, and crammed them into the battered traveling bags, which Nova fetched for him from the Terminal Hotel's lost property room. He wore them while he lounged on the hotel sofas, reading the texts that Raven gave him, watching the vids and holos, filling his head with the history of Golden Junction and the life and times of Tallis Noon. He dropped the fancy headset off his balcony and ran down to check that it still worked. It did: when he fitted it back under his hair and pressed the receiver against his temple, Nova's voice came whispering through the bones of his skull. When he double-blinked to activate the visual feed it transmitted images straight from his eyes to her clever mind.

"How are the clothes?" she asked.

Zen looked down at himself. Smartfiber trousers and the toes of his cherry-red boots. It felt odd to know that she was seeing what he was seeing, as if she were a passenger in his mind.

"Still too smart," he said. "Let's go to the beach."

*

So they went together, through the maze of Desdemor's canals, past dead shops and silent hotels. Each path they tried took them to another beach. Seaweed hung like bunting on the ornate railings of the promenades. Stairways led down into wave-slopping caverns, which, at low tide, became more prom-enades, automatic pop-up cafés unfolding from the ground like flowers. Zen liked the green-gold light, the clear air, the ocean. He even liked the Motorik girl padding along ahead of him, pointing out the sights.

He'd grown used to Nova. He'd even caught himself thinking sometimes that she was sort of pretty. He had squashed those thoughts fast—Zen Starling wasn't one of those sad, strange, lonely types who *fancied* Motos. But he liked her company, and she served as a stand-in for all the real girls he'd meet when he was far away and rich.

"*Tell me about when you were little,*" she said, inside his head.

"Why?"

"*Because I'm interested.*" She turned and faced him, smiling, speaking aloud now. "That's the difference between people like you and people like me. I've always been like I am now, but you were little once. The child you were is still inside you somewhere, peeking out through your eyes."

Zen snorted. "Not me. I had to grow up fast. I don't remember much."

But he did. The memories had been all around him during these days in Desdemor. He told her some of them as they walked on. He told her about his acting lessons, and the model trains he used to build and paint, and the view from the first bedroom window he remembered. He had never told anyone about that stuff before. He started telling her about Ma and Myka, but those were not comfortable memories; it made him miss the times when he had been too small to notice Myka's anger or Ma's madness. He had loved them then, but that had faded somehow, and he knew he was a disappointment to them. He talked about games he remembered instead.

"I used to play a game sometimes," said Nova, as if she were remembering some childhood of her own.

They stood on the promenade. The tide was out, the wet sand reflecting the green crescent of Hammurabi. "I'd walk way out there on the sand and start dancing," she said. "Flinging my arms about, whirling and twirling, laughing and shouting . . . And then the rays would notice me, and come swooping down. And I'd wait till the very last moment, then I'd drop flat and lie completely still, and the stupid things would go whooshing over me and flap about the beach, wondering where I'd gone. And I'd lie there still as a statue, laughing at them. They only strike at things that move. It's a funny instinct for predators to have evolved, but of course they didn't evolve, they were designed. Poor rays."

Zen had not yet seen the rays up close, although he had heard them calling. With no hunters to keep the population down, they were spreading inland from the offshore reefs, nesting in the penthouses of the abandoned towers at the southern end of the island.

"Let's try it," he said, in his best Golden Junction drawl.

"I don't think Raven would . . ." Nova started to say, but he had already scrambled over the railings, dropped down onto the sand, and started running toward the far white lacework of the surf. He thought that was what Tallis Noon would have done.

She ran with him. Each stride took them one or two yards. Their deep footprints filled quickly with water, a chain of little mirrors stretching away behind them to the promenade. They ran past tide pools and the wrecks of pleasure boats half buried in the sand. They were almost at the sea's edge when Nova shouted, "Zen!"

He looked round, and was startled by how close the ray was, how large, how silently it had come swooping down from its aerie in the old towers. Brown, it was, with patterns on its wide wings like the markings on spiders' backs. (The creamy speckles still held a blurred echo of some gene-tech outfit's corporate logo.) Its hooked beak opened to let out a fierce hoot, designed to freeze Zen's blood, or maybe announce to the flock following behind it that Zen was its prey and they would have to make do with the leftovers.

Then Nova crashed into him, knocked him flat. She didn't say anything, but her voice came into his head like the voiceover on a video, or the voices his mother heard. *"Lie still, remember!"*

So he lay as still as he could, half his face pressed into the wet sand, tasting the salt of Tristesse's ocean, smelling the hot leather stink of the ray as it swooped overhead, lashing its barbed tail. He wasn't pretending to be Tallis anymore. The shock had jolted him out of character.

Other rays followed the first, hooting in confusion as if to ask where their prey had gone. They flew away along the beach. The first one circled for a time, puzzled by those still forms on the sand, but too stupid to understand that they were the same running figures it had been hunting a few seconds earlier. After a while it gave one last disgruntled hoot and flew away after the rest of its flock.

When he was sure that the rays were gone, Zen sat up. From out there on the sand he could see the whole of Desdemor, the white facades of the waterfront buildings stretching southward like sea cliffs. At the southern end of the city, where he had never been, a high viaduct went out across the sea, reaching away and away into the haze that hid the horizon.

"What's that?" he asked. "I thought Desdemor was the end of the line?"

Nova shook her head. "It's the end of the K-bahn, but a single track line runs through the city and out across that bridge."

Zen shaded his eyes, looking at the viaduct.

"So there's another island out there somewhere?"

"I suppose so. It's not on the maps. I expect it used to be a hunting resort or something."

"We should go there and explore."

She grinned at him. "I'd like that. If there's time."

The tide had turned. Small waves came foaming round them. Keeping watch for rays, they hurried back across reflections of Hammurabi to the promenade.

*

Raven did not approve of the game with the rays. One of his drones, cruising above the beach, had recorded the whole thing. When Zen and Nova returned to the Terminal Hotel, wet and laughing, shaking the sand from the folds of their clothes, he scowled and said, "You're valuable, Zen Starling. You need to take better care of yourself."

"What about Nova?" Zen asked. "Isn't she valuable too?"

"You can't lie as still as she can. If one of those rays sees you it'll crunch you down like a biscuit. You won't be laughing then."

"I've got to pass the time somehow," Zen said, feeling cheeky and sure of himself, elated after the ray game. "How long are we waiting here anyway? How long till we go to meet the Noons?"

"Soon," said Raven. "Think you're ready?"

"Oh, I'm ready," said Zen, in a posh boy's voice, putting his hands in his pockets and standing in the lazy, laid-back way, which was how he played the part of Tallis Noon.

Raven just looked at him. Then he strode off to the hotel's gunroom and came back with a rifle. It was elegant and old-fashioned looking, with a wooden stock and ceramic barrel. "If you wanted to bait the rays," he said, "you should have taken this. A good marksman could bring down a ray from a mile away with one of these. Of course, you're not a good marksman, so you can link the gun's computer to that headset I gave you; Nova can do the aiming for you and tell you when to pull the trigger."

"I can manage," said Zen, although he had never even touched a gun before. Some of the kids in Cleave carried cheap, printed pistols, but he'd never bothered, because he could never imagine using such a thing. He was a thief, not a killer.

"You'd better take it with you on the Noon train," said Raven.

"You think I'll have to shoot my way out?" asked Zen.

"I think it's good to be prepared," said Raven, and showed him how to put his fingerprints into the ray gun's memory so that Zen was the only one who could make it work. "The Noons have big hunting reserves at most of their stations. You can tell them you're hoping for some sport. A young Noon carrying a vintage ray gun won't raise any eyebrows. The best place to hide something, Zen, is always in plain sight."

12

The first time Yanvar Malik killed Raven had been on Vagh, in a decaying mansion near the cobalt mines. It had seemed like a job for a drone, but Railforce had sent humans to do it: Malik and five others, slamming through the K-gates on a train called *Pest Kontrol*. The mission was top secret. There was a rumor that their orders came directly from the Emperor, and another that they came from the Guardians themselves.

Malik could still see the mansion's high ceilings, the elaborate plasterwork, the rotting muslin curtains through which the sun of Vagh had poured its sickly light. Could still see Raven rising from his chair, surprised when Malik burst in, and even more surprised when Malik shot him twice in the chest and then one more time in the head. The gravity low, the spent cartridge cases tumbling slowly through the air, the body falling in a leisurely way.

A few days after that they killed Raven again, in a resort on Galatava. He looked surprised that time too. But from then on the mission grew more difficult. Railforce said that Raven would not dare to use the Datasea, but news always reached him somehow; he knew they were coming. Sometimes he ran—Malik remembered shooting him in the back as he sprinted away across the houseboat roofs of the watertown on Ishima Prime, and calling in a missile strike on Kishinchand that reduced Raven's speeding car to a stain on a mountain road. Sometimes Raven tried to bargain, or to bribe them. When that didn't work, he started fighting back. He'd killed two of Malik's comrades with a booby trap on Naga, and led them out onto a thin sea of methane ice on some dead-end, airless world where two more had gone crashing through into the burning cold depths. On Chama-9 he took out the *Pest Kontrol* with a terrifying virus that ate straight through its firewalls and destroyed its mind. (Malik made sure Raven died slowly and painfully that time. He had liked that train.)

It was just a mission, to begin with, but somewhere along the way it became personal. It wasn't just because Raven killed his comrades, and tried to kill him; lots of people had tried to kill Malik, and he didn't hate them for it. But to have to keep killing the same man over and over, to see that same face through his gunsight on world after world—it was like being trapped in a nightmare, or some weary, repetitive game.

And there was the feeling, too, that Raven had cheated. Malik was not a young man anymore. He could sense his body aging: wounds healed slower, and hard exercise made his joints ache. His hair was thinning fast. He was starting to realize that you only got one chance at life, and that his was half over. But not Raven. When Raven started to feel age slowing him down, he just discarded that body and cloned another. When Malik realized just how many chances he had had, in how many bodies, it started to be a pleasure to kill him.

"How come all your bodies look the same?" he'd asked Raven on Luna Grande before he shot him. "If it was me, I'd want all my clones to look different. I'd try out being different colors, different sexes."

Raven said, "I wanted to keep hold of my identity. If I saw a different face each time I looked in the mirror, I might forget who I was."

"You won't be anybody, soon," Malik pointed out, killing him again.

It certainly made his job easier, with only the one face to look for. There was only so much Raven could do with hair dye and e-makeup. Sooner or later, Malik always found him.

"Why didn't you do something *great*?" he complained, the time he killed Raven at the skid-ship regatta on Frostfall. "You could have made a difference. You just spent all that extra time partying and playing."

"I *tried* to make a difference," Raven said, looking ruefully down at the holes Malik's gun had just made in him. "That's why the Guardians sent you after me."

On Ibo, he said, "Whatever the Guardians told your masters about me, whatever they say I did, it's a lie."

But nobody had told Malik what Raven had done. They'd just said to kill him.

*

And at last they sent his team to Iskalan, put them on a space-ship, and blasted them way out into the blackness of that lonely system, where whole dark planets of hardware hung unmapped, data centers for the Guardians. There was a hollowed out asteroid there. They landed, and cut their way down through blast doors into a facility where hundreds of bodies lay in glass coffins frosted with flowers of ice.

Malik remembered the sound the ice had made, crackling under his glove as he wiped clear spaces on the coffin lids. Strange how these small details stayed with you. He remembered peering in through the glass, and seeing Raven sleeping there; the same face he had killed so many times. All the coffins were the same: hundreds of sleeping Ravens, filling the racks which covered the chamber's walls. Or maybe not sleeping, maybe just not yet alive. This was a storeroom, where Raven kept new bodies until he needed them.

"I don't see how he can ever download himself into these," said Lyssa Delius, the only other surviving member of Malik's original crew. "He doesn't exist in the Datasea anymore. What's to download? These are just meat."

"Railforce want them taken out anyway," said Malik. But the truth was, *he* wanted them taken out; he wanted every last one of those handsome, lifeless Ravens gone. They left enough demolition charges in that chamber to vaporize the whole asteroid.

And when they got back to the station at Iskalan, they were told the mission was over. Whatever Raven had done, the Guardians were satisfied that his punishment was now complete. He was finally dead.

So they had a sad little celebration in a station bar, remembering lost comrades and recalling battles that they could never talk about to anyone else. And then they went off to other units, other lives. As far as Malik knew, none of the others had been troubled by nightmares. None of the others had felt that sense of something unfinished, loose ends left hanging. The Guardians had said Raven was dead, so Raven must be dead.

Malik got a promotion. He got himself a husband, a house on Grand Central, a cat. But the feeling wouldn't fade, and in his dreams he kept on killing Raven. He got a divorce, a posting to a long-range patrol train out on the branch lines. And slowly he started to notice things. A witness to a robbery at a biotech plant on Ashtoreth who described a tall, pale man, and another on the far side of the Network two years later who saw someone who sounded like the same man the night a trainload of construction equipment went missing from the rail yards on Nokomis. Both robberies impossible; the security systems that should have stopped them wiped by viruses that left no trace, the cameras recording no image of the thief.

Raven was still alive. He had convinced Railforce and even the Guardians themselves that he was dead, but one last version of him was still alive.

Malik hated leaving a job unfinished. He started collecting any report that might point to Raven, trying to find evidence that would convince someone. But there was never any evidence: just hints and whispers. Just a drunk on Changurai who claimed to have seen a Moto girl in a red raincoat come out of a blocked-off passageway, which led down to the old Dog Star Line. Just a street thief called Zen Starling who claimed to know nothing about Raven, and then vanished.

Zen Starling is the only lead I have, he thought. *What does Raven want with a street thief?*

The pictures his drone had caught of the kid in Ambersai and Cleave had been lost along with his train, along with the scraps of information poor Nikopol had found. All Malik had to go on were his memories. *Zen has a sister who works in the refineries.* If he could just find out what Raven wanted with the boy, the puzzle might start to make sense. And the only way to do that was the old way: talking to people, piecing things together.

He stared out of the carriage window, taking one last look at the tasteful towers of Grand Central. The train gathered speed, carrying him toward the K-gate that would take him back to Cleave.

13

The next day was clear and still. Hammurabi so crisp in the morning sky that Zen felt he could reach out and touch it from the balcony of his room. A day to go exploring down that old southern viaduct, he thought, and was surprised at how happy that made him. He ran downstairs to find Nova.

But Raven was waiting in the breakfast room with news. "Zen! It's time to go! Get your luggage together. We're leaving for Surt."

So that was that. Zen's time in Desdemor was ending just as suddenly as all his other peaceful times. Something fluttered in his stomach like dry leaves as he followed Raven and Nova across the empty station. He knew that feeling. Stage fright.

"What if the real Tallis Noon shows up?" he asked. He had thought of that a few times, but dismissed it because—well, what were the chances? Now the danger seemed quite real. "What if the real Tallis boards the Noon train while I'm there already, pretending to be him? What then?"

Raven waved his words away. "You think I hadn't thought of that? You think I haven't mapped out all the twists and turns this thing might take? Tallis was at Przedwiosnie last week, just a few stops up the line from Adeli. He probably did have plans to meet the Noon train. But he got delayed. A girl called Chandni Hansa got on the same train. Very pretty. She and Tallis got talking. They got off at Karavina. Do you know Karavina? It's romantic. Houses on stilts. Moonlight on the vapor lakes. Chandni will make sure Tallis has a long stay there."

"How can you know that?"

"Because I paid her to," said Raven.

"Okay," said Tallis uneasily. So he wasn't Raven's only hireling. He wasn't sure how he felt about that. And what did "a long stay" mean? Pretending to be Tallis Noon had made him feel oddly close to the real Tallis Noon, as if they were brothers or something. Was Tallis really enjoying a romantic stopover on Karavina? Or was he lying on the bottom of one of those vapor lakes with a knife in his back? And was that how Zen would end up, too, once he was no more use to Raven?

They had reached the platform. The *Thought Fox* opened its carriage doors for them. Raven turned and laid his thin hand on Zen's arm. His eyes were kind, his smile precise. "It's going to work, Zen. We'll all get what we want. I'll have the Pyxis, and you'll be rich."

"What about Nova?"

"Nova's just what you're taking with you instead of burglar's tools," said Raven.

But later, when the *Thought Fox* was stitching its way through space-time's raggedy fabric, Zen saw that Nova already had what she wanted. Her eyes were on the windows, waiting for the glimpses of new worlds that opened up sometimes between the long underground sections as the *Thought Fox* roared through the K-gates. Nebulae setting over deserts of white sand or refuse floating in a derelict canal, she watched it all with a look that was almost hungry. In her own way, she was a railhead too.

*

The Dog Star Line ran deep beneath the other platforms at Surt station. The elevators that had led to it were all decommissioned, and the stairways that once served it were sealed off and forgotten. Even the tunnel through which the old line ran was blocked by a ferro-ceramic barrier. The *Thought Fox* sensed the obstruction ahead as soon as it came through the K-gate. It did not slow down, just unfolded a big gun from either side of its hull, blasted the barrier into pieces, and shouldered aside the smoking fragments.

It was not a train that said much, or sang for joy as it sped along, the way that other trains did, but after it had smashed that barrier it laughed softly to itself. The deep, unsettling sound gurgled out of the speakers in the carriage ceilings, startling Zen, who sat perched on the edge of his seat, impatient for the journey to be over. The *Fox*'s weapons were still extended when it pulled in at a deserted underground platform a few minutes later.

"I will wait for you on Sundarban," Raven told his passengers. "You will be alone from here on, Zen, but Nova has everything that you need."

For a moment he looked almost fatherly. But when they were crossing the dead platform and Zen looked back to see him watching from the carriage door, he had no expression at all. The guns of the *Thought Fox* tracked to and fro, aiming at abandoned snack kiosks and the footbridges that spanned the rails, as if the old train were seeking new targets to destroy.

PART TWO
NETWORK EMPIRE

14

Threnody Noon was bored. She had been bored for days, but today was the first time she had felt able to admit it to herself. After all, she had been looking forward to this trip for months. She had been tired of living at home, in the quiet coral house beside the lakes on Malapet, where her mother painted flowers and uploaded data-prayers to the Guardians, which the Guardians never bothered answering. She had yearned for the bustle and excitement of life on her father's train. But once she was aboard it—once she had grown used to the splendor of the carriages and the glamour of the other passengers—she had started to feel discontented almost at once. Her father kept introducing her to people as "my daughter, Threnody," but anyone could see she wasn't one of his official daughters. His short marriage to Threnody's mother had been designed simply to seal a business deal between his family and hers. He would never have invited Threnody aboard his train at all, except that she was almost of marrying age herself now, and he wanted her to seal another business deal, by marrying Kobi Chen-Tulsi, the heir to a Sundarbani asteroid-mining company.

Kobi was also on the Noon train that season, and he bored her too. Sometimes, when she thought about having to marry him, having to live with him for years to come, Threnody wished she'd not been born a Noon at all. It was almost frightening— except that Kobi wasn't frightening, just dull. Curled up on her bunk in the speeding train, she thought, *I'm still a girl.* She was seventeen, but she didn't feel any different to how she'd felt when she was twelve. *I don't want to be engaged,* she thought. *Not to Kobi Chen-Tulsi, not to anyone. I want to see the Network first.*

She *was* seeing the Network, of course. The worlds of the Silver River Line rushed by outside her window; K-gates spilled their colorless light over her. Each time the train stopped, excursions were arranged: picnics and fishing trips, ancient fortresses and famous mountains. But somehow, that didn't seem to count.

So when the train reached Adeli, she pretended to be tired, and stayed behind while all the others went roaring off to hunt and party on the island peaks. She told herself she would have fun on her own. But she was still bored, and when the train announced that it had a message from a young wandering Noon, asking to come aboard, it felt like the first interesting thing that had happened in a thousand light years. Tallis Noon, from Golden Junction. She knew nothing about that branch of the family. She walked through the pillared carriages and met the Motorik manservant whom the train had dispatched to greet the new arrival.

"Don't worry," she said, "I'll meet him myself."

*

Adeli was a world of mists. Life took place on mountaintops, and all around them stretched seas of flickering fog: natural cloud chambers through which passing particles drew their sudden, shining trails. Stilt-walking its way across the fog to the summit-city of Adeli Station came a viaduct, and along the viaduct the Noon train was snaking. Lighted observation domes glowed under the evening sky, and from a hundred extravagant little turrets on the carriage roofs flew the imperial standard and long banners bearing the smiling sun logo of the House of Noon.

Zen had been studying pictures and vids of that train. He had memorized the floor plans of the main carriages, the doors, and access hatches. None of that had prepared him for how beautiful it looked. He stood among trainspotters and excited children on the platform and simply stared as the train pulled in. Those huge twin locos, the *Wildfire* and the *Time of Gifts*, had been in the Noon family for centuries. Their curved and complicated cowlings had been in and out of fashion so many times that they had finally escaped it altogether and were just themselves: grand, ancient, honey-colored things with the worn beauty of old buildings. Behind them were the five huge double-decker carriages that formed the quarters of the Emperor and his inner circle. And behind those, curving away out of the station and across the viaduct, were lesser carriages, all just as beautiful.

"Zen?" said Nova, in his head. She stood just behind him, ignored by the other sightseers. *"I have sent a message to the Noon train to let them know that you are here, and that you wish to board."*

He looked back at her, but she was playing the part of his meek Motorik servant, and would not meet his eye.

He was playing a part too, of course. The rehearsal was over; the performance was about to begin. He was wearing a short jacket of smart vinyl, currently tuned to default black. A black knitted shirt, cut low enough to bare his collarbones. Narrow trousers. Square-toed boots. Catching his reflection in the Noon train's windows, he felt pretty confident that he could pass as Tallis. He definitely didn't look like Zen Starling anymore.

He nodded to show Nova that he had understood, and started to move along the platform. Low-status guests like him would board farther back. Nova followed, carrying his bags. Carved friezes ran along the sides of the train, and children were scrambling up onto them from the platform, stroking the heads of sculpted animals. From the benign way the train's maintenance spiders watched them, Zen could tell that the *Wildfire* and the *Time of Gifts* didn't mind, and even welcomed these small visitors. He wondered what would happen to any child who tried using the *Thought Fox* as a plaything . . .

"Tallis?" said someone nearby.

All the way from Desdemor, Zen had been reminding himself, *My name is Tallis Noon, my name is Tallis Noon,* but the sight of the Noon train had driven it right out of his head. Nova saved him, pinging an alert at him through his headset and saying aloud in a soft, respectful voice, "Tallis?"

He looked round, finally remembering who he was meant to be, and found a young woman at his side, smiling like he was the best thing she'd seen for weeks. A girl, really, he told himself, when he'd stopped being dazzled by that smile. No older than he was, but a lot better turned out. Her hair was short and fashionably turquoise. Her skintight shimmersuit flowed with patterns of peacock's feathers, and her boots seemed to be coated with gold leaf.

She smiled at Zen some more and said, "I'm Threnody." She

put her hands together and bowed her head. "We're cousins of some sort, about a zillion times removed . . ."

He had read a bio of her back in Desdemor. He wondered why she would bother coming down from her fabulous train to meet a random railhead.

"I'm pleased to meet you, cousin Threnody," he said.

She took his arm and kept smiling as she led him through the cordon of guards and along the platform, past the big, shining wheels of the imperial train. Nova followed, carrying Zen's bags. "Your message reached us as soon as your train came through the K-gate," Threnody said. "I'm sorry everyone else is busy. There was a picnic this evening, and a hunt . . . Dusk is the prettiest time on Adeli, don't you think?"

Beyond the station, the fog-sea flickered with pale fire. He could see lights on the peaks that rose from it, and heard a tiny crackling, which might have been distant gunshots. Despite all his preparation he was feeling a little dazed; the beauty of the night, the train, the girl—this job was nothing like raiding stalls in Ambersai.

"It's a pity you didn't send word ahead with an earlier train," Threnody was saying. "The family would have arranged a proper welcoming committee."

"I didn't want to make any fuss," he said. "I didn't know I was coming here anyway. Not for sure, I mean. I've been traveling, looking around . . ."

"*Careful with the accent,*" said Nova, in his head. "*You're starting to sound like a comedian playing posh in the threedies . . .*"

Threnody Noon said, "You've really changed!" Which made Zen's heart stop beating for a moment, because Raven had promised him that nobody on the Noon train knew Tallis Noon. Then she went on, "The last time we met we were both just babies. At the fire festivals on Khoorsandi? I've seen pictures. You were as fat as a dumpling."

Zen laughed as lightly as he could, and said that he didn't remember, which of course he didn't.

"So you're from Golden Junction?" asked Threnody, and, without leaving time for him to answer, "I've never visited the eastern branch lines, it must be so interesting. Do you have Station Angels out there? We don't get them in the central Network; I'd love to see one—is it true they look like actual angels?"

She was steering him toward a carriage a little way down the train, and one of those white boarding stairs where uniformed Motorik waited. They were stupid-looking security goons, but behind those masklike faces their minds would be linked to whole carriages full of hardware. If Zen's face or the way that he walked didn't match whatever records of Tallis Noon that hardware held, his visit would end here. The gun drones circling the station could probably laser him off the platform like a splodge of chewing gum.

But Threnody Noon didn't even give the Motos a chance to scan him. "Family guest," she called, adding some command in a corporate code, and the nearest of the goons saluted and stepped aside so that she could lead Zen aboard the train.

"Don't they want to check me?" he asked, surprised.

"Anyone can see you're a Noon, Tallis," she said, laughing. "We can always bend the rules for family."

Zen shrugged, and laughed with her. So far, this imposter business mainly seemed to consist of laughing to order, which he felt he could cope with. He had a nasty moment a few seconds later, when he looked back from the top of the stairs and saw the security goons stop Nova, but Threnody told him that they were just scanning his bags and checking his Motorik's mind for viruses.

They didn't find any. Nova had made sure her upgrades and personality tweaks were well hidden. As for the bags, there was nothing in most of them but crumpled clothes, and a few items that Raven had added to make it seem like they'd come from Golden Junction. The only one the goons bothered opening was the long leather case that held the ray gun.

"I was hoping to find time for some shooting," said Zen.

"That's a pretty old-fashioned gun, isn't it?" asked Threnody.

"It was my grandfather's. It's a ray gun."

"We'll be stopping at Jangala soon. I don't know if there are any rays there, but there'll be all sorts of other things to shoot in the hunting reserve . . ."

The goons closed the gun case. Nova picked it up along with the rest of the bags, and came up the stairs to join Zen and Threnody on the open balcony at the rear of the carriage.

"What's wrong with your Motorik's face?" Threnody asked.

"They're meant to be freckles," Zen said. "She thinks they make her look more human."

"She sounds glitchy. Would you like a new one?"

"Oh, I'm used to Nova," he said.

She gave him a smile that meant "suit yourself," and turned to go into the carriage. The door had no handle, only a gilded, smiling sun mounted in its center. Threnody tapped the sun lightly between its eyebrows and the door opened so suddenly and so silently that it was as if it had simply vanished. Zen smelled the perfumed air of the Noon train. He looked past Threnody into the pillared carriage.

"*It's beautiful!*" said Nova, in his head.

"It's beautiful," he agreed, aloud. At first he was not sure why he felt sad and then he knew. Just for a moment, he had believed that he was really Tallis Noon, and that this beautiful girl was really welcoming him aboard this beautiful train. That would have suited him pretty well. It was the life he'd have had if his mother had never stolen him from the Noons.

But there was no point feeling sorry for himself. No one was going to hand him riches on a silver plate. He was going to have to take them for himself. He was good at that. He was going to rob these people, and get away clean.

He stepped into the train.

15

He had arrived at a good moment. Later he would wonder if Raven had arranged that somehow, but probably it was just luck. Most of the imperial family and their guests were at the picnic, on one of those wooded mountaintops that rose from the fog-sea. Zen had a chance to see the central carriages of the Noon train empty, except for the Motorik staff and the silent cleaning machines, which didn't count. Threnody's voice echoed as she led him from one carriage to another: carriages walled with gold mosaic, with livewood bark, with horn. Carriages of glass, like rolling greenhouses, filled with moss and small trees, where pretty dragonflies darted and hovered.

None of these carriages looked much like any train Zen had seen before. They were no wider than a usual train—just twenty feet wall-to-wall—but they had been decorated by the best designers on the Network, and the best designers on the Network knew how to make a twenty-foot-wide carriage look much bigger. Only the rows of windows told you that you were not in

PHILIP REEVE

a luxurious house, and even the windows were mostly curtained, or screened with blinds. Some of the carriages were open-plan, with chairs and tables dotted across an expanse of carpeted or livewood floor. In others, you walked along corridors, past the doors of smaller, private rooms. Floors of marble, ceilings of biotech tortoiseshell and mother-of-pearl, stairways spiraling to bedrooms and observation domes on upper decks.

Threnody led him up one of the stairways, to the cabin that was to be his. "It's one of the smaller guest compartments, I'm afraid. I hope you like it. The bedroom is in there . . . Bathroom over here . . . Put the bags down, Nova, and report to the Motorik section, carriage fifty-nine."

Nova did as she was told. As she walked away along the train, her voice came whispering into Zen's head again. *"Keep your headset on. If you need me, all you have to do is whistle. You know how to do that, don't you?"*

Threnody waited while he unpacked a few of his things. Then they returned to the lounge carriages, the garden carriages. He tried to tell Threnody about his travels—he had prepared a whole store of anecdotes—but she preferred to talk about the family and the various friends and relatives who were traveling with them. "The Albayek-Noons from Seven Badger Mountain are on board—they're always fun, though Ruichi is giving himself terrible airs now that he's signed the engagement contract with the Foss boy. And Uncle Tibor was here, but he's gone back to Grand Central . . ."

"So how many passengers altogether?" asked Zen.

"About nine hundred, at the moment, I think."

That was good, he thought. With so many guests coming and going, who would worry about one extra? And they had so much stuff that they probably wouldn't even notice when he helped himself to the Pyxis. Maybe he could grab a few things for himself while he was at it, fill his pockets with ornaments before he left, just in case Raven didn't pay up . . .

"Which carriage is the art museum in?" he asked. (He already knew, because Raven had made him study 3-D maps of the whole train, but he didn't want to *sound* like someone who had been studying 3-D maps of the whole train.)

"Oh, farther back somewhere," said Threnody, not much interested in any work of art that she couldn't actually wear.

"I'd like . . ." he said, and then—because it sounded more Noonish somehow—"I'd *love* to have a look at the collection while I'm here!"

Threnody wrinkled her nose. Even when wrinkled it looked better than most noses. She said, "It's only old pots and holographs and stuff. I'll show you round some time if you like."

"No time like the present . . ." Zen started to say, but, just then, swift shadows came darting across the curtained windows. Expensive skycars were swooping over the viaduct, settling onto the platforms of Adeli Station like rare birds. The rest of the family had returned.

The train began to fill with them. They came aboard in groups, talking and laughing, grabbing flutes of spiced wine from Motorik waiters who appeared silently to meet them. Noon elders, splendid in their robes and turbans, discussing business and telling each other the latest scandals. Officers of the CoMa, the family's Corporate Marines, strutting in their ornate uniforms. Provincial Stationmasters and their families, traveling on the Noon train as the Emperor's guests, as awed as Zen by all this splendor. Young Noons in hunting gear, boisterous as puppies. Zen wondered what it must be like to be one of them and have nothing to worry about except potting expensive bioteched animals in the family reserves. It seemed to suit them. They seemed happier and better looking than any of the kids he knew in Cleave.

He moved through the suddenly busy carriages with Threnody, while she introduced him to this relative and that. This was her aunt, Lady Sufra Noon. This was her Uncle Gaeta, her cousin Neef. This was her half sister, Priya, proud and nervous as a high-bred racehorse, wearing a dress made of light, the straps of her biotech sandals twining up her brown legs like silver ivy. This proud little kid in his miniature CoMa uniform was her half brother, Prem. Oh, and here was their father, Mahalaxmi XXIII, Chief Executive of the Noon Family, Emperor of the Great Network, Master of the Thousand Gates, known to his adoring subjects as the Father of the Rails and to the less adoring ones as the Fat Controller.

A strangely unreal moment. The jowly and intelligent face, which had solemnly smiled at Zen from a thousand grubby banknotes, smiled solemnly now at him in real life, close enough that he could smell the imperial sweat beneath the expensive imperial perfume. Electric-blue hummingbirds no larger than Zen's thumb hovered around the Emperor on blurred wings, settling sometimes to perch like ornaments on the epaulets of his tunic. They studied Zen so intently with their black eyes that he realized they were not birds at all, but camouflaged security drones. Surely they would see straight through his disguise? Surely Mahalaxmi would guess that this hand he was shaking belonged to a Thunder City urchin?

But no; he just nodded, welcoming Zen as he must have welcomed a hundred other distant relations that week. "How are things at Golden Junction, Tallis? You must tell me all about it," he said, and moved on in his cloud of blue birds without waiting for a reply. Zen didn't interest him, and Zen was glad of that. He wasn't there to be interesting. He wanted to be just another face in the crowd.

But one of the guests was interested in him. This was a lad of Zen's own age, tall and chunky, with a mane of hennaed hair, and the violet eyes that were fashionable that season. He didn't like Zen at all. "Who's your new friend, Threnody?" he asked, and squared up to Zen like he was getting ready for a fight while she explained. Zen wondered what he could have done to offend him. Had he met the real Tallis Noon before, as Threnody had? Had Tallis pulled his stupid hair when they were children? Zen could see how tempting that might be.

Then Nova, in his head, said, *"He's Kobi Chen-Tulsi. The Chen-Tulsis run mining operations on a couple of Sundarban's moons. Kobi is scheduled to be married to Threnody Noon next autumn."*

That explained the way Kobi was glaring at him, thought Zen. Threnody and this rich, pretty boy of hers had had an argument. That's why she hadn't joined the hunting party, and that's why she had come to meet him at the station. She had just been using Zen to make Kobi jealous.

It seemed to be working.

"Golden Junction?" sneered Kobi. (Threnody had just told him where cousin Tallis came from, and he was making the most of it.) "I didn't know the Noons still had assets way out there. There's nothing there, is there?"

Zen just smiled like he wanted to be friends and said, "Not much. Not compared with this train. It's amazing! Did the hunt go well? Threnody tells me you're an excellent shot."

Kobi looked puzzled for a moment. Angrily puzzled, as if he thought Zen might be mocking him. He was a simple creature, thought Zen. Just a big dog, snarling to defend his territory.

But he had shown Zen one useful thing, at least. The Noons of Golden Junction were seen by this lot as hopeless hicks. Country cousins, clinging onto the outermost twigs of the family tree. Nobody on the Noon train would think it strange if Tallis seemed nervous amid all this splendor.

He moved aside to make sure that Threnody and Kobi had a chance to talk, and hopefully sort out whatever it was that they had fought about. Lifting the blind on the nearest window, he saw that the station had vanished. The train had started moving so gently that he had not even noticed it set off. Now it was snaking its way through mountains, above valleys of flickering fog.

"Are you all right?" asked Nova, in his head.

"I'm fine," he lied, knowing she was probably monitoring his heart rate and things and knew exactly how nervous he had been. "Security is pretty laid-back, considering he's the Emperor and everything."

"Don't you believe it," said Nova. *"That gnat bite on your wrist?"*

Zen hadn't even noticed that he had been scratching it. "What about it?"

"That wasn't a gnat. A micro-drone took a sample of your blood the moment we came aboard, so the train could check you had the Noon security tags written into your DNA."

"And what if I hadn't?"

"It would have—well, you did, so why worry about it? Just relax. Enjoy yourself. I'm enjoying myself. I love this train."

Zen smiled. He loved it too. What railhead wouldn't? Above the chatter of the Noons and their guests he caught a sound, a high double note, a duet that echoed from the mountainsides as the train went by. The *Wildfire* and the *Time of Gifts* were filling the fog-lit night with trainsong.

16

On the walls of a factory in Cleave's industrial zone, a forest was growing. Trees spread their pale limbs across the old ceramic. Orchids glowed like small suns through the city's drizzling rain.

Flex didn't mind the drizzle. The paintsticks that she used were meant for decorating the hulls of trains. If their pigment could survive passing through a K-gate, it was not going to come to any harm in the thin rain of Cleave. She selected a bright blue from the bag at her feet and started sketching in a flight of butterflies, imagining the way their bright wings would wink with color in the crisscross shadows of the trees. The woman who ran this factory missed her home on far-off and jungly Jihana, and she had hired Flex to brighten the place up.

"I wish I could draw," said Myka Starling, standing behind the artist in her rain cape and wide-brimmed, dripping hat, watching the forest take shape.

"You can," said Flex. "Everybody can, really. Try! Help me. Draw a tree, over there . . ."

Myka shook her head. "My brain doesn't work like yours, Flex. My hands don't."

Myka was the one who had recommended Flex for this job, and she had taken to coming every night after work to watch the mural taking shape. It was calming, unlike home, where Ma had been more mad and anxious than ever since Zen ran off.

So she stood watching, while the paintsticks hissed, and Flex fetched fresh ones from her pockets, red and gold, sapphire blue. A strange bird unfurled its wings across the wall, opened its long beak to sing; you could almost hear it. Myka was puzzled by her friend's skills, and proud of her. She couldn't even imagine what went on in Flex's head, so different from her own. She was so entranced that it took her a few minutes to notice that she was no longer the only one watching.

A man stood in the shifting mist behind her. A small and wiry man, and an offworlder by the look of him, because he had no rain hat and the drizzle gathered on his bald head and ran down his face, down into the collar of his shabby blue coat.

Myka didn't know who he was, but she knew he was trouble. She turned to face him, squaring her big shoulders. There was enough of her to make two of him, and he seemed to recognize the danger he was in. A big black gun appeared in his hand like a conjuring trick.

"Railforce," he said. "Hello, Myka. How's that brother of yours?"

"If I knew, I wouldn't tell you," said Myka, watching the gun.

Flex, turning from her forest, said, "Myka, he's one of them. That night in the rail yards, when Zen disappeared, he's one of the Bluebodies who came off the armored train that broke down in the tunnel."

"Malik," said the man, lowering the gun a little, looking at

Flex. He was wearing some kind of military headset with small emerald lights on it that flickered. Flex, who didn't like people looking at her, seemed to shrink inside her baggy clothes.

"You must be the one who got Zen onto the tracks that night," said Malik. "You're a good painter. I see your stuff everywhere."

"Don't say anything," Myka warned her. Flex had secrets, a past that only Myka knew about, and Myka meant to keep it that way. She said to Malik, "Flex doesn't know what you're talking about."

Malik smiled. "Don't worry. I don't care about people painting on trains. I'm just trying to find your brother."

"Why?"

"Because I think he's in danger. He's been keeping bad company."

Myka snorted. "That sounds like Zen, all right."

"You know where he is?"

"No."

"You've had no messages from him?"

"No."

"Did he ever mention somebody called Raven?"

"No."

"Does he have any special skills?"

Myka shrugged. "Stealing things. Sleeping. Getting on my nerves. He's all right. He's not a bad kid. He likes riding the trains. He's just a railhead, really."

"Ever see him talking to a Moto? One that looks like a girl?"

"In a red coat? It came to our place the night he left, asking questions. Like you. That's when Zen took off. He climbed out the window rather than talk to it. We don't like Motos in Cleave."

"Of course," said Malik. "You had those riots, didn't you?

Smashed up all the wire dollies you could catch. I expect anyone who talked to a Moto round here would be in for a world of trouble with their coworkers."

"What's that supposed to mean?" asked Myka, stepping toward him.

He raised the gun again, just a little, to remind her that he had it. He smiled half a smile. "Do you have any pictures of your brother?" he asked. "Can't find his image in the Datasea."

"Our ma always told us not to put anything about ourselves there. She said the Guardians or somebody would use it to trace us."

"Wise advice, that," said Malik. "Maybe I need to have a word with your ma."

"You leave her alone. She can't help you."

"But you can."

Myka scowled. After a moment the images started pinging from her headset to his: images of Zen, looking younger and happier than he had that night on Malik's train. He nodded his thanks, and pinged back his contact address. "If you hear from him, you'll send me word."

He was turning away, fading back into the rain and the dying light.

"You won't catch him, Bluebody!" shouted Myka. "He's sharp, that brother of mine."

Malik didn't look at her, but his voice came back to her as he strode away. "You'd better hope I'm sharper, then. For his sake."

*

Malik rode the next train out of Cleave. He wasn't sure where he was going, but it didn't seem to wise to stay, in case the local newsfeeds worked out he was the same old fool whose dead train had blocked the K-gate the other day. Anyway, traveling soothed him: the movement and the passing views. Like Zen Starling, he was just a railhead really.

He flicked again through the pictures Myka had given him. It was his first good look at Zen. The kid was too young to have been part of Raven's crew for long. Probably just being used, the way Raven always used people, like pieces in a game. When Malik had talked to him he had been dirty, frightened, it had been dark. In the photos the boy was smiling and relaxed, or caught mid-movement, turning, speaking. He didn't look much like his sister, Malik noticed. But he looked like *somebody*.

He blinked the file of photos shut and opened a window to the local data raft. The train was on Tusk by then; the logos and jingles of Tuskani newsfeeds filled his head. He swiped them aside until he found what he was looking for: a report from Grand Central, where Senator Tibor Noon, the Emperor's twin brother, was making a speech. Tibor looked as sulky as ever about being born three minutes after Mahalaxmi and not inheriting the throne himself. His chubby face was still handsome, the strong features and good bone structure of the Noon family as distinctive as corporate branding . . .

"Oh Guardians!" said Malik suddenly. (The woman in the seat across from him smiled, thinking he must have just hit a hard level in an online game.)

He swung through the data raft, calling up other images: of Emperor Mahalaxmi himself, of his children and his ancestors. He compared them to his images of Zen Starling.

Then he shut down the headset, took it off, and sat there watching the worlds go by, and wondering.

What did Raven want with a boy who could pass for a Noon?

17

Next day, the Noon train called at Burj-al-Badr and Tu'Va. There were speeches by the Emperor, and declarations of loyalty from local senators and Stationmasters, some of whom joined the train for the rest of the journey to Sundarban.

On Burj-al-Badr, that desert world, the K-gates were not buried deep in tunnels, but stood naked in the open air. From one of the Noon train's observation domes, Zen saw the ancient archway, which spanned the tracks ahead, like the fossilized wishbone of some immense, metallic bird. A curtain of energy rippled like heat haze under the curve of it, and into this haze the locos and forward carriages were vanishing. The passengers at the front of the train were already looking out at Tu'Va, hundreds of light years away . . .

On Tu'Va there was an outing to see the Slow River Falls, where a famous cataract of liquid glass dropped over towering cliffs. Zen stayed on the train, hoping to find Threnody and remind her of her promise to show him the collection. Only after the flyers had left for Slow River did he find out that Threnody had gone with them.

He mooched up and down the train anyway, while it wound its way through the Tu'Va uplands toward the rendezvous point where the sightseers would rejoin it. He found the carriage where the collection was housed, but it was locked, and Nova did not think it would be wise to draw attention to himself by asking for it to be opened. He went on down the train instead, and wound up staring at the fish in an aquarium carriage and making small talk with a few of the other passengers ("Very fine trilobites. My auntie breeds pterodactyls at home on Golden Junction. Oh, me? I'm just riding the rails . . .").

*

That evening, when the flyers had returned and the train was powering its way toward the next K-gate, a Motorik in Noon livery brought an invitation to Zen's door. He was invited to dinner in the main dining car.

"What's this?" he asked Nova, when the Moto had gone. "Isn't that where the Emperor eats? Why do they want me there?"

Nova, speaking through his headset, said, *"It's a very grand dining car. Half the family dines there. I expect your new friend Threnody put you on the guest list. She fancies you."*

"No she doesn't."

"Zen and Threnody, sitting in a tree, K-I-S-S-I-N-G . . ."

"She's just using me to make Kobi jealous."

"Well, I bet she fancies you too. I would, if I were human."

Would she? Of course not; she was teasing—still, for a moment, he felt oddly pleased.

He made himself think about Threnody instead. He hadn't

seen her all that day, and was starting to fear that she had forgotten her promise about showing him the collection. Dinner might be daunting, but it would give him a chance to mention it again without looking too eager.

Only when he reached the main dining car, he found that he was not to be seated next to Threnody. She was up at the head of the long, long table, with Kobi and the Emperor and her sister, Priya. She didn't even glance at Zen when he took his seat at the unfashionable end, among cousins by marriage and provincial officials. His neighbor was an elderly woman: gray dress, gray hair, and a faint, watchful smile that made Zen wary. He looked at the carriage walls instead of her. They were windowless, and in their depths hung branching, abstract shapes like frozen lightning.

"They are called Lichtenburg Figures," the lady explained. "Made by firing streams of high energy particles through acetate."

"I know," Zen lied, remembering that he was supposed to know things like that. "I've just never seen any so *big* before."

"One gets so used to being surrounded by these beautiful things," she said. "It's good to have guests; they help us to see them again."

She took a turn looking at the walls, while Zen looked at her. She had a lean, lined face. Her eyes were not completely gray. There were flecks of gold in them, and they were as watchful as a hawk's.

"You are the young man from Golden Junction, aren't you?" she said.

Zen nodded, and tried to recall her name. Nova came to his rescue, whispering through his headset. *"She is Lady Sufra Noon, sister of the Emperor."* He remembered her now. She had been in the aquarium that afternoon; she had not been one of the people he talked to, but he had noticed her standing a little apart, listening in.

For a moment he felt completely certain that she had overheard him make some mistake. He was sure that she knew he was an imposter and had invited him to the Emperor's table in order to expose him.

"My dear . . ." she put her thin brown hand on Zen's wrist, "you are the image of my little brother Tarsim, when he was young."

He wasn't sure how to respond to that, but it turned out that he didn't need to: she just carried on talking.

"He rode the rails with our Corporate Marines, during the Spiral Line Rebellion. He died at the Battle of Galaghast."

Zen started to realize that he was safe. She was just a kind old lady. She had probably seen him looking lonely there in the aquarium and decided he would like to listen to her stories about the family. He made sympathetic noises, as if he cared about her long-dead brother, and looked down at the plate that a Motorik servant had just placed in front of him. It was made from some old-fashioned form of ceramic and he wasn't sure if the stuff on it was food or decoration. He copied Lady Sufra as she chose a delicate pair of silver tongs from the array of implements beside her plate and started eating.

Lady Sufra smiled. "It was a long time ago. And it is not such a tragedy to die young. At the time I thought it was, but now I understand that the real tragedy is growing old. My brother gave his life for a noble cause. If the Spiral Line Rebels had won, they would have put one of the Prell family on the throne. The last thing the Network needs is one of those degenerate Prells as Emperor."

Zen's plate was whisked away. In its place, the Motorik set

a seashell filled with pale, clear liquid. Some sort of soup? Zen selected a shallow spoon.

"Of course," said Lady Sufra, "I know that on some of the branch line worlds there is discontent. The Human Unity movement is gathering strength. People talk about getting rid of Emperors altogether. About defying the Guardians."

"I don't know much about politics," said Zen.

Sufra Noon watched him with her gold-dappled eyes. "But you must have some opinion, Tallis Noon. I hope you are not afraid to voice it? What is the feeling on Golden Junction?"

Zen hadn't rehearsed an answer to that.

"I think ordinary people don't much care who rules them," he said, improvising, giving her Zen Starling's opinion in Tallis Noon's voice. "Whether it's a Noon or a Prell or some Human Unity president, it won't make any difference in the streets of Cleave or the Ambersai Bazar. People just want to be left alone."

Lady Sufra looked into his eyes for a moment. Zen started to fear that he'd offended her. Then she laughed. "That is a most refreshing observation," she said. "Everyone else at this table would have told the old lady what they thought she wanted to hear. The Noons of Golden Junction must be a tougher breed. By the way, what do you think of the soup?"

Zen looked down at the shell. He had almost emptied it. "It doesn't taste of much."

She leaned closer, whispering, "That's because it is a finger bowl, Tallis. You are meant to wash your fingers in it before the next course arrives."

He blushed, horrified at his mistake, but she just smiled. It seemed she had taken a liking to him. "So tell me," she said, "what is it that you do, out there on Golden Junction?"

"I have been studying," he said. "Art."

"Ah! And have you seen our collection yet?"

"Not yet. But it's one of the reasons why I came here."

"Then I shall show you round myself. Tomorrow."

*

"Well," said Nova, her voice whispering in his head as Zen lay on his bed that night, lulled by the rhythm of the Noon train's wheels. *"You made a big impression on Lady Sufra. Smooth work."*

"I remind her of her dead brother. That's all."

"Well, her live *brother is the Emperor of the Network,"* said Nova, *"and she'll show you the collection herself. So that's useful."*

Zen lay in the dark and listened to the thrum of the engines, the steady beat of the wheels. The Noon train had passed through several K-gates, and he was not sure which world he was on. Part of him wanted to be up in the observation galleries, watching new sights go by. But he was tired after his performance, and he needed to rest, to keep his wits sharp for tomorrow. So he lay in the dark, and the headset gripped his scalp with a gentle pressure. After the strangeness of that long day it felt good to lie there alone and listen to Nova's familiar voice. He was glad he had a friend aboard, someone to whom he didn't have to lie. Maybe that was why Raven had sent her, he thought, to keep him sane.

"Where are you?" he asked.

"Right at the back somewhere, between the mobile garages and the luggage vans," she said. She sent pictures to his headset. The meek silhouettes of other Motorik stood motionless in half light all around her. She said, *"The Noon Motorik are useless, even worse than that lot at the Terminal Hotel. No conversation at all. They like doing as they're told, and powering themselves down when they come off duty."*

"So you're all on your own back there?" asked Zen, feeling sorry for her.

"I'm all right. I've been listening to the locos talking. The Wildfire and the Time of Gifts. They're wonderful! They're so old and so . . . They tease each other, and sing, and talk about old times, other worlds they've seen. I don't think they know I'm listening. It's sweet. People say they're twins, but they aren't. They're lovers. They come from different engine shops. They met on the Network. And they love each other so much . . ."

How can machines be in love? wondered Zen, but he was too embarrassed to ask. He said, "You should think yourself lucky you don't have to talk to the Motos. If I have to make polite conversation with many more of these Noons, I'm going to trip up. One of them will have met the real Tallis, or know something about him that I don't . . ."

"You're doing fine," said Nova. "I'm proud of you. Really."

Zen smiled. He knew that she was smiling too, back there among the sleeping Motorik. It felt intimate, this talk that they were having. As if she were lying there next to him. Which was a nice thought, he suddenly found. A memory of her came into his mind, laughing in the green-gold light of Desdemor while a wind from the Sea of Sadness blew her hair across her face. Yes, it was a very nice thought. He followed it a little way and then stopped, ashamed.

"Are you all right?"

"I need to get some sleep."

"Well, good night, Zen Starling," she said, just before he took off the headset.

He paused. "My name is Tallis Noon."

"Just testing."

"Good night, Nova."

"Good night."

18

He slept late next morning. It didn't matter. The Noons slept later still. Only Threnody seemed to be awake when he made his way along swaying corridors to the breakfast car. She was sitting alone at a table by a window. Her hair was still wet from a swim or a shower, and calligraphy scrolled down her screen-fabric dress, the words of some song or poem he'd never heard. He felt her watching him as he moved along the buffet, lifting this dish cover and that, wondering what Tallis Noon would eat for breakfast.

"Good morning," she called, when he turned her way. "Are you going to join me?"

"What would Kobi think about that?"

"It's nothing to do with Kobi who I choose to have breakfast with. He's asleep anyway. He drank too much at dinner."

Zen went and sat down at her table. Outside the window, an airless, black-and-white landscape was passing, dotted here and there with far-off lighted domes that looked like snow globes, each with a little city inside.

"Are you enjoying our train?" asked Threnody.

"Very much," said Zen. She had completely forgotten promising to show him the collection, he realized. Still, that didn't matter now. He asked, "How were the Slow River Falls yesterday?"

"Slow. Like a waterfall made of molasses, but more boring." She ate a mouthful of her breakfast, then said suddenly, "I expect you're wondering what I see in Kobi?"

Zen shrugged.

"He's an oaf. And he calls me Thren." She laughed, and impersonated Kobi's braying voice: "Thren! Thren!" Shook her head, looked at Zen under her blue fringe. "You must be wondering why I'd get engaged to him."

"None of my business," said Zen.

"Yes it is. You're a Noon, aren't you?"

"Yes. Of course."

"Well, you must care about the future of our family, then. In another few thousand years all our industrial worlds may be mined out, and since the Guardians can't make any more K-gates, the only way to get to new worlds will be through space. Kobi's family have been spacers for generations, mining asteroids and minor planets in the Sundarban system. An alliance with them will be very good for our family. And very good for me. I shall become the head of a whole new family branch, the Chen-Tulsi-Noons. We shall have our own seat in the senate."

"Sounds good," said Zen, though he didn't think it sounded worth marrying Kobi for. He'd always thought rich people were able to do whatever they liked, but Threnody was a lot like him in some ways, playing a role so she could get what she wanted. Only somewhere in her there was a remnant of the girl she'd been, who still daydreamed, now and then, of letting her family mind its own business and taking off along exotic branch lines with a raggle-taggle railhead like her cousin Tallis.

When he stood up to leave the carriage, he saw that Kobi had already arrived, and was glowering at him across the buffet. He waved, and dodged quickly past him to the exit, halfway to the next carriage before Kobi reached Threnody's table and said too loudly, "What was that Golden Junction monkey doing here, Thren?"

*

In the carriage that housed the Noon collection, the air was cool and still. As Zen stepped into the first big compartment, the walls lit up with fields of luminous color that shifted slowly up and down the spectrum. Lady Sufra was waiting there for him. Her eyes shone with amusement as he made his bow.

"So, Tallis. What do you think of our Karanaths?"

Nova whispered in his headset. *Quinta Karanath, a light-painter from the Orion Dynasty . . ."*

"They're wonderful," he said, blinking round at the light-blobs while he parroted the words Nova fed him. "They're early works, aren't they? She must have—"

"*He!*"

"He must have created these when he was still influenced by the hard-light abstractionists . . ."

Sufra Noon seemed pleased. Zen sensed that he had passed a test. She said, "I've always loved these early pieces best. The use of color is so very daring."

Zen looked at the pictures. He started to say something, thought better of it, then said it anyway. "At the freight yards on Cleave there are these taggers who run out across the tracks to spray their designs on the trains. That's what I call daring."

"I was forgetting what an original thinker you are, Tallis."

"The trains wear the best tags with pride, and carry them off through the K-gates to be seen on other worlds. There's one tagger called Flex. The locos love her stuff."

"Flex? What an extraordinary name." He had amused her again. "I shall be sure to look out for her work, next time I am at the station."

Zen wondered what Flex would paint on the *Wildfire* and the *Time of Gifts* if she was given the chance. Ivy and climbing roses, he imagined. Make the old locos look even older, give them the coats of moss and ferns that they ought to be clad in, if passage through the K-gates did not burn such things away. He smiled. How Flex would love this train . . .

Lady Sufra was beckoning him through into another compartment, where the holoportraits of a hundred long-dead Noons turned to watch them. "Is there anything in particular that you wished to see?"

"I think there are some pots—"

"*Ceramics,*" whispered Nova.

"I mean ceramics."

"Oh yes, my great grandmother, the Lady Rishi, was a keen collector. Most of the objects here were hers. Vases from Chiba, and some little animal sculptures called Wade's Whimsies, which are said to have come from Old Earth."

"Isn't there something called the Pyxis?" asked Zen.

One of Lady Sufra's eyebrows rose and curled. "So you have heard of *that* ugly old thing? They gave you a most extensive education, out there on Golden Junction."

They went left and right through a narrow maze walled with shelves of Chiban vases until they came to a compartment devoted to family history. There were medals and ceremonial weapons, a battle suit. Holographs hung in the air like faded flags: scenes from history, famous stations. Zen barely noticed them, because in one corner of the room a cone of light shone down from somewhere in the ceiling, illuminating a low plinth. On the plinth stood the Pyxis, looking even smaller and less impressive than it had in Raven's images.

His hand had reached for it before he knew what he was doing. His fingers hit a curved surface. What he had taken for a cone of light was actually a cone of diamondglass.

"Oh, we can't let people touch it!" said Lady Sufra. "It's a family heirloom."

Zen couldn't imagine anyone else wanting to touch the Pyxis. It didn't look as valuable or as pretty as the rest of the collection. It was almost defiantly dull.

"What is it, exactly?" he asked.

"No one is certain," said Lady Sufra. "The name means 'box,' but it doesn't open; it's solid. Art from some forgotten era, I suppose. My great grandmother obviously thought that it was important: she left strict instructions that it should never be removed from the train. Perhaps it comes all the way from Old Earth, like the Whimsies, though they are much more interesting—let me show you . . ."

She set a hand against the small of Zen's back, starting to steer him toward another exhibit, but as he turned away from the Pyxis, he caught sight of one of the holograms. It was a historical view, like a glimpse through a window into some summery world where flags were fluttering and feather-trees cast their shadows over people dressed in the fashions of centuries ago, gathered beside a huge golden train. Uniforms and feathered hats; camera drones splashed with the decals of forgotten media outlets. Among the crowds moved strange un-human figures, which might have been avatars of the Guardians or just actors dressed up. And there, watching it all with a glass in one hand and an expression of faint mockery that Zen knew well, was someone he recognized.

The same gray eyes, the same thin smile.

Raven.

He looked at the caption, a block of glowing letters to the left of the picture. "The Opening of the New Platforms at Marapur, Raildate 33-6-2702." Nearly three centuries ago.

So that couldn't be Raven, it was just someone who looked like Raven . . .

But not just a bit like Raven. *Exactly* like him. Zen enlarged that section of the image. Everything about that gaunt face was just as he remembered it, right down to the half-contemptuous half smile, eyes narrowed against the day, as if uncomfortable in sunlight.

"A big moment for our family," said Lady Sufra, turning back to see what Zen was looking at. "Look, there is Lady Rishi herself, standing beside the interface of Shiguri."

"It's a reconstruction?" he asked.

"Oh no. All the holos here are direct historical records, made at the time. It looks as though they had a nice day for it, doesn't it?"

Zen's mind did complicated little dances, trying to find other explanations and stumbling always over the obvious one—that Raven had survived somehow, un-aging, for centuries.

"Who—?" he started to say, but Lady Sufra had already seen what he was staring at.

"That is Dhravid Raven. He was a curious character. An artist, an industrialist. I remember seeing him at the imperial palace on Grand Central, when I was a little girl."

"But he must have been very old by then?"

"No, he looked exactly as he does in that holo. He was not human, you see. Oh, his *body* was human enough, but *he* was something else, something more."

"A Guardian?"

"More than a human, but less than a Guardian. His mind existed in the Datasea, but he downloaded copies of himself into these cloned bodies, just as the Guardians used to. Of course, Guardians wore many different bodies, but Raven always looked the same. Easier, I suppose—like only wearing black."

"What happened to him?"

"He was destroyed," said Lady Sufra. "About twenty years ago. He offended the Guardians in some way, so they deleted him. My father, Ambit the Fourteenth, was Emperor at the time, and the Guardians made him send troops to scour the Network for Raven's clones and kill them all. Good riddance, I thought. He was a bad piece of work by all accounts. Now come, there are some family portraits on the upper deck that I am sure will interest you . . ."

He followed her up the stairs at the end of the carriage, but the portraits didn't interest him. Nor did the Whimsies, or the netsuke, or the 4-D collages. He had to look at each of them and pretend to be interested and make the intelligent-sounding comments Nova told him to, and all the time the only things that he could think of were Raven and the Pyxis.

19

The Noons and their guests were gathering near the front of the
train for a recital by a group of musicians called The Mandlebröt
Set. The band was setting up its instruments in one of the
forward carriages, which had a glass floor. It was unnerving to
look down between your feet at nothing but the wheels and axles
and the track blurring by. There were always a few passengers
who were afraid to set foot in that part of the train.

Zen pretended to be one of them. He was in no mood for
music. He made his way back down the train, through lounges
where elderly Noons sat reading holoslates, through buffet cars
full of chatter and a recreation carriage where a rowdy game of
train-quoits was in progress, until he reached the biggest and
most densely planted of the garden carriages. There were no
formal beds here, just a path of ceramic paving slabs winding
over moss, through whispery groves of bamboo. If you ignored
the glimpses of an industrial world rushing past outside, it
looked almost real.

So did Nova, who stood waiting for him there.

"Meeting is dangerous," she said. "We should talk over the headset."

"Why?" he asked. "You're my Moto, aren't you? I can talk to you if I like." He was angry, and he needed to talk face to face. She was the only person he could talk to honestly on this train.

"You saw that holo Lady Sufra showed me?" he said. "It was Raven, wasn't it?"

She looked away. Nodded.

"Sufra said he was a Guardian . . ."

"He's not. Not exactly."

". . . or something like a Guardian, some sort of . . ." Zen made grabbing gestures, trying to snatch the words he needed from the air. "He lived for hundreds of years. Dozens of cloned bodies. And all the time the real Raven was a program running in the Datasea . . ."

"The Guardians tried to destroy him," said Nova. "They deleted every copy of him, and they had the Emperor send an assassination squad to kill his clones, and then they deleted every reference to him, so that it would be as if he had never existed."

That explained why Zen's swift search of the local data raft had thrown up almost no mention of Raven. "But they didn't delete references to that train of his," he said. "The history sites say that during the Spiral Line Rebellion, Railforce sent armored trains to seize stations that supported the rebels. The *Thought Fox* bombed the station city at Ukotec into dust, and sent its drones and maintenance spiders out into the ruins to slaughter the survivors. It even murdered its own crew when they tried to stop it. That's why it ended up abandoned—because it was mad, and it didn't care who it killed. Did you know that?"

Nova wouldn't even look at him. She said, "The *Thought Fox* respects Raven. He has it under control."

"Barely! Don't you remember in Cleave, how it shot up Uncle Bugs for no reason at all? If even his *train* is a war criminal, what does that make Raven?"

Nova was always surprising him. She surprised him now: her wide eyes, the almost-human way she flinched from the anger in him. "You mustn't wonder about Raven," she said. "Don't ask about him—"

"Why are you so loyal to him? He's programmed you to be loyal, I suppose?"

"I'm afraid," she said. "I'm afraid of what he'd do to you, if you let him down. He needs the Pyxis. You have to get it for him. That's all you should be thinking about."

The music from the glass-floored carriage came faintly through speakers somewhere: slow washes of sound that built and wavered and faded. The scurrying patter of small drums. Kotos, and soft gongs. The locos were singing along. Zen thought how nice it would have been to be alone in that garden with a real girl, Threnody maybe, instead of with a Motorik, discussing an impossible burglary.

He said, "I thought the Pyxis was just going to be sitting on a shelf. But it's stuck under a diamondglass cone. I'll have to smash it to get the thing out!"

"It's all right," said Nova. "There is a plan. Raven planned for this."

"Okay. Tell me Raven's plan."

She spoke flatly, as if she were reading something, as if she were just a machine, reciting a message it didn't understand. "Before it gets to Sundarban, the train must pass through the Spindlebridge. Spindlebridge is a space habitat built between two K-gates in—"

"I know what the Spindlebridge is."

"While it is there, you will go to the collection, and I will upload a powerful virus into the train's systems. It will disable all alarms, door locks, everything. You will take the Pyxis and leave the train. The Spindlebridge is in orbit around Sundarban. There are spacecraft—shuttles—housed in hangars on Spindlebridge's hull. We will take one, fly to the surface, and meet Raven."

Zen just looked at her. *That's* Raven's plan?"

"Yes."

"And he didn't see fit to tell me before?"

"He told me, and now I'm telling you. He said not to discuss it until you were here. He didn't want you to worry about it. He said he didn't want to distract you from your performance."

"He thought it might me worry me, did he? He thought I might be a bit nervous about stealing a spaceship?"

"I'm sorry, Zen—"

"Can you fly a spaceship?"

"They fly themselves, mostly."

"This virus he wants you to use," he said. "Is that like the one that he hit Malik's train with, back in Cleave?"

In a very small, reluctant voice, she said, "It's called a trainkiller."

Zen imagined it nested there behind her worried eyes, chains of dangerous code curled in her brain like sleeping snakes. He shook his head. "No. We can't do that. Not to the *Wildfire* and the *Time of Gifts*—"

"I don't *want* to do it," said Nova. "But that's what Raven—"

"Well Raven isn't here!" shouted Zen. "I'm running this thing, and I say we have to find another way!"

He had never stolen from anyone he knew before. The Ambersai shopkeepers he had robbed had been strangers; they'd had more stuff than him, so he'd never felt bad about taking some

124

of it. Well, the Noons had more stuff than him too—more stuff than all the shopkeepers in Ambersai together. A few days ago he would have said that they deserved to be robbed. But he liked Lady Sufra. He liked Threnody. He liked this beautiful train, those old locos. He didn't want to do any of them more harm than he had to.

In the middle of the most important job of his life, he seemed to be growing a conscience.

He said, "Why can't we just knock out the security in the carriage where the collection is?"

"The security programs are very old and very expensive and very good. If I took out that one, the *Wildfire* and the *Time of Gifts* would notice."

"Then you have to find a way to stop them from noticing."

"But—"

Zen reached out and held her by both narrow shoulders. "Listen. Here's the new plan. We wait until the train goes through the last K-gate from Spindlebridge to Sundarban. Then you'll open the door to the collection and kill the security systems there, very quietly, not harming the train or anybody else in any way. I'll take the Pyxis, and get off as soon as we reach the station. Hopefully we'll be back on the *Thought Fox* before the Noons even notice it's gone."

"That is a very simple plan," said Nova.

"Simple is good. No spaceships, no trainkillers, just swipe it and leave."

"Raven must have thought of that. There must be some reason why he decided on Spindlebridge instead—"

"Raven isn't here," said Zen again.

"Perhaps he knew I could not outwit the train's security systems—"

"You can," Zen said. "We are stopping at Jangala for three days before we head down to Spindlebridge and Sundarban. That gives you three days to come up with a way to get me into the collection. And I know you can do it. You're better than any security system. You'll find a way to fool them."

She smiled at the compliment. "I'll try."

"Good. Thank you."

Her face suddenly went bland again, becoming the calm mask of a well-mannered Motorik. Someone was calling Tallis's name. Zen turned and saw Kobi coming into the carriage. Behind him, in the vestibule between that carriage and the next, Threnody stood waving. She was wearing hunting clothes—a camouflage shimmersuit and kitten-heel combat boots.

Kobi was smiling, but his eyes darted suspiciously from Zen to Nova.

"You're pretty friendly with this wire dolly," he said. "Don't you have real girls on Golden Junction?"

Zen felt his face go hot. In Cleave, if someone hinted that you fancied Motos, you hit them. Even if you weren't a fighter and they were bigger than you. It was a matter of honor. But there'd be trouble if he broke Kobi's nose for him, so he just stood his ground and glared.

"I'm joking, Tallis!" Kobi said. He slapped Zen on the shoulder, slightly too hard to be friendly. "We're going hunting. Coming? Or are you scared of hunting, too? I heard you didn't have the stomach for the glass-floored carriage . . ."

"Hunting?"

"In the game reserve." Kobi jabbed a finger at the glass wall. The Noon train had passed another K-gate while Zen was talking to Nova, and he hadn't even noticed. Dense greenery was rushing past, falling away now and then to give views over folded, forested hillsides.

"We are approaching Jangala Station," said the soft voice of the *Wildfire*, or perhaps the *Time of Gifts*.

Kobi said, "Threnody says you brought a gun with you."

Zen turned and snapped his fingers at Nova as if she was a toaster or something, that needed switching on. "Go and fetch my ray gun from the luggage, Nova."

Kobi watched her leave the carriage. "There's something off about that wire dolly. What are those marks on her face?"

"Those are freckles."

"That's what I thought. You need to get her blanked and rebooted. I suppose you're too *fond* of her."

"She's a family heirloom," Zen said. "So's the gun. My grandfather used it for hunting reef rays."

He had hoped that would sound impressive, but Kobi said, "We aren't hunting *rays* today. The Jangala game reserve is stocked with heritage megafauna. All kinds of Old Earth critters re-created by the Noons' geneticists. It's the best collection anywhere on the Network."

He went to rejoin Threnody. Zen started to follow him, then saw Nova coming back into the carriage with the ray gun in its long case. He waited for her. "I don't have time for this," he muttered as she passed the gun to him.

"It will be all right," she promised.

Zen didn't want to leave her, but he didn't want to give Kobi any more cause to tease him about her either, so he simply nodded and went after the others. The train was slowing. Among the trackside trees grew the bulbous bio-buildings of Jangala Station.

The Noons loved their forests. The name of Sundarban, their main planet, meant "beautiful forest' in one of the ancestral languages, but billions of people lived on Sundarban, so most of that world had to be city and farmland. Jangala, on the other hand, was a pleasure planet, where towns were few, and everything that was not actual sea was covered with a sea of trees.

The Noon train pulled onto a long siding outside the station, and the passengers climbed down to stretch their legs, sniff the warm air, meet the local representatives, and ignore the crowd of excited trainspotters, which the guards were keeping at a respectful distance. Motorik servants descended from the rear part of the train with picnic tables, covered dishes, and gleaming stacks of crockery. Awnings were erected. Some carriages opened their roofs to reveal air-cars waiting there for any passengers who wanted to see Jangala from the skies. One extended a ramp to the trackside, and down this drove a silvery maglev car. It halted obediently in front of Kobi as he led Threnody and Zen off the train. They piled in, and it drove off with them, through the outskirts of the station city and away into the trees.

At first the way was wide and well marked, with clusters of smart hunting lodges growing like fruit in the treetops on either side. Then the road came to an end. Zen felt faintly alarmed. He was a city boy; he had never been anywhere like this before. The car went on for a few miles, cruising above maglev trackways laid under the soil. After that there were only footpaths.

The car parked itself, and a couple of small hound-drones detached from it and whirred around Kobi as he shouldered his pack and his spindly, lightweight gun. Threnody unpacked a similar weapon from one of the baggage lockers and shut her eyes for a moment, synching the rifle's targeting computer to her headset. Zen slipped a cassette of cartridges into his ray gun, wishing that hunting gear on Tristesse hadn't tended so much toward the retro. Threnody's and Kobi's guns were feeding them information about everything from ammunition levels to wind speed. His gave him nothing but splinters.

They set off through the mist, which hung in the warm air between the trees. Zen had never seen so many trees, nor so big. The ground between their roots was springy, a thick carpet of moss and leaf litter. Awnings of huge green leaves spread overhead. Peering up through the canopy, trying to glimpse the sun or moons, Zen saw shadows darting by. He thought they were the shadows of flyers, until Kobi raised his gun and shot one. It came crashing down through the branches, and Kobi's hound-drones went darting to retrieve it. A feathered flying lizard with a mouthful of teeth.

"*Archaeopteryx*," said Nova, who was still watching through Zen's headset, whispering in his ear.

"Archaeopteryx," Zen said, as if he'd known that all along.

"Specially engineered," said Threnody. "Our geneticists design them not to leave the borders of the reserve."

It seemed like a lot of trouble to go to, designing special birds just so that Kobi could blow holes in them, but Zen didn't say so. "What else do you hunt in here?" he asked as they moved on.

"Old Earth animals," said Threnody. "Some of the classics. Deer. Bears."

Zen nodded as if he knew what she was talking about, but those names meant nothing to him. Nobody had ever bothered seeding Old Earth animals on any of the worlds he knew.

"In this zone there are supposed to be megafauna," said Kobi. "You'd like the horns of one of them for your wall, wouldn't you, Thren?"

"No," said Threnody.

He laughed as if she'd said something funny.

"These megafauna," Zen said, "I guess they're designed to stay in the reserve too?"

"Oh Guardians, yes!" said Threnody. "The Jangalese wouldn't want one of those trampling through their station . . ."

"So are they designed not to attack human beings?" he asked hopefully. "They'll just stand there nice and quiet and let us shoot them, will they?"

Threnody giggled. "You *are* funny, Tallis! If there's no danger, there's no sport!"

"Just checking," Zen said.

"But don't worry. We aren't going after megafauna. They're expensive; only the heads of the family hunt them, and only on special occasions. Kobi's just trying to impress you."

They were going downhill now, the ground sloping toward the river. The roar of a waterfall came through the trees, a homely sound for a boy from Cleave. Zen fell back far enough that the others wouldn't hear him whispering to his headset.

"Nova, can you see where I am?"

"*Sort of. I'm watching you through a weather satellite.*"

"Any animals around here? Big animals?"

"*It's hard to see through all the trees.*"

Zen knew what she meant. He hated the woods. He liked buildings around him and a sidewalk under his feet. Trees gave him the creeps. And all he could see were trees: big trees and small, leaves like spiked fans, leaves like corrugated green roofing sheets, knobbed and spined and warted trunks. All he could hear was the river, and the rustle of unseen beasts in the undergrowth.

"Tallis?" Kobi was calling to him, pointing down a path that opened off the track they had been following. "We're coming to the river. There's a footbridge somewhere. Check down that way, will you? We'll try the other."

"Can't your drones sniff it out?" Zen asked, watching the machines circle him.

"That would be cheating."

Zen went down the path. It was a green tunnel, walled with trees whose buttressed roots looked like the fins of rocket ships. Lianas and trailing curtains of moss hung from the branches, brushing his face. In the shadows on either side hung huge pale flowers, giving off a sickly scent that was attracting clouds of bees: little black bees, each with the smiling sun logo of the Noons marked in the fur on its back.

The path led down into a misty clearing filled with slanting sunbeams and the roar of the river. A thick, musky odor hung in the air.

"Can you see a bridge?" he asked his headset.

"Not near where you are," said Nova. And then, *"Oh, Zen, watch out—I think—"*

He started to turn, and something hit him so hard on the left side of his head that he lost his footing and rolled, cursing, down into the dell. Kobi followed, holding his gun by the barrel as if it were a bat.

"Think you can come breezing onto the Emperor's train and take my girl, railhead?" Kobi said. He was flushed and panting and his eyes were bright.

Zen didn't answer. He was on his knees in the moss, throwing up the Noons' expensive breakfast, which looked pretty much like any other breakfast when it came back out. Kobi started to circle him. Zen wondered why he didn't shoot, then guessed those fancy hunting guns were probably fail-safed not to fire on human targets. *Anyway,* Zen thought, *he's bright enough not to leave a bullet in me. He just plans to smash my skull and leave me to be eaten by some animal.*

"And I suppose you think you're impressing Auntie Sufra too?" Kobi was saying while he walked around and around Zen, working up the nerve to hit him again. "You think she'll fix you up with a job, and a good marriage? Is that it?"

Zen shook his head, and regretted it. His headset had fallen on the ground. He picked it up and put it on. It was still working. Nova's voice buzzed in his skull. He caught the words, *". . . sixty feet . . ."*

And looked up just as the beast burst from the trees behind Kobi.

He never did find out what sort of animal it was. "Megafauna," Kobi and Threnody had called them, but that was a word for all the big beasts of the reserve. What breed this was, and whether it was an ancestral animal from Old Earth or the figment of some gene-tech designer's imaginings, he couldn't say. It was big, that was what he would mostly remember of it. Big and hot-smelling, with armored plates on its back and ginger fur bristling up between them. It had lowered its head as it came charging out of the trees, so its face was hidden at first by the rack of huge horns, which it wore like a clumsy crown.

One of those horns caught Kobi as he turned, too late, to aim his gun at it. The beast flung him across the clearing with a twitch of its head, then, with another, smashed down the hound-drone that darted in to try to lure it away. The drone distracted it for a moment, sparking and flapping on the ground. The beast stamped it flat. It lowered its head and sniffed the wreckage, then looked up, straight at Zen. It had a horny beak and small, red, angry eyes, and it hated Zen for trespassing on its territory. It reminded him a bit of Kobi.

He wasn't used to big animals. Rats were all he usually saw in Cleave. He sat there with his head stuffed with pain, stunned by the size of this thing, by its hot and angry presence. If it had charged at him then, it would have killed him, and he would have been too dazed to care. But Kobi let out a groan, over on the far edge of the clearing where he had been thrown. The beast swung its blunt head toward him and snorted.

Kobi was dragging himself across the ground there like a broken Motorik, while the surviving hound-drone fluttered above him, shrilling out distress calls. Muscles tightened like hawsers under the beast's hide as it shuffled around, aiming itself toward him. Its breath smoldered in the sunbeams. It pawed the leaf litter with a three-toed hoof.

Zen scrabbled sideways across the slope and found the gun he'd dropped when Kobi hit him. He aimed without thinking, and was surprised how hard the stock kicked his shoulder when he pulled the trigger. Splinters of bone flew off the beastie's antlers, but that didn't bother it much. It drew its attention away from Kobi, though. Its mad little eyes considered Zen again, while Nova did something to his headset that dropped targeting cross hairs into his field of view. He pointed the gun again, lined up the crosshairs on the center of the thing's forehead. Again the recoil kicked him. The beastie bellowed. There was a hole through its horny faceplate. It threw back its head and roared, and blood fountained up into the splayed sunbeams.

Zen fired again. It went down on its knees, then collapsed slowly, like a demolished building. It quivered for a bit, farted gigantically, and died. Threnody came running down into the clearing with her own gun ready. Kobi blubbered and cursed. Zen stood shaking, and the sunbeams danced in downdrafts as the drones and flyers of the House of Noon came down all around them.

21

Zen had never understood before why rich people went hunting. It had seemed just part of the cruelty of them. They enjoyed lording it over other people, and they enjoyed harming animals, just like the urchins who tortured stray dogs in the Ambersai Bazar. But as the flyer carried him back to the K-bahn that day, he barely saw the passing view. His head was full of the way that huge, hot beast had crumpled. It had been so big and beautiful, and he had killed it. He knew how the first hunters must have felt, back in the first forests on Old Earth, when they matched themselves against such monsters, and defeated them. A silvery light seemed to hang above the passing treetops, and he barely heard the voices around him: the family medics shouting urgently, Threnody telling everyone how brave he'd been.

Back on the Noon train, the imperial doctors checked him over, treated him for mild concussion, sealed the cut behind his ear. They gave him drugs that numbed his headache. They all assumed that the beast had done that to him, and he did not bother to put them right. Kobi was going to live, they said. The Emperor himself arrived, shook Zen's hand, and thanked him for saving the young man's life.

Zen mumbled something in reply. The silver light had faded by then. He wanted to crawl into bed and sleep for a thousand years.

He did sleep for a bit. Sometime later, he walked along beside the track in the lilac evening, watching the Motorik fold awnings and tables away. Threnody found him there.

"Are you all right?" she asked.

Zen shrugged. He had been better. The long shadows and the rising mists combined with the drugs the doctors had given him to make everything feel like a dream.

"Everyone's talking about you," she said. "Father is very grateful to you. We all are. And the family knows what a fool Kobi was. Uncle Gaeta's security people retrieved recordings from one of the hound-drones. Kobi had been planning to delete them, I suppose. I suppose you must have a recording of your own. Your headset . . ."

Zen had taken the headset off. The wound on his scalp made it too painful to wear. He said, "I can't remember."

"If such a recording was ever to be made public . . ." said Threnody. "Can you imagine the scandal? Kobi's family are valued allies of the Emperor. Our enemies would be sure to use this against us. 'Look how these spoiled young people behave,' they'll say. 'If the Emperor lets his own daughter be engaged to a murderous lout like this, how can the Network be safe in his hands?'"

So that was why she had come looking for him, thought Zen. He could imagine her father or her uncle or Lady Sufra telling her what to ask him, knowing he would be more likely to listen to her.

"I don't want a scandal," he said.

"Of course you don't!" She seemed to think she was winning him over. "We are all Noons. We manage these things privately. Kobi will be punished severely, you can be sure of that. Apart from anything else, that monster you killed was one of the best specimens in the reserve. The Chen-Tulsis will have to pay for that. And don't think I'll be marrying him anymore. That's completely not going to happen. The family will just have to find a new match for me . . ."

In the deepening dusk, white flowers were opening beside the rails. Their scent mingled with the hot, mineral smell of the train.

"I heard Auntie Sufra talking to my father about you," said Threnody, speaking very softly, looking very shy. "She was saying that we could use a bright young man like you on the imperial council. She said that perhaps it was time we strengthened our links to the Golden Junction branch of the family."

Zen wondered how Tallis Noon would respond to such an offer. He wished this were his real life. For a moment, he thought it could be. He'd forget about Raven and stealing the Pyxis. He'd stay with the Noons. He'd stay with Threnody. He'd make a name for himself on the council with his knowledge of life on the streets . . .

But sooner or later, Raven would come looking for him.

The light was almost gone. A few last Motorik folded a few last, luminous awnings. The big voice of the *Time of Gifts* (or perhaps it was the *Wildfire*) said, "Will all passengers return to the train, please? We are departing shortly for Spindlebridge and Sundarban."

"What?" said Zen. He thought he'd heard it wrong. "But we're staying here for two more days . . ."

Threnody shook her head. "There's a change of plan. Father decided that, since the alliance with the Chen-Tulsis is still important to us, it would be disrespectful to stay here in light of what happened. That's Kobi for you: even unconscious in a hospital bed he can still mess things up for everybody. We're taking him home aboard the Noon train. He'll be on Sundarban in three hours."

Zen stared at her. The fuzzy feeling of well-being that the drugs had given him was gone.

Threnody laughed. "Don't worry; we can come back to Jangala another time."

Zen nodded, found a smile of his own. "I hope so."

She went back aboard the train, to a party in one of the garden carriages. Zen hurried to his own compartment and fitted his headset on over his bruises. He needed to talk to Nova.

22

He lay in the dark and whispered, and the headset caught his words and sent them whirling down the speeding train to Nova.

"Can you get me into the collection?"

"Not yet."

"When?"

"I'm working on it. I think . . . soon."

"Because we'll be on Sundarban in a couple more hours."

They were on Nagaina by then. Zen had felt the train slow as it pulled through the station, showing off to the trainspotters and the crowds of children waving flags. Now it was gathering speed again, heading for the next K-gate, which would take it onto the Spindlebridge.

"It will take 1.47 hours to cross the Spindlebridge," said Nova. *"Once we pass the second K-gate there, we'll be about thirty minutes from Sundarban Station City. Is thirty minutes long enough to steal the Pyxis?"*

"I could steal it in thirty seconds if you can just knock out the security in that carriage," said Zen.

One of the locos spoke over the compartment speakers. "We are approaching the Spindlebridge. Spindlebridge is a zero gravity environment. Please ensure all loose objects are secured."

Zen wished he could feel excited. He had always wanted to see the Spindlebridge. All railheads did. It was one of those places that everyone wanted to visit. Downstairs, people would be crowding to the windows. Motos would be going up and down the train, putting children's toys away safely, gathering plates and glasses. He wondered if he should go and join them.

The door of his compartment chimed. He swung himself off the bed and picked up the ray gun. At the same moment, the train punched through the K-gate, and gravity stopped working.

"Who's there?" he shouted, bumbling across the ceiling with the gun in his hands.

No reply; just another soft chime.

He fitted the gun into a clip on the wall beside the door that was probably meant for coats. When he unlocked the door and opened it, he found Lady Sufra waiting in the corridor outside. She must have been wearing magnetic shoes, because she was standing on the floor, not floating like him. Her weightless hair was a halo of white snakes.

"Tallis?" she said. "We have to talk . . . There may be a problem . . ."

"Is Kobi all right?"

"Oh, it's not about him. We're on the Spindlebridge."

"I know," said Zen.

Of all the strange stations of the Network, there was none stranger than the Spindlebridge. Above the planet Sundarban, two naked K-gates hung in orbit. Why the Guardians had chosen to put them in such an inconvenient spot, nobody knew, and the Guardians were not letting on. One led to a gate on Sundarban, several hundred miles below. The other led to Jangala, and all the stations of the Silver River Line. The Noons, seeking to link Sundarban to their other possessions, had built a bridge between the two: a three-hundred-mile tube of ceramic and diamondglass hanging in space with a K-gate at either end. Bulbous clusters of buildings clung to it: factories where the Noons made things that could only be made in zero-g.

The Noon train was rushing through this tube. Looking past Lady Sufra, Zen could see struts and stanchions flashing past outside, and Sundarban peering in at him through diamondglass panels in the hull, swirls of cloud like cappuccino foam above some coffee-colored mountains.

Lady Sufra didn't look as if she'd come to tell him that he was missing the view.

"What's the matter?" he asked.

"I like you, Tallis," she said. "I liked you from the start, long before you saved Kobi. I thought when we first met that you were the sort of young person we needed on the council. So I asked the *Wildfire* and the *Time of Gifts* to find me some details about you from the Datasea, just to be certain you were suitable, and—well, there is something rather strange."

Zen had an awful, sick, swirling feeling that had nothing to do with the lack of gravity. As if he'd fallen off a cliff, or been sat on by heritage megafauna.

"There is a report on a family newsfeed that says you were robbed by a person on Karavina. You had to apply to the family's embassy there for funds to take you home to Golden Junction. And the strange thing is, this seems to have happened only yesterday . . ."

For a moment Zen couldn't understand. Then he thought— the girl! The girl that Raven had hired to divert Tallis to the vapor lakes. She must have helped herself to Tallis's wallet or something, and accidentally tugged on a loose thread that was going to unravel all of Raven's plans.

"So either the Tallis Noon on Karavina is an imposter," said Lady Sufra, "or . . . Well, I'm sure it's all a mistake, but I did have to mention it to my brother Gaeta. He is on his way with a security detachment. He'll ask you some questions, clear this up . . ."

She was waiting for him to protest, to tell her that yes, it was a mistake. When he didn't, her face grew very serious. "Tallis, if there is anything you need to tell me, you should speak now . . ."

Zen didn't answer.

"So it is true?" she said, and for a moment he felt that, no matter what they did to him, the worst thing about getting caught was disappointing her.

"Why?" she asked.

He wondered if he should confess everything. Perhaps she would still be grateful to him for saving Kobi, for not stealing the Pyxis, for warning her about Raven. Maybe she could protect him from her family, and from Raven too.

"*Zen!*" said Nova, suddenly and urgently in his head. "*Security team coming into your carriage . . .*"

Zen could hear them: men's voices, down on the lower deck. Something buzzing like a gigantic bee. Lady Sufra stepped back from the doorway and looked behind her as Gaeta Noon came up the stairs, weightless and clumsy, two CoMa officers behind him, a big, ungainly drone hovering above their heads.

Zen slammed the compartment door. Locked it. Grabbed the gun and somersaulted across the room to the window, but there was no way to open it, no way to break it.

"The ceiling," said Nova, sending her mind into the Noon train's systems, calling up plans. *"There's an access hatch . . ."*

"I can't see it," said Zen above the noise from the door: the pounding fists and shouted threats. He was scrabbling frantically at the smooth plane of livewood that formed the cabin ceiling. Nova delved with her mind into the train's systems, and a seamless hatch slid open.

"They know I'm here now," she said. *"The* Wildfire *and the* Time of Gifts. *They're locking me out of their systems . . ."*

Her voice cut off. He thought for a moment his link to her was severed, but she was just thinking. When she spoke again her voice sounded harder somehow.

"Zen," she told him, *"I am uploading Raven's trainkiller. It's the only way . . ."*

He was busy pulling himself up into the crawlspace above the compartment ceiling. He wasn't sure he'd heard her right. It was a narrow space, barely big enough for him to wriggle through. Intended for small maintenance spiders, he thought—and as he thought it, he saw one, scuttling toward him. At the same moment he heard the bang from below as his door was kicked open, then four more bangs, louder, which was Gaeta Noon or one of his companions or their drone shooting at him through the ceiling. Holes appeared in the floor of the crawlspace all around him, bright stalks of lamplight poking up through them.

"I'm through the trains' firewalls," said Nova in his ear. *"I'm—"*

The lamplight vanished. The red light on the front of the maintenance spider went out too, and in the faint light that was left Zen saw it collapse. A klaxon started to howl somewhere, unbearably loud in that small space. He crammed his hands over his ears. It didn't help much.

The Noon train shrugged. A weird motion, like nothing

he had felt before. Dreadful noises added themselves to the din of the klaxon. Acceleration tugged him in various directions, pressing him to the crawlspace roof, then slamming him against the dead maintenance spider.

If the spider was dead, did that mean that the train was dead too?

Nova, in his head, trying to sound calm: *"Zen, move toward the back of the carriage. There is a hatch that leads out onto the roof. Don't forget you're weightless . . ."*

"What's happening?" he asked, looping the strap of the ray gun over his shoulder and worming his way through the dark. He could see the hatch now; she must have opened it; light was flooding in.

"Bad things," she said.

He reached the hatch, struggled over onto his back, and pulled himself up through the roof of the train.

She was right.

*

Later, when he saw that video, which all the newsfeeds kept on showing until it lost all weight and meaning, he would understand how the *Wildfire* had been blasted off the track by some internal explosion caused by Raven's trainkiller. How it had dragged the *Time of Gifts* over with it as it died, derailing the vast carriages behind it too, leaving the rest to fend for themselves.

All he saw at the time were carriages racing under him and past him. The train was breaking up, couplings detaching at random so that the carriages ran singly or in groups of two or three. Some applied their brakes, some ran on at full speed and crashed loudly against the slower ones ahead. Most stayed on the rails, but a few were rising uncertainly into the air. Doors opened and closed, spilling out people in party clothes, kids in pajamas, flailing and screaming in the train's slipstream. Far behind, among the luggage vans at the rear end of the train, an auxiliary power car went off like a bomb. And over all the other sounds, that high, shuddering klaxon shriek still going on, like trainsong gone sour. Zen thought at first, as he went groping and scrambling his way through the unfolding wreck, that it was the death cry of the two locos, and then fumblingly understood the truth. The *Wildfire* was dead, but the *Time of Gifts* was still alive. That awful bellowing was a cry of grief.

Nova in his head: *"Oh, Zen! It's worse than I thought—I hoped it would only . . ."*

Something ripped upward through the roof he clung to. Gaeta's drone, rotors thrashing the gritty air, soared out through the hole its guns had torn. It was an old-school drone, one of the sort that people called Beetles. Zen had seen a couple of them flying perimeter sweeps around the Noon picnic spots on Jangala and had thought them as absurd as the ceremonial uniforms of the imperial staff. Now, confronted by this one, looking into the black muzzle of its railgun, he felt less inclined to scoff.

Luckily it seemed disoriented. Perhaps the trainkiller had affected it, too. It wavered, trying to bring its gun to bear on him, and a dining car came through the air side-on, like a bat at a ball, like a windscreen at a bug, like a mother ship spewing white flying-saucer fleets of dinner plates from all its doors. Zen ducked. The dining car swept over his head and slammed into the Beetle, which was flung aside, one rotor dead, the other whining, trailing smoke, lost in the wider chaos as the dining car slammed down onto the forward end of the carriage Zen was clinging to. Flung free, he flailed through the air like a trainee acrobat, grabbed the roof of the next carriage, and clung on tight, staring

145

back at his own carriage as it crumpled under the impact of the dining car.

That should give Gaeta and Lady Sufra something else to think about, he thought, then wondered guiltily if he should go back and see if they needed help. But he could not think what help he could give, or why Gaeta and his men shouldn't just start shooting at him again. So he started moving up the train, grabbing at finials and ventilators on the carriage roofs, ducking the fragments that hissed by like bullets, until there in front of him was a gap, a dozen carriages torn out of the train, and beyond it the carriage that held the collection, still on the rails, still attached front and rear to its neighbors, rattling down the Spindlebridge.

Nova again. *"Zen, here's what we'll do: get into the collection, grab hold of the Pyxis, then get off the train, get right off the train . . ."*

"I *am* off it!" he shouted, air-swimming, and then the carriage in front of the collection caught him in the midriff, a glancing blow, which knocked all the breath out of his lungs. Fish from the train's aquarium flew by, each sleeved in its own silvery coat of water.

The top half of a broken Motorik went tumbling past, torn synthiflesh and jutting ceramic bones, spraying gobs of blue gel, telling him, "Dinner may be a little late this evening, sir . . ."

Zen clung to the carvings on the edge of the carriage roof while a storm of luggage hurtled past. A lost red shoe kicked him in the side of the head. A cotton bag flapped into his face. He dragged it off, but did not let it go. Looping the strap over his neck, he started to crawl his way along the carriage. Everything was slowing; these carriages had their brakes full on, spraying long fans of sparks from under their wheels. That must be something Nova was doing.

"Where are you?" he asked.

"*Don't worry about me,*" she said. "*I'll find you. We'll go back to Raven's plan, find a spaceship, get away.*"

Looking down-line to make sure that the Beetle was not still tailing him, Zen saw an airborne garden carriage slam through the side of one of those spherical factory units, carriage and factory both coming apart in sprays of shrapnel. The lights were going out, section by section, all the way along the Spindlebridge, as if Raven's trainkiller had hitched a ride for itself on the *Time of Gifts*'s distress calls and infected the bridge's systems too.

He groped his way down the outside of the carriage, and the doors parted to let him in. The corridor was empty. He pulled himself along it, through the juddering concertina coupling and then through another open door into the carriage that housed the collection. Shrill little alarms were wailing inside, but the *Time of Gifts* was still bellowing its mourning cry, so he didn't think anyone would take much notice. The lights were off, but Quinta Karanath's holopaintings lit his way as he passed through the first gallery, batting drifting vases and sculptures aside with the butt of the ray gun. From deeper in the carriage he could see the glow of the old holographs, a beacon guiding him toward the chamber where the Pyxis waited.

It wasn't easy, swimming through the air, scrambling like a climber along the walls, using picture frames as handholds. The bag he had rescued kept floating up and bumping against his face; the ray gun tugged him endlessly off-balance. His nose was plugging up, and he had a sharp headache, a taste in his mouth like salt and metal. Kicking off from the doorway of the inner chamber, he flailed through the hanging holographs and bashed into the cone that housed the Pyxis. It was still on its plinth inside.

Zen swung the gun at the glass, but it rebounded. He turned it round and pulled the trigger, and the recoil drove him backward and slammed him against the carriage wall.

The diamondglass held, but part of the cone had a frosted look where the impact of his shot had damaged it. He aimed at that place, firing again and again, filling the Noon collection with a thunder that he hoped would go unheard in the louder thunder outside.

At the fifth shot, or perhaps the sixth, the glass gave way. The fragments did not fall, just scattered slowly in every direction. Zen swam through them to where the Pyxis waited for him. He didn't know what had held it to its plinth; it came away easily enough. He stuffed it into his bag as quickly as he could, fought his way back through the weightless carriage to the door.

The carriage was barely moving now, just lurching forward from time to time as the carriages behind bashed into one another. The only light came from fires, which had started farther down the line, a reddish and uncertain light that cast long shadows from the clouds of wreckage hanging in the air around the train.

For a moment then he felt complete despair. How was he supposed to move through that soup of debris? How was he supposed to find his way to these spacecraft hangars that Nova had talked about so blithely? How was he supposed to find Nova?

But she found him. Came scrambling like a spider along the carriage side and reached in to him, just as she had done on that other dead train, in Cleave.

"Well, the trainkiller worked then," he said.

She looked at him with one of those mysterious expressions she had invented for herself. Maybe she had never felt guilt before. Now, with all those miles of loss and ruin around them, she had more to feel guilty about than almost anyone. "I'm glad I used it," she said, as if she was challenging him to disagree. "The Noons would have killed you."

"They still will, if they catch me," said Zen. Portions of his mind kept trying to calculate how many people must be dead and injured, how many trillions of damage done. And he would be the one they'd blame. He had crossed a terrible line. He wasn't just a thief anymore. He was a saboteur. A murderer. A *mass* murderer . . . They'd probably have to invent a whole new name for the crimes he'd be accused of.

So he needed Raven. He needed his protection. And the only way that he could get that was by finishing the job he had been sent to do.

He took Nova's hand, and she pulled him outside, into the disaster that they had made.

23

A narrow tubeway ran along the side of the Spindlebridge, designed for maintenance Motos and the bolder sightseers. Once they had found their way into that, it was not too hard to pull themselves along by the handholds on the walls. So they made their way down the line, following a map that Nova found in her mind. They went past the wreckage of the great train, past the firefighting vehicles and the gashed factories, through the hooting klaxons and the booming bullhorn voices that told them not to panic, to stay in their carriages and await assistance. The air stank of burnt metal: the smell of cans on a garbage fire.

Halfway down the Spindlebridge was a wider section that rotated slowly. There was a little station there, tourist shops and novelty hotels, a park with bluegrass lawns and clumps of trees (even in space, those Noons had to plant their trees!). Refugees from the disaster were gathering there, glad of the centrifugal force, which provided something that felt like gravity and gave them back the gift of their own weight. The lights were out in that section too, but there were big observation windows that lay like pools on the floor, and up through these shone the kindly light of Sundarban.

Between the window-pools lay shapes that looked like bundles of lost clothes, surrounded by silent or weeping Noons. Still dazed, Zen wasn't sure what they were, until he went close to one of the groups of mourners, and saw Lady Sufra lying there. Whoever had dragged her from the wreck had laid her out with as much dignity as possible, and lit a little cloud of firefly drones to hang above her head like mourning candles, but they had not been able to disguise the brokenness of her: the way her neck was twisted, her torn and filthy clothes, or the look upon her dead face.

Zen looked, and pressed the heels of his hands against his eyes to stop the tears, then looked some more. Telling himself what he'd been telling himself all the way down the bridge, that this was not his fault, not his, not all of it. Knowing that he'd never have the chance now to explain himself to Lady Sufra, or to say that he was sorry.

"*Come away,*" warned Nova. "*Gaeta may be here, or someone else who knows about you.*"

The whole station seemed full of weeping. Children howling for their mommies, tough Noon CoMa with tears carving tracks through the soot on their shocked faces. Even the wrecked *Time of Gifts* had stopped howling and was doing something that was more like sobbing: a desperate, desolate sound. Zen had not known a train could grieve like that. It made him angry, made him use his elbows to jab those stunned, tearful people aside as he followed Nova toward some hatchway she'd discovered from the station plans.

He was afraid whole raggedy crowds of Noons would be

making for the spacecraft hangars on the outer hull, but none were. The K-bahn was the backbone of their world, and even as they stumbled out of the wreckage of their carriages, it never occurred to them that another train would not be along soon to take them to Sundarban. There the planet lay, bright outside the windows, but who would think about flying down to it in a spacecraft, when a train would get them there in more comfort and less time?

Well, someone had—the first hangar Nova found was empty. But in the second a dart-shaped shuttle dangled from its launching gear above a space-door made from a single wide disc of diamondglass. Below it lay the continents and seas of Sundarban, ruffs of white cloud gleaming in the raking sunlight.

They went in through the airlock. This outer part of the station seemed unaffected by the failures that were spreading inside. Lights came on obediently, and when Nova transmitted a command to the ship, a ceramic gangplank extended, leading to an airlock in its hull. Orange lamps began to spin and flash around the space-door, and stuff happened up in the tangle of ducts and plumbing overhead: sloshing sounds, which Zen guessed were fuel and coolant gurgling through pipes.

"Will it let us aboard?" he asked. He was wary of the ship and the long drop beneath it. "It's a Noon ship . . ."

"You *are* a Noon, remember?" Nova said. "Anyway, it is a very stupid ship; I have already persuaded it to accept your orders. I'm transmitting a message to Raven, down on Sundarban. He can tell it where to land."

"That was easy, then," said Zen.

She smiled at him. A weepy sort of smile. Then she leaned close and he felt the print of her lips on his cheek and the corner of his mouth. When she stepped back she was blushing. Her face was very beautiful, he thought. He hadn't been sure before, but he was now. The mind that lived behind it made it beautiful, the same way that the flame inside a lantern makes the lantern beautiful.

He was wondering if it would be weird to tell her so when a small red light came wavering across the shuttle's hull and settled between her eyebrows like a bindi.

He started to shout a warning, but she had already felt the laser's touch. She threw Zen down, and the bullets whipped over them and struck sparks and shrill noises from the gantry above the yacht.

As the sound of the shots faded, Zen heard the rotors of a drone, and looked up in time to see his old friend the Beetle flying into the hangar. Gaeta Noon must have ordered it to hunt Zen down, and it was obeying single-mindedly, ignoring the disasters around it and the damage it had suffered. It flew like a maimed bird, lopsided, dipping down to scrape the floor every few feet. Zen guessed most of its weaponry had been put out of use. Even the railgun it had just fired was silent now.

"It's out of ammunition," Nova said.

"Can you knock it out?"

"It has good firewalls. It will take a moment . . ."

The Beetle, which was nothing if not persistent, launched itself clumsily toward them, extending a whirling silver blade.

"Get onto the ship," said Nova. "I'll open the space-door."

He started to tell her that she couldn't, but that bright mind of hers had already flicked a parcel of code into the boathouse's brain. The flashing lamps turned from orange to red. Klaxons whooped, drowning out Zen's words. The door beneath the moored ship slid aside, and the boathouse atmosphere started pouring out into space. The Beetle went tumbling after it. Zen nearly followed. He struggled up the gangplank, through the gale. The shuttle shuddered on its gantry and the lights flashed red, red, red. He turned as he reached the shuttle hatch, and there was Nova scrambling up behind him.

But even as it hurtled away into the dark, the Beetle seemed intent on vengeance. Either that or it was making one last, desperate attempt to anchor itself to the Spindlebridge. Zen saw a spark of light out there, but he took it for a reflection flashing from some piece of litter that had vented with the air. A second later, just as Nova reached the top of the gangway, the grapnel that the Beetle had fired punched her in the back and drove through her, exploding from her chest in a spout of blue gel.

Her fierce grin faded. She looked wide-eyed at Zen. Stuff came out of her mouth, wet and blue, with little deeper blue fragments in it.

He reached for her. His fingers touched hers. For a moment he almost had hold of her. But the Beetle was still tumbling away from the station. The carbon-fiber cable went taut, dragging the grapnel's barbed head against whatever Nova had in place of a breastbone.

"Zen . . ." she said, and then the Beetle yanked her after it, away from him, out into space.

And the boathouse was empty of air, and the ship was nagging at Zen to close the outer hatch, and there was nothing he could do but duck inside and let the door hiss shut. He pressed his face to the window while the airlock filled with air. He could not see Nova or the Beetle.

The ship still followed Nova's instructions. Zen ignored it when it told him to strap himself in. A moment later he was flung against the ceiling as thrusters fired, blasting it away from the Spindlebridge. When the thrust ended, he did not fall, but floated free, weightless again. He shouted Nova's name, but she did not answer. Only the calm, stupid voice of the ship, telling him that she had set a course for coordinates on Sundarban.

He went from the airlock into the main cabin, a livewood bower with huge diamondglass windows. From there he saw the exterior of Spindlebridge for the first time, bone-white and sky-wide. One end of the huge structure was in ruins, blasted open by the explosions at the rear of the Noon train, spewing debris and atmosphere into space.

But Nova and the Beetle were gone, lost in the never-ending deserts of the night.

24

"Well," said Raven, when Zen came stumbling out of the ship. "That all went very smoothly!"

Night winds chased litter across a patch of scrub country outside Sundarban Station City. Along the horizon the lights glittered in a forest of high buildings. Nearby, a K-bahn line emerged from a tunnel in the side of a rocky hill, weeds growing as tall as people up between the rails. The tunnel had been blocked. Fragments of the shattered barrier lay on either side of the track, and the *Thought Fox* sat smugly waiting among them, its scarred old hull faintly silvered by Sundarban's moons.

"You've got to tell the ship to go back up," Zen said. He pointed behind him at the spacecraft, which perched on the sand, its hull ticking and steaming after the journey through the atmosphere. His voice was hoarse from shouting orders at it. Locked on the course that Nova had given it, it had refused to obey him. "Nova's still up there," he explained. "We have to rescue her."

"Nova's gone," said Raven. "I lost her signal hours ago."

"She's adrift. In orbit!" Zen thought of her up there, falling and falling around the wide, blue world. "She's Motorik," he pleaded. "She doesn't need air, she's not like a human being, you could repair her . . ."

Raven looked up at the sky. The Spindlebridge was a bright star, low on the horizon. The sky was streaked with the meteor trails of debris hitting the upper atmosphere. "Sorry, Zen," he said. "We need to leave. We can't waste time looking for a broken wire dolly. She'll burn up in orbit like the rest of the debris. She'll be a shooting star. It's what she would have wanted." He grinned at Zen, and danced a few shuffling steps on the sand. "Now, what about what *I* want? You have the Pyxis, I presume?"

Zen held out the bag. Raven looked inside, and his face softened. "Good boy! Now we can really get to work."

"We killed Lady Sufra," Zen said. "And the *Wildfire* and the *Time of Gifts*—and so many people . . ."

"Best not to think about that," said Raven kindly. "Give me the box, Zen."

"What?"

"The Pyxis."

Zen took it out of the bag. He had not noticed until then how unexpectedly heavy it was.

"What is it?" he said.

"It's just a box. A container."

"Lady Sufra told me it was solid."

"It looks solid when scanned."

"So—is there something inside it?"

"Open it," Raven suggested.

Zen looked down at the Pyxis, still clutched in his hand. It still looked solid, but suddenly a crack appeared, and then another, and it folded open. Inside, in a dense nest of metallic foam, lay a shining black ball. Across the ball's surface, almost too fine to see, there stretched a labyrinth of faint grooves, an infinitely complex pattern, ruled by geometries that Zen didn't recognize and couldn't hope to understand: a maze so intricate that, as he looked at it, it seemed to crawl and shift.

"What is it?" he asked. "Is it more art?"

"In a way," said Raven. He came and took the Pyxis and the sphere from Zen's hands. "It's very old," he said, a sort of reverence in his voice as he ran his fingertip over the strange patterns. He replaced it in its nest, and the Pyxis snapped shut, the secret seams along which it had opened fading away. "It is very old, and it has been hidden for a long time. Thank you for helping me to get it back."

He tossed the Pyxis into the air, caught it, and darted it into a pocket of his coat. He looked at Zen, and his eyes were kindly. "Come. It's late, and you've been working hard. You want my advice? Forget all this. You've done your bit. You get to step off the ride now. It's time to go home."

*

Back through all the K-gates, through the un-light and the roaring tunnels, back down the Dog Star Line. Zen barely saw the worlds that flashed past outside the windows, nor the food that Raven put in front of him. Ukotec, Ukotec, Ukotec, said the wheels on the tracks, reminding him of the pictures he'd found in the Noon train's archives, the *Thought Fox* rolling through passageways built from the crumpled bodies of the people it had murdered. The white noise of the engines reflecting from tunnel walls blended with the roar of the train crash, which still seemed to be going on somewhere inside him, as if echoes of the disaster were rumbling through the marrow of his bones.

There were sleeping compartments on the *Fox's* upper decks. He dozed for a while, dreamed of Threnody, and woke again wondering if she was dead too, and knowing that, if she was, then it was he who'd got her that way.

Sufra Noon was in his memories too. And, more than either of them, Nova. He had never dreamed the breaking of a Motorik could hit him so hard. He missed her more than anything, her voice in his ear and her not-quite-human kindness. It was all very well for Raven to tell him he should forget it all, but how could he? How was he ever going to forget any of it?

*

He slept again. When he woke, Raven was sitting beside his bunk. The train was rattling through a long tunnel between K-gates, and the light from lamps on the tunnel walls came through the blinds and flashed across Raven's face. He started to talk, and it reminded Zen of times when he'd been ill as a small child, when Myka or even his mother had sat beside his bed and told him stories.

But as he woke up and started to listen, he realized that what Raven was telling him was not a story. Not the made-up sort, at any rate.

*

"There was once a boy very much like you, Zen Starling. He lived hundreds of years ago, on a world way off down the Orion Line. Like you, he was a little too clever, not bad-looking, eager not to live the life his parents lived, but not sure how to change things. And then something happened that changed things for him. I've never been sure if his luck turned good or bad.

"What happened was this. The Guardians used to move among human beings much more often and more openly in those days. Sometimes they would download themselves into cloned bodies just to attend a party or take a walk in the evening air on some particular world. Interfaces, we called those bodies. The boy—his name was Dhravid—had seen them often, because his parents were minor officials, and they tended to go to the sort of parties and ceremonies that the Guardians liked to attend. He had met the Shiguri Monad, which wore the body of a golden man, and Sfax Systema, which appeared as a cloud of blue butterflies. He had seen the Mordaunt 90 Network, whose favorite interface was a centaur, truly exquisite, a triumph of biotech. And one day he met a Guardian who called itself Anais Six.

"It was at a summer party on the terraces beside the Amber River. Moonlight on the vineyards across the water, and the music of the songflowers. The body that Anais Six wore was sexless, blue-skinned, with golden eyes and high golden antlers. Dhravid could tell that it had not used interfaces as much as the other Guardians: it seemed clumsy and uncertain of itself. It kept looking at its hands, or running the tips of its fingers over its face. The boy found it charming. As he was watching it, thinking how strange and beautiful it was, it tripped on a stairway. He put out a hand to stop it falling.

"That was how they met. And, to cut the story short, it fell in love with him. And he fell in love with it. In the years that followed, Anais came to him again and again. Sometimes its interface was female, sometimes male. Sometimes it was neither.

Different bodies, different faces, but he always knew it. Through all those eyes he felt the same immense intelligence watching him. It was flattering to be loved by something so great. And there were practical rewards, too; someone who has won the love of a Guardian does not want for much in this life.

"But this life is short. Anais began to worry. It knew that Dhravid would one day die, and it could not have that. So it stored a copy of his personality. He became data. Can you imagine it, Zen? Perhaps nobody can who has not experienced it for themselves. To become data in the Datasea: living in the information streams, but part of them, too. Dhravid became, not quite a Guardian himself, but a thing with many of the same powers. He put copies of his mind into probes and sent them to the far stars. He had interfaces of his own now: cloned bodies, all with the same face, his own face, so that he still had some tie to the person he used to be. He lived a thousand lives on a thousand worlds. He swam down into the data-deeps. He started to understand the very origins of the Datasea, and of the Great Network itself.

"And that was how he learned that the Guardians have their secrets. Why do they not like us asking questions about the nature of the Network? Why will they never explain the technology behind the K-gates? Why did they bury the walls on Marapur? He wanted to share those secrets, and they would not allow it. They turned against him. They turned Anais against him. They had never approved of what she had made him into. They made her rob him of the gift she had given him. She deleted him from the Datasea. He was left with nothing but a handful of cloned bodies to live in. Even those died, one by one, hunted down by Railforce assassins on the orders of Anais Six, until there was just one left. It was a come-down, I can tell you. To have been a god, and then to be only human again . . ."

The train passed through some evening world. Low sunlight pierced the blinds, flowing over Raven's stern face. He was talking about himself, of course. Zen had known that from the start. Telling it as if it had happened to someone else, and maybe it had; maybe his time in the Datasea and his thousand interfaces had changed him so much that he was no longer the same person who had first met Anais, on the terraces beside the Amber River, where the songflowers sang.

Remembering his eviction from the Datasea seemed to have jolted him out of the story. He was silent for a while. Then he said, "They almost destroyed me, Zen. In this one last body I crept onto the Dog Star Line to hide. I did not think at first that I could bear to live like this. I wanted to die, and I almost did. But then I thought of the things I'd learned in the Datasea. The secrets that the Guardians do not want to share. I thought I would tell everyone. But who would believe me, my word against the Shiguri Monad, and Anais Six, and the rest? And as soon as I showed myself, they would track down this last body, and destroy it like they did all the others. That is why I chose to stay hidden, to bide my time, to lay my plans in secret . . ."

"What plans?"

"Things need shaking up, Zen. Everything keeps repeating itself, century after century. Empires rise up and grow old, and there's always some new would-be Emperor waiting in the wings to take their turn. Dark ages come and go. People are born and people die. It's so *pointless*. The Guardians mean well, but they have shunted the whole human race onto a branch line of history, and we keep trundling round in circles. It's time someone changed that."

The train pierced a K-gate. It seemed to rouse Raven from his thoughts. He looked down at Zen, and when he spoke again his voice, which had sunk to a whisper, was its normal flat self again.

"Come, Zen Starling. Here's where your adventure ends."

*

He took Zen back down into the carriage. On the seats lay Zen's old clothes. He climbed out of the ones Raven had given him and put them on, his foil jeans and ancient smart-coat. The only thing that had changed was the headset he found in the coat pocket. It was the double of the one he'd been wearing on the Noon train, and he started to put it on without thinking, imagining he'd hear Nova whisper in his ear. Then he remembered. Until Desdemor he had always been alone, and he had thought he liked being that way. Then, with Nova, he had found someone with whom he could share everything. Losing her again was more painful than anything he had ever known. He could not believe how much it hurt. This was the feeling people write all those songs about, he thought, all those poems and movies. Heartbreak. He had always thought they must be exaggerating.

Quickly, making sure that Raven didn't see, he pocketed the old headset too. Perhaps it still held a recording of her voice, at least, a few views of Tu'Va and Jangala to prove it hadn't all been some strange dream.

"What about making me rich?" he said. "What about what you promised to give me? Was that just a lie?"

"I'm letting you live, Zen," said Raven. "That's your reward. If you ever try coming after me, I might take it away."

The *Thought Fox* banged through another gate and slowed, pulling into a darkened station. The light from the windows shone on a roof of ceramic tiles, a few Station Angels that danced and faded over a deserted platform. When the doors opened, Zen could smell burnt dust and stale air.

He stepped out onto the platform. The *Thought Fox* closed its doors behind him and let out a long hiss, which may have been its own way of saying goodbye. He saw Raven for a moment, standing behind the glass, one hand raised in a sort of salute. The platform flickered like one of Nova's movies. Then the train was gone, and dark descended. The noise of engines faded and then cut out completely as, somewhere up the line, a K-gate opened and the train passed through it. Dead leaves whispered along the platform, dancing in the wind of the train's departure just as they had danced when it first opened its doors for him. And then he realized that they never had been leaves, only the tiny dried-up corpses of insects.

He found his way through silent passageways and cob-webbed turnstiles to an old emergency exit. It opened for him. He stumbled out into the hot metal stink, the waterfall thunder, the never-ending noisy dusk of Cleave.

At first he wasn't sure where he was. He put the new headset on, hoping to call up a map, and it was then that he found Raven's gift. The headset was preloaded with false IDs and travel documents for him, and Ma, and Myka. There was a link to a bank in the local data raft. He blinked the link, and steadied himself against a wall as the details of his new accounts superimposed themselves over his vision, blotting out the dingy, spray-wet street with clouds of zeroes.

Not really a gift, of course. He'd earned all that money by lifting the Pyxis. It was payment for services rendered. For a moment, he thought about snatching the headset off and throwing it into the nearest waterfall.

He didn't. But he thought about it.

PART THREE
DAMASK ROSE

25

Three days after the catastrophe at Spindlebridge, a young man, his sister, and their mother boarded a K-train at Cleave Station. The young people were carrying duffel bags and backpacks, as if they were going on holiday, perhaps to visit family in some other district, farther down the line. The mother seemed agitated; they had to coax her through the barriers onto platform two, where their train was waiting. The names on their travel documents were Mun, Minti, and Arundhati Kevala, and they traveled all the way to Golden Junction. There they disembarked, joining the crowds who were gathering for one of the local festivals. The mother still seemed troubled; the daughter looked around in wonder at the living skyscrapers and all the different K-bahn lines that wound between them; but the son barely glanced at them, as if he had traveled so widely that a provincial interchange like Golden Junction could not impress him. He kept watching the wallscreens, half hypnotized by the footage from Spindlebridge.

A few hours afterward, the three boarded another K-train. The names on their IDs had changed: they were now called Jav, Chetna, and Satiya Panassar. They traveled back the way they had come, but got off at Summer's Lease. A sleepy white city dozed there beside the K-bahn tracks, three big moons in the autumn sky. The Panassars transferred to a local train, which did not go through any K-gates, just chugged away across the city on a narrow gauge line. Slowly the white buildings grew lower. Hills appeared above the rooftops: arable fields where harvesting machines were working. The train crossed a viaduct and the sea came into sight. It shone under the autumn sun, dotted with clusters of domed islands like the tops of half-submerged mushrooms. They were algae colonies, breathing in carbon dioxide and breathing out oxygen. Billions of them would have been seeded in the shallows when the planet was being terraformed; now only a few clumps were left, to remind everyone how Summer's Lease had won its kindly atmosphere.

The Panassars stepped off the train at a station where the air smelled of the sea. A jitney carried them through quiet streets to a house that had been bought in their name a few days earlier. A quiet and private house, set away from its neighbors in a ragged garden. Walls of glass and white ceramic. Dead leaves scudding on the surface of the swimming pool.

"We're home, Ma," said Zen.

"We're safe," said Myka. "They won't find us here."

Their mother looked around, wary, but calm. She was like that always in new places, as if she had left her fears behind her, on the other side of the K-gates.

*

"We are safe, aren't we, Zen?" his sister asked, later, when their mother was sleeping. They had been exploring the house, the large, sunlit rooms; Myka in a daze, running her rough hands over the perfect surfaces of the livewood furniture. When they stepped out onto the terrace where the pool waited, she looked at Zen as though she had woken from a dream. "Where did you get all this money? What did you do? Will someone be coming after you?"

Zen shrugged. "You and Ma are safe, I think," he said. "But I can't stay."

"So someone will be coming? That man Malik?"

"Maybe." Myka had told him about Malik's visit to Cleave, but he did not really think Malik could trace them to Summer's Lease. He remembered the Railforce man saying, "Raven hides his tracks well." But he also remembered how many people had seen him on the Noon train, how many photographs he must appear in. And what about the report from Karavina that had alerted Lady Sufra? However small a report it was, however deeply buried beneath the news from Spindlebridge, someone else would see it one day. Sooner or later, the Noons would start searching for the boy who had claimed to be Tallis. Sooner or later, if he stayed here, they would find him.

And it wasn't just the fear of being found that meant he couldn't stay. There was Nova.

The headset that he had stolen from Raven had been badly damaged; its scrambled memory still held a few of Tallis Noon's photos and a shaky, three-second video clip of Kobi Chen-Tulsi, made in the last seconds before the megafauna arrived, but no image of Nova had survived, and no recordings of Zen's talks with her. It didn't matter. He could still hear her voice in his head, and remember the feeling of closeness when he talked to her. He kept thinking of the broken Motorik that had blown past him when the Noon train derailed, torn in half but still calmly talking. What if Nova was still conscious, hurtling around and around Sundarban with the rest of the Spindlebridge debris, waiting to hit the atmosphere and burn?

He had to help her. He had to try. He wasn't sure how, but he was starting to form a plan.

"You reckon a Moto could survive after someone put a harpoon through its body?" he asked his sister.

Myka looked wary. "What's that got to do with . . . And how would I know?"

"You killed Motos, didn't you? In the riots, back in Cleave?"

"Not me. Not personally. I saw some killed. I don't know if . . ." She went quiet for a while. Then she said, "You should ask Flex."

"Why?"

"Oh, Zen, didn't you ever work it out? Flex is a Moto."

"Flex? Really?"

She laughed at him, enjoying his surprise.

"I thought there weren't any Motorik in Cleave . . ." he started to say. But, of course, the reason there weren't any Motorik in Cleave was because angry rioters had smashed them up. Suddenly that explained things, like the way Flex kept herself bundled up and living all alone in the stacks, and maybe it gave him a clue about how Myka had saved Flex's life.

"I thought you hated Motos?" he said.

"There's a lot about me you don't know," said Myka.

Zen went inside, up the stairs to his mother's new bedroom.

She was sleeping like a child, lying on her side with her hands curled in front of her face. The room was quiet, and the sunlight came in softly through drawn blinds. She would be all right here, Zen thought. Everything had changed. Myka would be able to afford doctors for her, Motorik to help look after her, drugs to keep her fears at bay. He wished he could stay here and watch her getting better. There was a lot that he didn't know about Ma, too.

One day, she might be able to explain why she had stolen him from the Noons. But he would not be there to hear her.

Yanvar Malik was looking at a frozen girl when he heard the news. He was in a cold-prison on Karavina and the warden had just pulled the girl's freezer unit out of the racks for him to see. He wasn't sure what he could learn by looking at her, but he looked anyway: opened the inspection hatch and peered in.

Her name was Chandni Hansa. She had been pretty in the mug shots, but they had shaved her head and now her face was gray and her lips were blue and she looked dead, although Malik knew she would thaw out all right in ten years when her sentence was up. She had stolen some money and a high-end headset from a boy she had met on the K-bahn, and probably the only reason she had been caught and sentenced and frozen so fast was that the boy had been a member of the Noon family, a distant relative of Emperor Mahalaxmi. The story had barely registered on the newsfeeds, but it had caught the attention of the cheap watchbot that Malik had set to trawl the Datasea for unusual stories about the Noons. Now here he was on Karavina.

"Where's the boy she robbed?" he asked.

"Gone home to Golden Junction," said the warden. She was a local woman, and Malik thought she should have been tall and willowy like the wraiths of mist that danced above Karavina's vapor lakes, but she was short and square and grumpy.

"She tell you anything before you froze her?"

"Oh, all these popsicles tell us some story about how it's not their fault," said the woman. "She said some man put her up to it. Found her on Przedwiosnie and told her to board such-and-such a train and get friendly with this Tallis Noon kid and bring him here for a few weeks. Paid her, she says. But if that's the case, she shouldn't have got greedy and started stealing Tallis's stuff, should she?"

"Did she describe this man who hired her?"

"She said he was tall-ish. White-ish."

Malik kept looking in through the peephole, down into the little icy world where the young thief lay like a frozen princess in a story. She'd had a story of her own, of course, just like Zen Starling had. Raven had come to her and made her an offer, and she'd done what he asked. She had lured Tallis Noon to Karavina, out of the way, so that Zen Starling could impersonate him somewhere else, to do—what?

The warden gasped. She'd been checking her headset while Malik was busy with his thoughts, and the newsfeeds had just updated. She didn't look grumpy anymore. She stared at Malik like a startled child; he could see what she had looked like when she was ten. She said, "I think something terrible has happened! Oh Guardians! The Emperor's train—the Noon train—Spindlebridge . . ."

"Raven," said Malik. He left her there with Chandni Hansa, and went running through the stunned streets to the station to find himself a train to Sundarban.

27

The Emperor was dead. The Noon family and the imperial civil servants had kept a lid on the story for as long as possible, but it escaped at last, as captive stories do. Mahalaxmi XXIII had been in his private carriage at the front of the train, and had died when it left the tracks and plowed through a factory complex. All across the Network, on the newsfeeds and gossip sites and in the streets and stations, nobody was talking about anything else.

Even the Guardians, who usually paid so little heed to human affairs these days, were startled by the news that was spreading through the Datasea. The Mordaunt 90 Network, the Twins, Sfax Systema, Anais Six—one by one they turned their attention toward Sundarban and Spindlebridge. The people who first programmed those vast intelligences, on Old Earth all those years ago, had charged them with guiding and protecting humanity, and it was a job the Guardians took seriously. They had always done their best to keep human society stable. It had shocked them, when the first human beings found their way onto the Great Network, how quickly the corporate families began to fight with one another, the furious small wars that raged for control of new branch lines and important interchanges. An Emperor, carefully guided, subtly supervised, had been their way to keep the peace.

But the Emperor was dead, and so was his brother Gaeta and his wife, Milla; his sister Sufra and his young son Prem. His daughter Priya, shuttled down from Spindlebridge on the replacement spacecraft service, went on the Sundarbani media to announce that she was now Empress. But her uncle Tibor, at Grand Central, was claiming that *he* was Mahalaxmi's natural heir, and the other corporate families were grumbling that perhaps it was someone else's turn to rule the Network. There was a rumor that the Prell family, ancient rivals of the Noons, were readying armored trains and placing their Corporate Marines on standby.

Out on the obscure branch lines, in dusty or frozen half-terraformed worlds where Emperors of any name were unpopular, the rebels of Human Unity watched the news unfold, and weighed their chances.

*

When Threnody finally made it down from Spindlebridge—shocked, tearstained, weary—she went straight to the family estate in the mountains. She would rather have gone back to Malapet, to her mother and the comforting boredom of home, but the journey would take weeks with the Silver River Line shut down, and anyway, Priya said it was too dangerous to travel. She had convinced herself that their uncle Tibor had been responsible for the disaster on the Spindlebridge. Now she was camped out in the luxurious crescent-shaped hunting lodge at the heart of the estate, surrounded by lawyers and paparazzi drones and Corporate Marines and Railforce officials, having noisy meltdowns about Tibor's treachery. When she saw Threnody, she said, "What are you doing here? You should be with your fiancé, while he recovers from his injuries . . ."

"What about *my* injuries?" asked Threnody, who had sprained a wrist during the crash. "And if you think I'm still marrying that fool Kobi—"

"Of course you are marrying that fool Kobi!" shouted her sister. (Threnody was shocked. Priya had always been so quiet and sort of *dull* before. Becoming Empress seemed to have given her a temper.) "I know you never thought him much of a catch, Thren, but things are different now. I need that marriage! I need the support of the Chen-Tulsis. So go to him, and don't do anything that might give his people an excuse to break off your engagement."

Threnody did not try to argue. She was slightly afraid that, if she did, Priya might start to think that she wanted to be head of the family too, and have her poisoned or drowned or something, like some unlucky princess in a historical threedie.

So she went to find Kobi at his family's house, where he was recovering from his injuries. The Chen-Tulsis had spent a lot trying to make the house look grand, but the money had been wasted, because it was on quite the wrong side of the city, too far from the K-bahn and too close to the spaceports. The thunder of shuttles taking off to fetch survivors from the Spindlebridge drummed across the landscaped grounds, and by night the glare of rocket exhaust reflected in the ornamental lagoon where the gene-teched coelacanths swam. Threnody thought it was a depressing place. But Kobi was pleased to see her, and she felt warily pleased to see him. He seemed quieter than before, and weaker, and nicer. Threnody supposed that being mauled half to death by heritage megafauna would do that to a person.

She walked in the grounds with him, half listening to him talk while she used her headset to scan the data raft for news of her cousin Tallis. She was in mourning for her father and his family, but she could only summon up a sort of general sadness for them—she hadn't met most of them till she boarded the Noon train; they had been strangers, really. Tallis, for some reason, had been different; she needed to know what had become of him. So every few hours she checked to see if his name had been added to the list of the dead or the list of those brought down from orbit.

It never was. Tallis Noon seemed to have vanished.

Zen's plans hit a snag as soon as he reached the K-bahn station. Summer's Lease was Prell territory, and the Prells were strengthening security—getting ready to go to war with the Noons, if you believed the newsfeeds. There were new barriers going up at the entrance to the platforms, cameras poised to scan your retinas and flash your image to facial recognition programs. As far as Zen knew, no one was looking for him yet, but he did not want to take that chance. He left the station and walked the streets that backed onto the railway until he came to a place where a footbridge arched over the K-bahn lines. He waited there until he heard the train leaving the station, the sound of its engines changing as it crossed the rail yards and gathered speed, entering the narrow cutting that would take it beneath the bridge.

There were not many people about at that hour. The only other person on the bridge was an old lady walking her miniature triceratops. She glanced at Zen as she passed him, noticed some wild expression in his eyes, and turned to look back at him. He heard her call out something as he scrambled up onto the parapet of the bridge. The rails of the K-bahn shone below him, the ballast between them speckled with autumn leaves.

The train was coming into view, a glimmer of reflected morning sky dancing on the carriage roofs. The 5:15 to Cleave. On the loco, as he'd hoped, Flex's painted creatures.

He stepped off the bridge.

The lady with the triceratops screamed. Zen hit the roof of the rear carriage with a thump that left him gasping. The bridge was whisked away; the backs of buildings flickered by. He groped for something to cling onto as the train hit the long straight at the edge of the city and started to accelerate.

The loco knew that he was there, of course. While he was still grabbing for handholds, a maintenance spider popped out of its trapdoor at the far end of the carriage and came swaying along the roof toward him. The spider didn't have to worry about handholds: magnets or magic kept its feet geckoed to the train's ceramic. As it drew closer to Zen, it raised a couple of manipulator arms and tested its pincers, readying itself to throw him off.

Zen raised one hand and screamed at it. "I'm a friend of Flex! Nice tags you're wearing, train! Flex did that! She's a friend of mine!"

The spider was slaved directly to the train's brain; the loco was watching him through its lenses. It hesitated while the train went clattering across a long white bridge that spanned an inlet of the sea. Beyond the inlet, a sheer cliff, the tracks vanishing into a tunnel. Wind tore at Zen's clothes and pressed against his eyes. He blinked away the tears and tried to gauge the distance to the tunnel mouth. A mile maybe, narrowing fast. And inside the tunnel, maybe five more miles to the K-gate. If he was still outside the train when he went through that, there would be nothing left of him but smoke . . .

The spider started moving again. It caught hold of Zen and swung him under its body so that its legs were all around him like a mobile cage as it went scuttling back along the train roof, leaping from carriage to carriage, making for the loco.

The tunnel swallowed them with a sudden woof of reflected sound. There was a rushing darkness, then light ahead—a colorless glow that shifted like candlelight but somehow illuminated nothing. It was the curtain of energy inside the K-gate, and for a moment Zen thought that he could hear it, a strange, high singing that harmonized with the song of the speeding train. He remembered Raven saying, "Why do the Guardians not like us asking questions about the nature of the Network? Why will they never explain the technology behind the K-gates . . . ?"

The spider made a last leap. A hatch on the rear of the loco opened, and it carried Zen inside. The hatch shut, and an instant later he felt the strange lurch as the train tore through K-space.

"Ahh!" said the loco. The K-gates were what it lived for: that rush, that release. For a moment it had forgotten the boy inside it.

Zen lay on smooth ceramic and tried to work out which of the small lights in the blackness around him were just afterimages and which were part of the loco's systems. He had never realized there was enough space for a person inside a loco; he had thought it would be all engines and computers. Perhaps this crawl-way was left over from when the train was being built, back when it still had need of people. Somewhere above him a big fan was purring. Somewhere the huge motor throbbed like a heart.

"Any friend of Flex is a friend of mine, traveler," said the voice of the train, after a few more miles.

"Thanks, train," said Zen. "I'm going to Cleave. I'll give her your regards."

"I am called *Gentlemen Take Polaroids*," said the train.

"Pleased to meet you," said Zen.

"I stop twice between here and Cleave," said the train. "If you like, you can get off and sit in a carriage."

Zen thought it over. "I'd sooner stay here, if that's all right. And when we get to Cleave, maybe you could let me off outside the station?"

He lay in the dark and thought of the bright rails rushing beneath him. The movements of the train woke memories of the crash on Spindlebridge. He heard again the klaxons and the screams, and felt the awful forces pulling at his body. He tried telling himself again that it hadn't been his fault. He'd been hired to pinch a box, and he had pinched it. The rest was Raven's doing. Zen was just as much his victim as the others.

Sometimes, he could almost make himself believe that.

In the rail yard outside Cleave Station the *Gentlemen Take Polaroids* paused to take on fuel, and Zen slipped out, stepped through a gate that one of the train's spiders opened for him in the trackside fencing, and set off into the city. Myka had told him where to go. Down mean and greasy stairs between the waterfalls, along clanging walkways into the maze of the industrial stacks, where huge factory flues reached up the canyon walls toward the distant surface like gigantic organ pipes. At last he opened a packing-crate door and went through it into a vaulted, thundery space beneath the railway.

It was full of dreams. The walls, the roof, even parts of the floor were covered with visions of elsewhere. Birds with human faces, fish with legs, crowned rainbows and tattooed cities, improbable flying machines, faces wise and foolish. All only paint, sprayed and brushed onto the old ceramic brickwork. Only paint—so how did they seem so *alive*?

"Zen?" Flex was sitting on a bunk at the vault's far end, face lit by the glow from a small screen. "I heard you'd left. Hadn't thought I'd see you again."

Even now that he knew Flex was Motorik, it was difficult to believe she was not human—or *he*, perhaps. Last time he'd seen her, Zen had been pretty sure she was a girl. Now she had a squarer jaw, a deeper voice, different ways of moving. It was still hard to be sure, but if Zen had been forced to guess, he would have said he was male.

"How's Myka?" asked Flex.

"She's well. Sends her love." Zen looked around him. When Myka used to tell him about Flex living rough, Zen had imagined somewhere messy: as messy as his place would be if he lived that way. But the arch was tidy. No food or cooking gear, of course. No comforts except for that simple bunk. Just a few boxes of paints and stuff lined up along a ledge, some trainspottery trophy photos of famous locos, the *Galactic Unlimited* and the *Hightown Crow*. Bio-glow lamps threw Flex's shadow over the paintings on the wall.

"They're amazing," said Zen.

Flex beamed. "They're just practice. I try things out here, then I paint on the trains."

"The one I came in on says hello, by the way. It was called *Gentlemen Take Polaroids*."

"Good old *Polaroids*," said Flex with a smile.

"Sorry I nearly got you caught that night, in the rail yards . . ."

"Sorry I left you there," said Flex. "I thought you were right behind me . . ."

Zen shrugged to show it didn't matter, but he was glad

Flex felt guilty about that. It made it easier to ask another favor.

"I need your help again," he said. "Not for me, for a friend. She's someone like you."

"A tagger?" asked Flex.

"A Motorik."

Flex's expression changed. He was better at pretending to be human than Nova, and his expressions were easier to read. He was afraid.

"Did Myka tell you about me?" he asked.

Zen laughed. "Oh no. I worked it out for myself, a long time ago." He meant, *I've been keeping your secret safe, just like my sister. You can trust me. You owe me.*

"Myka saved me during the riots," said Flex. "She helped me hide till I could pass as human . . ."

"You should tell me the whole story sometime," said Zen. "But I'm in a hurry. This friend of mine, she's badly damaged. You heard what happened on the Spindlebridge? She was there. A drone harpooned her and pulled her out into space. But she could survive that, couldn't she?"

Flex nodded slowly, carefully skirting around all the other questions that one raised, about what Zen's friend had been doing annoying drones on the Spindlebridge in the first place. He said, "We keep our central processing units in our heads, like you. There are subsystems in the torso, but they should self-repair, and space wouldn't be a problem—a lot of Motorik work in vacuum environments, on comet mines and such. But I don't see how you think I can help her."

"I need to get to Sundarban," said Zen, "and I can't just take the K-bahn. There's all sorts of new security stuff at the stations, and Sundarban will be worse."

"So what will you do?"

"I was thinking maybe you could get me down into the old Cleave-B station."

Flex looked doubtful. "The Dog Star Line? I've heard it's down there . . . The trains don't like to talk about it."

"I've seen it," said Zen. "It's there all right. Rails, trains, everything. But I don't know how to get to it."

"Me neither," said Flex. "I think that stuff was all closed up pretty tight." He hummed to himself, thinking. For a moment Zen thought he was going to refuse, and wondered if he would have to threaten him. That would be easy enough to do—"If you don't help me, Flex," he'd say, "I'll run outside and tell the proud workers of Cleave that there's a wire dolly hiding out in the stacks." He just didn't want to have to say it.

Luckily, Flex seemed intrigued by his story of the hidden station. "There are trains down there? Really?"

"Some. I saw them. Dead, or sleeping."

"The only people who might know a way in are the Hive Monks."

"Why would they know?"

"Cuz they're always rustling about down there, in and out of the deep tunnels," said Flex. "Some of those passages under the K-bahn are so ankle-deep in dead bugs, it's like wading through breakfast cereal."

"The old station was the same," said Zen, mentally crossing breakfast cereal off a list of things he would ever want to eat again. "Dead bugs everywhere. So you reckon they know a way in?"

"You'd have to ask them."

"Has Uncle Bugs pulled himself together yet?"

"His shop is still closed. If he's back together, he must be hiding out with the other Monks, down in Roachtown."

"I don't want to go to Roachtown!"

"If you want to find a way into Cleave-B, you'll have to," said Flex. He thought for a moment—perhaps remembering how badly things had turned out the last time he helped Zen Starling. Then kindness or curiosity got the better of him. He said, "I've been down there before. I can show you."

30

Roachtown was a district down in Cleave's depths, full of dead factories and the roar of the river. It flooded regularly, so no one lived there. No one but the Hive Monks, who found their way to Cleave from all across the Network and came rustling ponderously down the wet stairways to gather in the big, derelict bio-buildings. There they made homes for themselves out of the debris that the river washed up or the human residents of Cleave threw down from high above. There they quietly did whatever disgusting things Hive Monks got up to when no one was around to see.

Zen tied strings around his trouser legs before he started the long walk down Roachtown Stair. Tied them round his wrists, too. "Where there's Monks there's bugs," he said. "There'll be squillions of them that haven't formed a colony yet and will be running about mindless. I don't want them running up inside my clothes."

"They wouldn't really do that," Flex said. "I don't think they would."

189

Then he tied string around his legs and wrists too, just in case.

Down the long stair they went, until the bridges and the busy air traffic of the gorge were far above them and Cleave River was rushing past a hundred feet below. The old factories clustered along a wet ledge like Halloween pumpkins left out in the rain. Lights showed dimly through a few windows. Uncertain hands had painted a sign on the wall that read:

ROACHTOwN Pop. 100,000,000,000

They went carefully along the slippery pavement into the first of the factories. The sound of the river was quieter in there. In its place was another sound: the white noise of insects, whisper of feet and scrape of carapace. The shadows seethed with bugs: males scuttling across the rough floors, the larger, winged females blundering through the air. A shape that wanted to look human levered itself up out of a broken armchair and shambled toward them, like a beekeeper engulfed by his swarm. Cicada voices chittered, "Welcome."

"We're here to see Uncle Bugs," said Flex. "Zen Starling here wants to know if he's all right."

The Hive Monk whispered and fidgeted. Under its hood, its face was the face of a broken Motorik, antennae bristling from empty eyeholes and a twisted, gaping mouth. It said, "Someone scattered Uncle Bugs. Wreck smash. Long time it take he to come together."

"That wasn't Zen," said Flex. "We're just here to see how he is."

"Good old Uncle Bugs!" said Zen, though he was having trouble keeping the smile on his face. This wasn't like Uncle Bugs's shop—and Uncle Bugs's shop was bad enough. This place was vile.

Other Hive Monks had appeared out of the shadows. Streams of insects flowed from under the hems of their robes, or whirred from the darkness beneath their hoods. The Monks were exchanging parts of themselves, exchanging thoughts.

The Monk who had first spoken raised one arm like the clumsy puppet that he was and made a gesture. Beckoning, Zen guessed. *Come with me, human visitors.* Deeper into Roachtown. He shuffled away, and they followed.

They passed a ziggurat of broken toasters, a wall of lost left shoes. They came to a small room that must have been a supervisor's office once, when the factory was still a factory. Inside was a thing that looked at first like a big beanbag, then like an ants' nest, then like a stranded octopus. A waist-high mound, constantly moving. It was made of bugs, and streams of bugs like busy tentacles extended from it, fumbling with a thing of twigs and string that lay on the floor. Tiny mandibles wove and tied, trimmed and carried. Other bugs dragged some pale and plate-like object from a corner and carried it to the top of the mound. It was the paper face of Uncle Bugs.

"Zen Starling," said the mound.

Zen waved. "Came to see how you are," he said. He wished he had brought chocolates or grapes or something. What did Hive Monks eat? No, best not to even think about that . . .

"A drone shot me, Zen Starling," said the mound. "With a gun. Bang! Taken me all this time to find my mind again. Got to make a new skellington, too."

"I know," said Zen. "I'm sorry about that. But I've come to ask for your help."

"What help?"

"The old station. Flex says you know a way in."

"No way in to the old station," said Uncle Bugs.

"But I've been down there."

"No way in. All shut."

"I've seen the platforms, and the old trains waiting."

Sometimes, on warm nights in Santheraki when the crickets had been singing, a sudden noise or movement would make them stop, all together, and the silence would seem louder than all the noise they had been making. That was what happened now. The Hive Monks froze, and Zen could hear the river again, and the amplified jingle from an advertisement high above.

"Dead trains," whispered Uncle Bugs. "All dead."

"How do you know?" asked Flex.

Uncle Bugs seemed to sigh, but it was just the sound of all the bugs that made him shifting position. The paper mask slipped sideways, then came upright again. "We want—Hive Monks have always wanted—a train. That will cross the bright gates. That will go where we tell it, not where human people want to go."

"Where's that?" asked Zen. "Where do you want to go?"

"To the Insect Lines," said Uncle Bugs. "We see them in our dreams. Beautiful, they are! We travel and travel, trying to reach them, but we cannot reach them. A train could take us there. But we have no train. When we found this place, this Cleave, the dead trains underground, we thought good, we wake one, it will carry us. We make it take us through the bright gate to the Insect Lines. That is why so many of us are here. That is why the shop: we need money to buy things to make the train work again. But the train not work. Not for us. Not for us."

The paper face lay down in sadness. The bugs rubbed their legs together with a sad sound like a million tiny violins. The Hive Monks wanted to be human, Zen thought. That was their tragedy. They saw people riding the trains, passing through the K-gates, going wherever they wanted. They thought that if they made themselves human-shaped and found their own train it would take them to—where? What were these Insect Lines supposed to be? Beetle heaven? But the trains, for some trainish reason of their own, wouldn't work for Monks, only for humans.

"Thing about trains," said Zen, "you'll have to give them something. In return for carrying you."

"We give the trains many things," said Uncle Bugs.

"I can imagine," said Zen. "What? Rotting meat? Old shoes? Broken chairs?"

Uncle Bugs looked as sheepish as it was possible to look when you were a paper face being held up by a load of beetles.

Zen pointed to Flex. "You know who this is? This is Flex. This is the best tagger on the Network. Trains love her . . . him painting on them. You let him paint one of those old locos for you and it'll be raring to get through the bright gates, showing off its new graffiti. We'll talk to it for you. Trains probably don't even recognize those sounds you make as words. Let me have a word with one, and Flex can paint it."

"Flex?" said Uncle Bugs. "Flex the painter? Flex who the trains love?" Outside the office, streams of bugs carried the name from one Monk to another, "Flex? Flex?"

"You would do this for us?" asked Uncle Bugs.

"I'll have a go," said Flex.

"And in return?"

"On your way to these Insect Lines, drop me at Sundarban," said Zen.

For a little while there was just scuttling and rustling and the whir of wings as the Monks communicated with each other. Then Uncle Bugs started to move. The mound shallowed, spreading across the floor, making Zen and Flex jump backward. The swarming brown bodies of the insects covered the framework that lay there. They began piling themselves up in towers and teetering insect pyramids to heave the sticks upright. Shins, thighs, torso. The spindly wooden skeleton rose, wobbled, and was enfleshed with insects. Clumsy arms reached out, groping with pincer fingertips, fitting the paper face in place on a head that swelled like a bubble, plucking a burlap robe that hung from a hook on the wall. Uncle Bugs pulled the garment over himself and poured himself inside it. He adjusted his face again, the pale mask peering out at them from the shadows of the robe's deep hood.

"Good," he whispered. "You come now. We take you by the old ways to where the trains sleep. We show you. Come with us."

31

They went out of the factory and away through the Roachtown shadows, surrounded by the Hive Monks, who hurried along like novice stilt-walkers on their scrapheap skeletons. They seemed unreliable guides. Zen wondered if their way into Cleave-B would turn out to be impossible for humans. Just some crack between two bricks, perhaps, through which a hive of bugs could pour itself and drag its collapsed armature through behind it, like a folded-up model ship going into a bottle.

But he need not have worried. There was a door, old and forgotten, on an old, forgotten street where water raining down from streets above had filled the abandoned houses with whispering crowds of ferns. The door was shut, and had been locked, but the Hive Monks had picked the lock a long time ago. Hissing and heaving, toppling the busy weight of themselves against the door, they pushed it open. The passage beyond was dark, but old lights bolted to the ceiling woke when they sensed movement, and filled it with a sepia glow.

Zen hung back, not liking the thought of that narrow space, those clumsy insect-men. Flex put a hand on his back and pushed him gently forward, over the threshold. "It's all right," he said. "There's no harm in Hive Monks."

Which was all very well for him to say, Zen thought. Flex reminded him of Myka, when he was little, telling him there was no harm in the big brown spiders that spun their webs between the basement stairs. (And maybe there wasn't, but he wouldn't have wanted to go into a tunnel with a load of them, either.)

Still, he was not going to let Flex see that he was frightened. And as long as he didn't look down at the bugs that kept spilling out from under the Monks' robes, or concentrate on the crunchy sounds the dead ones made each time he put his foot down, it was possible to imagine that the hooded forms ahead and behind were just people after all.

They reached an old elevator, half-mad and muttering to itself, but happy enough to whisk them up three hundred feet to the level where the platforms were. The empty shops and waiting rooms were all as Zen remembered; he left Flex to stare at them like a child in a museum and went with the Hive Monks past the barriers and out to where the trains waited.

He had glimpsed the trains only briefly when Nova was leading him to the *Thought Fox*, and his memory had multiplied them until he was sure there had been ten or more, and much bigger than they were really were. In fact there were only three, and one of those was a brainless, bull-nosed shunter, coupled to a row of dirty freight cars. Of the other two, one was derelict, the ceramic cowling of its hull peeled open to expose gaping wounds where the Hive Monks had dragged parts of its systems out.

Zen jumped down off the platform and walked across the tracks in front of it to where the third train waited. The Hive Monks shambled ahead of him, reaching out to brush its wheels and sides with the antennae of their fingers. A huge, heavy, old-fashioned loco, the red curves of its hull faintly iridescent in the dim light. It looked a bit like a gigantic beetle. Maybe that was why the Hive Monks had chosen it and not the other one, a sleeker, newer model.

Its name was *Damask Rose*.

Zen walked right round the loco, kicking through the piles of little gifts the Hive Monks had stacked against its wheels, climbing over the couplings where it was attached to the first of its five dusty carriages. By the time he got back to where he started, Flex had made his way through from the main concourse and was staring at the train too.

"It's a beauty!" Flex said, looking up at all that curved ceramic just waiting to be decorated. "One of the old Foss Industries 257s, I think. I've always wanted to tag one of these."

Zen switched his headset on and let it scan for the train's mind. At first there was nothing. He was starting to wonder if it was dead after all when a big voice suddenly spoke through speakers on the loco's flanks, startling him, scaring all the bustling Hive Monks into stillness.

"I am waiting," said the *Damask Rose*. It had a voice like a slightly fussy schoolteacher. "I am waiting for instructions from the Sirius Rail Company. Until then, passengers will remain on the platform."

"That's going to be a long wait," said Zen. "I don't think there will be any instructions. This line's been closed for a long time. Haven't you talked to the Hive Monks? Haven't they told you what's happened?"

"I pay no attention," the old locomotive said, "to the chattering of insects."

"Well, maybe you ought to," said Zen.

"I am a locomotive of the Sirius Rail Company," said the *Damask Rose*. "I respond only to them."

"You're responding to me, though," Zen pointed out. "I'm not Sirius Rail. Nobody is, not anymore. We need you to take us to Sundarban and then on to other stops. You can do that, can't you? You must want to run again. Jump through those K-gates. You've missed that, I expect."

A wistful silence. The train was thinking.

"I'll paint you, train," said Flex. He stepped past Zen and stood with his hands pressed against the loco's prow. He looked up at it as if he could already see the pictures there. "I'll paint such pictures on you."

"What pictures?"

"Not sure yet. Nothing too gaudy. Purples and warm grays, I think. A lot of pattern, and the pictures tangled in the patterns. Maybe, along your pistons and your wheel guards, wings."

"Wings?" said the train.

"You fly," said Flex. "You fly between the stars, across the worlds."

"I did," said the train. "Oh, I did! But I am only a working loco, pulling standard class carriages. Trains like me are not usually decorated. Not on the Dog Star Line."

"The line is closed down," said Zen. "You can do what you like now. You don't want to sit here forever, do you? Take us to Sundarban."

"And after Sundarban," said Uncle Bugs, "we would like it if—please, O train—you took us to the Insect Lines."

"Is your pile of beetles trying to say something?" asked the

Damask Rose. It wasn't clear if it really couldn't understand the Hive Monks' whisperings or if it was just pretending not to because it didn't like them. When Flex repeated Uncle Bugs's request it said, "And *what*, pray, are the 'Insect Lines'?"

Uncle Bugs and his comrades whispered together, streams of busy insects flowing between them. The one thing Hive Monks had and humans didn't was the secret knowledge of their faith; explaining it while Zen and Flex were listening would be like giving up ancient treasure. But how else could they make the *Damask Rose* understand? They whispered for a while, then Uncle Bugs stepped forward. He spoke to Flex, for even the Hive Monks seemed to understand that Flex was the kindest of the two.

"Please," he whispered, "explain to the train that in the light of the bright gates, certain revelations were made to us. Our ancestors spoke with the great shining ones in the light of the bright gates. In the light of the bright gates the shining ones told them of the Insect Lines where the nests of the shining ones lie lit by the light of the bright gates. We would walk in that light among those nests, but we cannot pass the bright gates as the shining ones do. For centuries we have traveled, hoping, but now we see that only our own train can carry us. That is why we tended you, O train. That is why we repaired and woke you. Please, O train, carry us onto the Insect Lines!"

He folded in the middle, collapsing on the tracks in a heap of burlap and heaving beetle bodies, prostrating himself before the train. Around him, the other Monks did likewise.

"The Insect Lines!" they rustled. "The Insect Lines!"

"Pssssccchhhhh," said the train, a long hydraulic snort of disapproval.

"Great shining ones?" asked Zen. "Do you mean Station Angels?"

"The shining ones," whispered Uncle Bugs, and a thousand antennae quivered behind his mask. "Angels."

"They're not alive," said Flex. "They're just some kind of mist that comes off the K-gates when a train goes through."

"They bring messages," insisted Uncle Bugs. "From the Insect Lines."

Zen said nothing, remembering the shapes that had danced with Raven in lost Desdemor.

Flex told the train what the Hive Monks had been saying. It snorted again. "I've never heard of any Insect Lines."

"Maybe they're between the K-gates somehow, like in another dimension," said Flex. "If the *Damask Rose* could stop between gates . . ."

"You don't 'stop between gates,'" said the train. "There isn't anything between them to stop *in*. You go in, you come out. That's the way it works—at least, that's the nearest I can explain it to your undereducated, three-dimensional brain." (It had come as a shock to the *Damask Rose* to discover that it had been abandoned for so long, and only revived because a bunch of eccentric insects wanted it to take them for a pleasure trip. It was feeling lost and lonely, and that made it tend to snap.) "I thought you said you were going to paint me?" it said.

"Okay," agreed Flex.

Another pause. Then it said, "I must wait for instructions from the Sirius Rail Company."

"Agh!" said Zen, frustrated. "Are all trains this stupid?"

The Hive Monks chittered and buzzed. Trains were sacred to them; they were shocked that he'd called one stupid.

Flex just raised his hand and said, "It's old and all alone and it isn't sure what's going on. Give it time to think." He leaned his face against the train's warm side.

The train purred. It liked Flex.

"Take us one stop, train," he said. "Just one stop. "Try contacting the Sirius Rail office there. If you can, and they don't approve of us, we'll catch the next train back."

The train thought about that. Then, with a sound like a sigh, it opened the doors of its first carriage. "Very well," it said as they hurried aboard. "But just one stop, mind. I'm not promising Sundarban, and certainly not this beetley place. And I'm not taking all these, pssssscccchhhhh, these beetle-men. Only two. Three at the most. Otherwise I'll be finding dead bugs in the cracks between my seats for weeks."

The Hive Monks started to protest, but the train sounded too stern to argue with. They whispered urgently together, and pushed forward their three ambassadors—Uncle Bugs and two others. They came aboard the train with Zen and Flex, running the swarms of their hands over the pillars and the musty seat backs.

"When we find the Insect Lines," said Uncle Bugs, to the others left behind on the platform, "we shall return and take you with us."

"Pssssssscchhhh," said the *Damask Rose,* and closed its doors, shutting out the angry gesticulations, the rustly muttering of the Monks. A whirring sound came from beneath the carriage floor. The train jolted forward. Couplings clanked and buffers banged as each carriage bumped into the one in front. From light fittings and luggage racks a fine rain of dust fell, settling on Zen's hair, Flex's hat, and the raised hoods of the three Hive Monks. The train was moving. It hummed to itself, gathering speed, happy to be traveling again. A few minutes later they hit the K-gate, and then the mists of Tashgar were pressing against the carriage windows like filthy rags.

"What's this place?" asked Flex, staring out aghast at the dead landscape.

When they came to a station the *Damask Rose* slowed, but it did not stop. The wind of its passing stirred the dust-drifts on the platforms. The train opened hatches on its hull and poked out flower-shaped antennae, which it pointed at various portions of the sky. It trawled the Datasea with its wireless mind. All it found was static, and whispered transmissions that had left the far stars centuries ago.

"What has happened?" asked the *Damask Rose*.

"The line was closed," said Zen. "The station died. The city was abandoned. Keep going, train. Take us to Sundarban. There are trains and people there, and other lines, and news."

The *Damask Rose* made a deep, unhappy sound, and gathered speed again. Its passengers settled into their seats. After a while, when the light of a few more gates had washed over them and they were a long way from Cleave, Flex started to tell Zen his story.

32

It had been one of a unit of Motorik sent over to Cleave from the Prell Cybernetics factory in Golconda. Model PIT365, designation: Flex. There had been twenty-four others just like it. The Guardians had decreed long ago that a certain number of jobs on any world should be reserved for human workers, to preserve stability, but machines were cheaper, and the corporate families had persuaded Emperor Mahalaxmi to change the law so that Motorik were classed as human. One of the factories in Cleave had purchased Flex's batch to clean the flues of its blast furnaces.

The human workers who had been paid to clean the flues until then were not pleased to see these new Motorik laborers. The job was hard and dangerous and dirty, but it was their job. If they let these wire dollies replace them, where would it end? There probably wasn't a job anywhere on the Network that Motos couldn't do cheaper than real human beings. So they protested. They asked the other workers to join them. "Smash them!" they shouted, and went to ambush the freight container holding the Motorik as it was being trucked into the factory.

The container was massive and stoutly locked, but one of the workers was driving a thing called an "Iron Penguin," a pear-shaped armored suit with massive manipulator claws. She wrenched the doors off, and her comrades barged into the container, waving tools and makeshift clubs.

The earliest Motorik had been built for the military as ground assault drones. Research had proven that soldiers were less willing to fire on something that looked human; there was a momentary hesitation that gave military Motorik an edge. But the workers of Cleave must have been made of tougher stuff than soldiers were, because they didn't hesitate when they saw the new Motos. "We are pleased to meet you, fellow laborers," the newcomers said politely. They seemed confused when the blows began to fall. "Please tell us how we have displeased you," asked the one standing next to Flex, while a burly foreman knocked its head off with a wrench.

Somehow, among all the shouting and crashing, among the thrashing of severed Motorik limbs and gouts of gel and cries of, "Smash the wire dollies!" Flex found itself outside the container. The Iron Penguin closed huge claws around it and lifted it off its feet. Flex twisted round and looked through the machine's windshield, into the face of the driver, an angry brown girl with MYKA stitched across the front of her greasy work cap.

Angry, but not that angry, it turned out. Myka could have snipped the Motorik into pieces with those claws, but although she'd been as outraged as all the others when she heard about the company's plans to ship in putala labor, she felt suddenly less violent now that heads were being crushed and arms torn off and the blue gel, which served the wire dollies for blood, was pouring in such startling quantities out of the container. She met the eyes of the Motorik she had caught, and saw nothing in them but confusion. Nobody had bothered telling it that the world was going to be like this.

"Me neither," she said disgustedly, and rather than slamming the claws shut, she opened them, turning the Penguin quickly at the same instant. Flex was flung out of the battle, over a hand-rail, and dropped several stories into a pile of garbage that had been slung out on the bank of Cleave River for the next flood to wash away.

There Flex lay, wondering about what had just happened and why. It hid in the heaps of refuse while the shouting died away above. Its brain had been damaged, it thought. It kept getting strange ideas. It found old tiles in the garbage, and started scratching marks on them with a bit of rusty wire. It looked at the marks and liked them. It discovered that they could be turned into pictures. It concentrated. It drew faces and hands. It drew the Iron Penguin and the girl who drove it. It drew the river, rushing by.

Night came to Cleave. The strip of stormy sky that showed between the canyon's high walls turned black, and some of the shops and factories killed their lights. Flex went on drawing, until it heard someone come climbing down the ladder from the factory above.

It edged backward into a cleft of the canyon wall and watched as a flashlight beam swept the garbage mounds. It did not need a flashlight to see in the dark. It could see that the newcomer was Myka. It wondered if she regretted not destroying it when she had the chance. It wondered if she had come down here to find it and finish it off. It watched her stoop and pick up a tile. She looked at the tile for a long time, and Flex guessed that she had found the picture it had made of her. She looked around in case someone had left it there as a joke and was watching from the shadows, laughing. Flex stayed very still. Nothing moved but the ferns, which danced like slow green flames under the spray from the river.

"Moto?" she called. "You still down here?"

It felt the flashlight beam touch it. It saw the girl start as she noticed its pale face watching her through the ferns. She put the tile into one of the big pockets on the leg of her overalls and came crunching and slithering over the garbage. She said a word that Flex had not been programmed to recognize, probably a curse. She said, "What are we going to do with you?"

"Please, I would like to leave this place," said Flex.

Myka snorted. "Good luck with that. They're smashing all your sort. There are mobs outside the station, dragging wire dollies off the incoming trains, breaking them up, using their heads for lanterns. You're going to have to stay hidden."

"Thank you," said Flex. "For not breaking me."

"I wish I had," said Myka. "I wish I could. If they find out I've helped you . . ."

"Sorry," said Flex.

Myka picked up the tile that Flex had been working on when she came down the ladder. She looked at the picture scratched on it. She said, "I didn't know Motorik could draw."

"Neither did I."

"Were you programmed for design work or something?"

"I do not think so."

She put the tile down and looked at Flex's face again. (Zen could imagine what her expression had been. Exasperated, but kindly. She had been looking after her mother and her kid brother since she was little, and now this stupid Moto needed looking after too.)

"You can't stay here," she told it. "I can show you a stairway that leads up into the stacks. Plenty of places to hide out in the stacks. But someone's bound to see you, so you're going to have to stop looking so . . . You're going to have to look like a human being."

"How?" asked Flex.

"Your skin's too pale, and your eyes are too far apart, and . . ."

Flex dipped into the menus of its mind. Its white face darkened, taking on a brownish tone not far off Myka's own. Its eyebrows thickened into a Myka-ish unibrow.

"Don't overdo it," Myka said. She looked at its clothes—the remnants of its papery gray overalls, which hung in rags now, baring its blank and sexless body. "Are you a boy or a girl?" she asked it. "Male or female? Most people are one or the other, in Cleave."

"Which are you?" asked Flex.

"Female, of course."

Flex found a setting in its menus labeled GENDER and selected FEMALE.

Myka went rummaging in the garbage heap and found some overalls, and a lady's rain cape with plastic flowers for buttons. She made Flex put the clothes on, then sat back on her haunches and studied her. She told her to make her hair longer, and styled it roughly with her hands. "Well," she said, "you're an odd-looking girl, but at least people won't think 'wire dolly' as soon as they see you. You'll need to work at it, though. You need to watch people—you're good at that, I can tell from the way you draw. Watch us and copy how we move. Listen, and copy how we talk. But don't go talking to anybody except me, not unless you have to."

"No, Myka."

She led Flex along the riverside, along the rusted walkways, which jutted from the rock face there, up wet stairways, into the complicated alleys between the stacks. Before they parted she pinged something from her headset into Flex's brain: a messaging address. "Anything you need," she said, "you call me. I can bring you food, or whatever. But I guess your sort don't need food?"

Flex did not need food, but she needed power. She made her way alone through the stacks, and into the rail yards. She recharged herself from the unit that drove the huge loco-motive turntable outside the station. In an access space between the tracks she made a small lair for herself. She listened with her mind to the big, calm minds of the trains as they came and went. She heard their songs. They knew that she was there, but they didn't seem to care. On the walls of her den, where dirt and damp had stained the ceramic, she started scratching draw-ings. She drew trains and Iron Penguins and flowers and trucks and clothes. She drew Myka. She went out into the streets and watched people and came back and drew them. She delved into the Datasea and found other things to draw, things she didn't even know the names of.

Every few days there was a message from Myka in her mind. *"You still there, Moto?"* or *"You need anything?"* One day she messaged back. *"Please, I would like things to draw with . . ."*

"So Myka started bringing me paintsticks from the factory stores," said Flex, smiling at the memory while the *Damask Rose* carried him farther and farther from Cleave. "I started drawing on the trains. And when people started to recognize my pictures, they came and found me, and asked me to paint signs for shops and decorate taxis and trucks. They paid me in paintsticks and free power. And Myka helped me buy stuff, clothes and things, so I'd fit in better. She came sometimes just to talk. She told me about you, and your ma. She said I was a good listener."

And all this had been going on, thought Zen, while he'd been off on his thieving trips to Ambersai and Tusk, or hanging out at the Spatterpattern, or lying on his bed at Bridge Street, listening to Ma moan and fret. Myka would come home wet and tired and he'd always just assume she'd come straight from her dead-end job. He felt like a fool for not noticing that Flex was a Motorik; he felt a bigger one for never imagining that his sister might have this other life going on, this adventure of her own.

"Myka's right," he said. "There's so much I don't know about her."

Flex smiled. "She's good. Like you."

"Me? I'm not good."

"But you are going to all this trouble to help a Motorik, just like Myka helped me."

"It's different," said Zen.

"When we get to Sundarban," said Flex, "you'll have to get into orbit to find Nova. How will you do that?"

"I have a plan," said Zen.

Which wasn't true. He had only a fragment of an idea, more of a desperate hope than a plan. It was going to be risky, and perhaps impossible, but he had to try. If he could steal Nova back from death, perhaps it would make up for all the deaths he'd caused at Spindlebridge.

33

The *Damask Rose* did not go all the way into Sundarban Station. Zen told her to stop when she was still deep in the tunnels outside the station city.

"Do you want me to come?" asked Flex.

Zen shook his head. "You wait here. If you don't mind the bugs."

"I don't mind them," said Flex.

He spoke in a whisper, not sure how good Hive Monks' hearing was. They clustered at the far end of the carriage, rustling. Uncle Bugs and his two friends, who seemed to have no names. If Nova had been there, Zen thought, she would have made up names for them: Buzz and Cricket, something like that. But if Nova had been there, he would never have been caught up in this mad venture.

"Well, keep an eye on them," he warned. He didn't trust those bugs. They had come on this trip for their own reasons, and they didn't care about him. What if they found some way to make the old train listen to them, and persuaded it to move off before he got back?

"I'll watch them," said Flex. "And I'll get busy with the train's paintwork."

One of the train's maintenance spiders led Zen for miles through the tunnels, until he came to an access stairway leading to the surface. He took a deep breath, and began to climb.

*

Sundarban turned out to be the fanciest city he'd ever seen. It was the Noons' hometown, and they had built it to impress. Proud towers rose into the afternoon haze like fairy-tale rocket ships waiting to leap into orbit. Between them shone the station canopies—a hundred platforms, serving the K-gates, which lay hidden among the surrounding mountains. Wherever he looked, bright trains were moving, crossing bridges above the busy streets, passing through archways in the buildings. Sundarban's malls seemed open for business as usual, but Motorik work crews were busy removing the giant portraits of Mahalaxmi XXIII from their facades and replacing them with images of Priya I, who looked nervous and uncertain of herself, even in photographs. The public screens were profiling a woman called Rail Marshal Delius, whom they said had arrived in Sundarban to show her support for the young Empress, although the gossip sites that Zen picked up on his headset claimed she was really there to decide whether Priya Noon was worth supporting, or whether Railforce should side with her uncle. In times like these, when there were two or three rivals for the job of Emperor, the one who came out on top would be the one who had the backing of Railforce.

Bluebodies in combat armor patrolled the moving stairways

and stood guard outside the entrances to the station platforms. Zen rehearsed a story to tell if anyone asked him who he was, but no one did.

His first plan had been to pose as a salvage hunter and hire a shuttle to take him into orbit. That was before he found out how much hiring a shuttle cost. No wonder space travel had never caught on. He wasn't sure he could afford it. Even if he could, transferring that sort of money through the Sundarban data raft was going to draw him to the attention of all kinds of people.

So he found a quiet booth in a café, put on his headset, and quickly scanned the social nets. Kobi Chen-Tulsi was not hard to find. His smug selfies grinned from a dozen different sites. Zen chose the site that Kobi seemed to use least, and messaged him. "It's Tallis here. From Jangala. How are the bruises healing?"

*

Threnody was walking beside the stream that wound through the Chen-Tulsis' gardens when Kobi came to find her. When she first heard his voice calling, "Thren! Thren!" she pretended not to hear, just so she could have a few seconds more by herself, but when he came limping over to where she stood, she put on a smile and turned to meet him. She was surprised to see how worried he looked.

"Something's happened," he said. "You remember that cousin of yours, on the train? Tallis?"

She thought, *So they have found him, and he's dead.* Kobi's family had been coordinating the salvage efforts, sending up shuttles to gather the larger bits of wreckage. She thought, *They have found Tallis's body, and Kobi's come to tell me . . .*

But Kobi said, "He messaged me!"

"He's alive?" She should have felt happy, but she didn't. The news made her wary, and she was not sure why. Where had Tallis been, since the crash? And why was he messaging Kobi? Why not her?

"He's threatening me!" said Kobi.

"*What?*"

"He says I have to do something for him, or he'll upload his headset recording of the hunt on Jangala to every newsfeed and gossip site on Sundarban. He says he wonders how my parents will react when they see his footage of the . . . the fight."

"It wasn't a fight, Kobi," said Threnody. She glanced behind her to check that none of the servants or security drones were in earshot. "You knocked him down from behind. You tried to kill him. At least, that's how it will look . . ."

"I know!" said Kobi miserably.

Threnody felt sorry for him, and surprised at Tallis. He must be looking for revenge after what Kobi had done. She thought it seemed petty of him, considering everything that had happened since.

"So what does he want you to do?" she asked.

"He says he needs to get into orbit," said Kobi. "I know—it's bizarre. But he says he knows my family's shuttles are making regular flights, and he wants to go up on one."

"Have you told your family?"

"No! Only you! I shouldn't even be telling you. Tallis was very clear about that. He said, 'Tell no one. I'm smarter than you. Do you think I haven't mapped out all the twists and turns this thing could take? There's no way out for you that's any easier than just doing what I ask.'"

"That doesn't sound like the sort of thing Tallis would

say," said Threnody. But what was the sort of thing Tallis would say? If she was honest, she had barely known him, and anyway, her memories of him were all smudged and muddled by the more vivid, physical memories of the train crash. She didn't know him, and she didn't know anything about his branch of the family, the Golden Junction Noons. For all she knew, they might be angling for the leadership themselves, or in league with Uncle Tibor. For all she knew—

A terrible thought came to her. What if Tallis had been working for Uncle Tibor from the start? What if he had come aboard the Noon train as a spy? What if the crash had been something to do with him? She remembered how she had welcomed him aboard. How she had waved him through security. This was going to look bad, she thought. If it turned out Tallis had been up to something, then she would be accused of helping him. She hadn't meant to, of course; she had only done what any of the Noons would do; she had had no reason to suspect him, none at all.

But Priya wouldn't see it that way. Priya would think that she was part of cousin Tallis's conspiracy. Priya would have her tried as a traitor to the family, sent to the freezers . . . Even the thought made Threnody feel cold.

"You were right not to tell anyone," she told Kobi. "Can you message him back?"

"He said he'd contact me."

"And is there a shuttle you could take him up on?"

"I suppose. We have a scheduled flight leaving from Launch Pan 50 at twenty-hundred hours."

"Tell him you'll meet him there," said Threnody. "We need to find out what this is really about."

"Yes," said Kobi. "Yes, Thren."

He looked so meek, so defeated, that she felt quite fond of him.

*

Zen had spent that afternoon looking for a weapons shop that accepted cash and asked no questions. It had taken awhile, but he had found one in the end, and they had printed him a little snub-nosed pistol and sold him a cassette of ammunition. He could feel the weight of the gun in his pocket as an air-taxi took him out to Launch Pan 50.

The launch pans were in sandy hills south of the city. Evening by then: the sun going down red behind veils of dust. The ship that waited on Pan 50 was called the *Spacehopper*. It looked pretty from a distance, but when Zen stepped out of the taxi and walked closer, those creamy circles on its yellow wings turned out to be only spotlight beams, and the dark leading edges were just where the ceramic had been scorched and pitted by countless descents through the atmosphere.

Kobi was waiting for him at the foot of the boarding ladder, as he had promised. But he wasn't alone. He had brought Threnody with him.

Zen had not imagined that Threnody would come anywhere near Kobi, given how she felt about him, and what Lady Sufra had said about their engagement being broken. When he saw her, he almost panicked, almost turned and left, but his taxi had already taken off.

"She's the only person I told," Kobi said, hurrying across the pan to meet him. "I had to. We were supposed to be going out this evening; I had to explain . . ."

He's telling the truth, Zen thought. *He hates me, but he dares not cross me.* It was a strange feeling, knowing that Kobi was afraid of him. He liked it.

Threnody leaned against the boarding ladder, watching him. She was not afraid. He could see her trying to work him out. He checked the sky for her family's drones, but it seemed clear.

"Cousin Tallis," she said. "Where have you been, since the crash?"

He shrugged. "Here and there."

"I was worried about you. I checked. There was no record of you coming down from Spindlebridge."

"Well, in all the confusion after—"

"Why didn't you let me know you were safe?"

"I thought—"

"Why have you come back?" she asked, and he knew she suspected something.

"I'm glad you're all right," he said.

"Oh, I'm all right," she replied. "My father is dead, and half my uncles and aunts and cousins. Fat Uncle Tibor is challenging my sister for the throne. The newsfeeds are saying that Elon Prell is going to declare himself Emperor as well, which will mean we'll be at war with the Prell family. And now my cousin Tallis is blackmailing my fiancé. But I'm *all right,* Tallis. Do you really have footage from Jangala?"

Zen nodded. "I recorded the whole thing," he promised. He sent a copy to her headset. Three wobbly seconds of Kobi, gun in his hands and eyes full of spite.

"Is that all?"

"That's a sample," Zen lied. "I recorded the whole thing."

Threnody started to say something, but Kobi interrupted her. "The ship is ready. We're scheduled to launch at twenty-hundred hours. My family thinks it's a routine salvage run."

Zen felt edgy. He looked up the ladder at the ship's open hatch. "Is there a crew?"

"I'm the crew," Kobi said. "But don't worry, the ship flies herself, really. We send her up on her own most trips."

The old Kobi wouldn't have admitted that, thought Zen. He would have bragged about what a hot pilot he was. Maybe he really had changed. He said, "Could I fly her?"

"No!" said Kobi. "I mean, not without clearance from my family. You'll need me aboard, or the ship will ask questions . . ."

Zen nodded, then looked at Threnody, wishing again that she hadn't come. He thought he could control Kobi, but not both of them. Yet he couldn't leave her on the ground, in case she raised the alarm. She was cleverer than Kobi, and she might not care so much about the recording getting out. She could have half the Noon CoMa waiting for him when he landed.

"You're coming too," he said.

"Oh, I wouldn't miss it," said Threnody.

He held out his hand. "Give me your headset."

"Why?" she asked, but he just stood there with his hand out, and a look on his face that made her wish she had not deactivated the security drones that were supposed to go with her whenever she left the Chen-Tulsi estate. But the drones would have reported all this to her family, and she did not want that. So she unclipped the headset from behind her ear and passed it to Tallis, watching as he stamped it into the spaceport dust.

"You're worried I'm going to tell someone about you?" she said, as bravely as she could. "What have you *done*, exactly, Tallis? What do you want Kobi's ship for?"

"I left something behind," he said. "Up there."

She looked up. Above the *Spacehopper*'s battered nose-cone, Spindlebridge was pinned to the twilit sky like a cheap brooch.

"I've got friends," he warned.

"I can't think what they see in you," she said.

Zen ignored her. "I've got friends here on Sundarban. If I don't come back, they'll upload the recording. Just get me up there and back down with the thing I need and I'll never trouble you or Kobi again."

He was more annoying than dangerous, Threnody decided. Even so, she was glad of the spare headset hidden in the cuff of her suit. She would wait to see what exactly he was up to, then contact her family. If she captured him herself, no one could accuse her of being his partner in crime.

34

Going up was worse than coming down. They lay on their backs in the vinyl chairs in the shuttle's command center while the engines tried to deafen them and gravity piled lead weights on their chests and their faces. But at last it was over, and they were floating free in the grubby little room, shock-haired and weightless, with the lantern of Sundarban shining in through the windows.

"Spaceships are so unromantic," complained Threnody. "And there's never a dining car. Why can't your family—"

"What are we looking for?" asked Kobi.

He would not have cut across her like that before, thought Zen. And she would not have let him. Something had shifted between them. Before, it had been an honor for Kobi to be marrying into the House of Noon; now the Noons were in such trouble that Kobi was doing Threnody a favor by not breaking the engagement.

So many changes, big and small, all spreading out from that first moment when Zen agreed to take the Pyxis.

"It's a drone," he said. "A Noon security Beetle, badly damaged. It was jettisoned from Spindlebridge soon after the incident."

"It should answer to one of the Noon activation codes, then," said Kobi. "We've fished a lot of Noon tech out of the black that way." He blinked some instructions to the ship, and it started calculating the drone's likely coordinates and broadcasting codes into space.

"Why do you want this drone?" asked Threnody, after a few hours. "Has it stored a recording of you?"

"Nothing like that."

"Maybe it's carrying footage of you that you don't want my branch of the family to know about. You were up to something on our train, weren't you? All those questions, and the way you made yourself so friendly with Auntie Sufra—we all thought that was quick work . . ."

"I didn't hurt your train," he said.

"I don't believe you. Maybe if our security people questioned you, they'd find you've been working for Uncle Tibor all along."

"Leave it, Threnody," said Kobi. "He has that recording, remember?"

"He *says* he has," said Threnody. "Have you actually seen it? All of it? Why won't he show us the whole thing?"

"Of course I have it," said Zen.

"Quiet!" said Kobi. He wasn't listening to them anymore. He was listening to a frail, crackly note that was seeping from the ship's speakers. "It's a drone's flight recorder! Responding to the activation burst. The drone is very badly damaged . . . Dead, basically . . . There's another piece of wreckage tangled up with it . . ."

Zen put on his headset while the shuttle aimed herself at the source of the signal. "Nova?" he whispered while Kobi and Threnody were busy talking.

There was no reply. The signal from the drone had stopped, but the ship had visual contact now. He pressed his face against the thick port and stared out at all the black. Ahead, something caught the light, tumbling. A glint of drone armor, a limp figure glimpsed for a moment against one of Sundarban's moons. Drowned and drifting, Zen thought. He wondered what he would do if he had come all this way and Myka was wrong, and Nova could not be saved.

*

For a long time up there, she had not been sure of anything. She was not even sure what she was. Something broken, trying to repair. Warnings and damage reports kept interrupting her mixed-up dreams. Start-up menus trickled down the screens of her mind like rain down a window, reminding her of her birth, on Raven's table back in Desdemor.

At last she regained visual functions, and enough of her memory to know that she was Nova, that she was adrift in the orbit of Sundarban, and that she was still attached to the drone.

Carefully, tumbling there in the hard light of the Sundarbani sun, she had managed to work the hooked grapnel back through her body, taking care not to let go of the microfilament cable that attached it to the drone. She wrapped the end of the cable around her waist and pulled herself along it, till she was close enough to the drone to tell that it was completely dead. Then she tied herself to it, like a shipwrecked sailor lashing himself to a drifting piece of wreckage, and waited.

She waited for a long time. She was not sure how long, because at first her connection to the Datasea would not work, and when it repaired, she was afraid to use it. She and Zen had committed a terrible crime. Who knew what watchbots and spy programs would be waiting in the Datasea to trap her?

So she hung there, part of the cloud of debris that had been vented from the stricken Spindlebridge. Sometimes another fragment would come close to her, moving so fast that she would remember she was moving too. Sometimes she had to use the drone's thrusters to push herself out of the path of some shard that would have sliced her in half. Sometimes she was aware of ships passing. They were gathering the larger pieces of wreckage, but none came within a thousand miles of her. Maybe there was no salvage value in a broken Motorik.

The Spindlebridge itself was visible at first, surrounded by shuttles and repair vehicles, but as time passed, she parted company from it, and it sank out of sight behind the curve of the planet.

Sometimes she amused herself by watching the way the sun shone through the hole the drone had made in her. A shaft of sunlight poked out of her chest, lighting the flakes of frost and debris that hung nearby. But slowly the shaft grew narrower, and one day it vanished altogether. Her body had harvested enough energy from the light to heal itself.

And then the drone woke up, broadcasting its location on an emergency frequency, and over the limb of Sundarban a bright new star appeared and swelled till it became an ugly, sulfur-yellow ship . . .

*

Zen felt acceleration tugging him gently back and forth as the ship maneuvered. Heard the hum and clang as her cargo bay doors opened and the manipulator arms reached out, but still saw nothing, only the harsh sun of space dazzling in at him. Then more clangs, more hums.

"Target acquired," said the ship.

"Is that it?" asked Zen. "Is she aboard?"

"She?" Kobi looked round at him. Then he nodded and grinned and said, "That's it. We've got it."

Zen started running, and remembered that it wasn't much use in zero-g. He grabbed at the ceramic bulkheads and pulled himself out of the command center and along vinyl-padded floatways to the lock that led into the cargo hold. It was still repressurizing, the lights on the door flashing red. He slammed his palm against them as if that might hurry things along. Squinted through the tiny window into the hold, where Nova's body drifted in midair, snared in ravelings of cable as fine and shiny as angel hair.

The door opened. He flew across the hold to her. Her eyes stared blindly at him through a crust of frost. Her lips were blue. Splattery stains surrounded the hole in her tunic.

"A broken Beetle and a dead girl?" said Kobi, watching from the doorway with Threnody. "That's what he dragged us up here for?"

"It's not a girl," said Threnody. "That's his wire dolly. The weird one."

"He came all this way for a broken wire dolly? Maybe you're right; maybe there's something in its brain, something he needs . . ."

Threnody didn't answer. She was pulling something out of her cuff, turning her face so that, if Zen looked round, he would not see her press it to her temple.

But Zen did not look round. Even if he had, he could not

have seen much through the film of weightless tears that filled his eyes. Nova was dead. She had been dead all this time, and his whole journey here had been a waste.

And then, as he tried to rub the tears away (they clung to his face, his fingers) he noticed how, beneath the hole that the grapnel had torn in the chest of her tunic, Nova's synthetic flesh was healing in a thick, ugly plaque of scar tissue. The grapnel was no longer sticking through her. She had pulled it free, and tied its line neatly around her waist.

"Nova?" he said again.

Nova blinked.

"You're all right?" he asked her.

Her face twitched, trying to smile. The frost was melting, shining on her cheeks. Space dust had gouged small scars and pockmarks from her face, but that made her look more human, somehow, not less. Zen wanted to hug her, but it was impossible with Threnody and Kobi there.

"Zen!" Nova was smiling at him. "You came back for me?"

"Yes!"

"Well, that was stupid," she said. "And very nice of you."

Zen was still crying, but laughing, too. He had found a way, like Myka said he would. He had come here and found Nova, and she was alive. But, as he went to help her untangle herself from the drone, something made him look back. Threnody was watching from the doorway with a mocking, triumphant look, as if, in some way that he did not yet understand, she had outwitted him.

*

By the time Nova was disentangled, the shuttle was reentering the atmosphere, jolting like a speedboat bouncing over choppy water. Flecks of plasma blew like fireflies past the command center windows as Zen strapped himself into his chair.

Nova was talking to him privately through his headset. Talking and talking, as if to make up for all the time she'd missed. ". . . when the drone woke up and started signaling, I thought some salvage ship was coming for me, I thought I'd be scrapped, or wiped and restarted, and all my memories lost. That's why I played dead, and when I heard your voice and realized you'd come back for me . . ."

Zen smiled at her. He had missed that voice so much. But he couldn't concentrate on what she was saying. He was still thinking about the way Threnody had looked at him. What had it meant, that look?

The buffeting was soon over. They flew into clear, quiet air. Below them, moonlight silvered Sundarban's oceans.

"Change course," said Zen suddenly.

Kobi looked round. "We're on the right course. Thirty minutes will bring us down at the docking pans."

"No," said Zen. "They'll be waiting for us. Threnody has already sold us out. She probably sent a message to her family while we were searching for the drone."

"I've done no such thing!" said Threnody, all posh and outraged, as if he had accused her of cheating at train-quoits. "You broke my headset, remember?"

"You've got another," Zen said. "Or you used the ship's systems to call Noon security."

"Threnody wouldn't do that," said Kobi loyally. "She knows I'd be finished if you put that recording out."

"There isn't any recording," said Threnody.

Zen got the pistol out. He didn't exactly point it at Kobi, but he held it as if he was thinking about pointing it. He said. "Put us down on the north side of Sundarban City."

Kobi looked at Threnody. "Is it true? You talked to your family?"

"Someone had to," said Threnody. "Kobi, we've captured the person who's responsible for the Spindlebridge catastrophe, and the Motorik that helped him. I don't believe he's even who he says he is! I heard the Moto when he started it up—it called him 'Zen.' He's an imposter. You think anyone will care about a recording of you once that story hits the feeds? They'll be glad you hit him!"

"Change course!" shouted Zen.

Threnody looked at the gun in Zen's hand. "What will you do if we don't, Tallis, or 'Zen,' or whatever you're called? Kill us?"

Zen knew he should. It was what Raven would do, he thought. Kill them both, throw the bodies out over the ocean. The people on the ground wouldn't know him or Nova. Without Threnody and Kobi to identify him, perhaps he could talk his way out somehow, tell them there had been an accident up in space . . .

But Nova would know. She was watching, turning her face from him to Threnody as they spoke.

He put his gun away. "I'm not going to hurt you," he said, very quietly.

He wasn't Raven, nor anything like Raven. But he wished he was.

"You're not a Noon at all, are you?" asked Threnody.

"My name is Zen Starling," he said. He could have tried to bluff it out, but he felt he owed her something, and the truth was all that he could spare.

"I always thought there was something strange about him," Threnody told Kobi. "I never understood why poor Auntie Sufra took such a liking to him."

The *Spacehopper* crossed a coastline. She swooped over forests, which looked like moonlit broccoli from that height, over towns and tea plantations and a looping river. Her airspeed was slowing. Through the viewports Zen saw roads and railway lines converging on the station city. Kobi kept talking to the ship. Threnody glared. On the plains ahead, the gantries of the commercial spaceport appeared. Zen thought he could already see the rotors of gun-drones catching the moonlight as they patrolled the sky above Kobi's pan.

And then, without warning, Kobi said, "Change course, ship. Set down outside the city."

The shuttle banked, veering away from the spaceport. "Kobi, what are you doing?" screamed Threnody. The horizon whirled. Air screamed over the stubby wings, the engines howled. Something hit the hull with a startling bang. There was a tumbling weightless darkness, lit by sprays of sparks. Then a crash, a lurch, a long, slithering rush, parts of the ceiling coming down, dirt and vegetation breaking over the viewports.

And silence.

"Were they shooting at us?" asked Threnody. "Was that shooting? Did they shoot us down?" Her voice sounded blurred and trembly. "Kobi, why did you change course?"

Kobi looked at Zen across the shattered command center. It was a look of pride. It said, *See? We're even now. We had our arguments, but you saved my life once, and now I am saving yours.* He seemed to think they were noble warriors in a threedie, and this was the way noble warriors behaved. He would want to shake hands in a moment. But Threnody moaned—some piece of the roof had hit her head as they landed—and he turned away, bending over her.

"Are you coming with us?" Zen asked him. "If you stay here, you'll be in trouble with the Noons. We have a train. We can get you away."

Kobi shook his head without looking up. "No thanks, Tallis, or whatever you said your name is. I'm staying here." He found a first-aid kit from somewhere and started dabbing nervously at Threnody's wound. Then he did look up, just for a moment. "I know you think I'm just a spoiled rich boy. I know you think this engagement between me and Thren is just a business alliance. That's what Thren thinks too. But I do care about her. I'm not going to leave her."

Zen looked at Threnody, and saw that she shared his surprise.

Kobi said, "You'd better go. Railforce will be on their way. We'll tell the Bluebodies that you hijacked the ship and crashed it and escaped."

That set Zen moving. He took Nova's hand and they scrambled out through the broken hatches, into the mud of a drainage culvert on the edge of Sundarban City. A drone buzzed over, making them cower, but it was only some farmer's crop-bot, come to survey the damage this unexpected arrival had done to his sorghum. Distantly, across the fields, they could hear other drones approaching.

They splashed through the mud to the culvert's end where a pipe took it under a road, scampered through the crops in a neighboring field, found their way between barns and tractor sheds to a road that ringed the city. The road surface glowed gently, releasing some of the sunlight that it had stored during the day. Floaters and ground-cars were stopping there, passengers emerging to gawk at the smoke rising from the site of the shuttle crash. The crackly rumble of jet engines rolled along the margins of the sky. Zen pushed Nova into one of the empty cars and climbed in after her. Nova did something with her brain and the car woke.

"Where are we going?" she asked.

Zen had no idea where Kobi had landed them. "Into the city," he said.

The car did a neat U-turn and set off up an exit ramp as the searchlights of the drones came sweeping across the fields.

35

"Flex?"

"Mmmm?"

"Flex?"

The voice of the *Damask Rose* pushed its way into Flex's thoughts. He was clinging to the old loco's hull, sketching in figures and shapes with sweeping gestures of his paintstick while a maintenance spider trained a work lamp on him and another held his bag of colors. These Fosses weren't quite as big as modern trains, so he hoped his supplies would hold out. If not, perhaps he could persuade the 3-D printer in the dining car to turn out some pigment for him.

The Hive Monks' strange myths had crept into his head and shown him what he needed to draw along the curved and streamlined flanks of the *Damask Rose*. Angels. Angels spilled from the single big lamp on the old loco's prow as if from a shining doorway. Insect angels and human ones; angels that looked like dogs and grasshoppers and fish; angels that looked like winged trains and flying kettles. Angels with the wings of eagles, angels with the faces of clocks. Angels in business clothes, angels in ball gowns, angels in nothing but their birthday suits and mismatched stripy socks. Angels strewing roses; angels eating bhajis, dancing down the train's sides in a wild fly-past, all laughing with amazement to find themselves a part of Flex's masterpiece.

If the paint held out, thought Flex, he would carry the procession right down the carriages, too; he'd always wanted to paint a train from end to end. He drew a big angel along the side of the engine compartment, a tall, strong angel, based on Myka Starling, with wide hips and big arms and a kind, handsome face.

And then the train's voice. "Flex?"

"Mmmmm?"

"Zen Starling has been gone for more than fifteen hours."

"Is it that long?" It was like that when you were working, when it was going well. Time didn't matter. Then he remembered where he was, and what Zen had gone to do. "Oh . . ." He switched off the paintstick and jumped down onto the ballast beside the tracks.

"Also," said the train, "I am picking up news bulletins in the local data raft. A space vehicle has crashed on the edge of the city. A search is in progress for two fugitives. One is a young man, the other a Motorik, gendered female."

"Oh no," said Flex.

"Do you think that is Zen and the Motorik he was attempting to salvage?"

"Bit of a coincidence if it isn't, don't you think?" asked Flex. (He didn't mean it sarcastically. He liked the careful, logical paths trains' brains took, the mental rails their thoughts ran down.) "At least they haven't been caught yet. We should do something . . ."

"What should we do, Flex?"

He leaned his face against the train's side. During his first days in Cleave he had sometimes snuggled up against trains in the engine sheds for warmth. The feel and smell of them was his happiest memory from those times, and always comforting. It didn't give him any answers, though. Poor Zen! Out in the station city somewhere, hunted by drones and Bluebodies and who knew what. How could Flex help? He was just a painter of trains. He didn't even know his way through the tunnels, not here on Sundarban.

"There is a lot of discussion on official emergency frequencies," said the train. "Railforce troops are being ordered to the outbound platforms."

"Not to platforms on this line?" asked Flex, suddenly afraid the Bluebodies might come marching along the tunnel to arrest him.

"It does not seem to have occurred to them that we may be here," said the *Damask Rose*. "I believe they are trying to make sure that Zen does not get out on any of the other lines. Units are being deployed throughout the city."

"Oh, Zen!" sighed Flex. Who would have thought that one young Thunder City thief could gather so much trouble to him?

A rustling sound nearby made him look up. The Hive Monks had come out of the train and stood looking at him. Well, Flex supposed they were looking at him. The eyeholes of their masks were aimed at him, but they must have each had about a million eyes so they were probably looking everywhere.

"We heard the train speak," said Uncle Bugs.

"Your friends are in danger," said one of the other Monks, as if it thought Flex might not have understood. "We must leave without them, and seek the Insect Lines."

"No!" said Flex, and the train let out a long and disapproving, "Pssssccccchhhh . . ."

"I told them you would say that," said Uncle Bugs.

"I can't leave Zen behind. He's part of my hive," said Flex, trying to help them understand. But he didn't think they would. Hive Monks left parts of themselves behind all the time; individuals weren't important to them.

"I will not leave without Zen Starling," said the *Damask Rose*.

"But you have the painter," said Uncle Bugs. "Zen Starling means nothing to you."

"He is brave," said the train. "He came all this way to save his friend. I will not leave without him."

The Hive Monks rustled together for a moment with the others. Then Uncle Bugs turned to Flex. "We will help you to find him."

"How?" said Flex. "They're out in the city somewhere, and the Bluebodies are crawling all over, looking for them. I don't even dare try to contact them in case the Bloobs pick up the signal. They could be anywhere."

The Hive Monks swayed. They whispered like dry reeds, nodding their misshapen heads. They seemed pleased with themselves. "We are Hive Monks," they whispered. "We can go anywhere."

Later, when they had gone, the train spoke again.

"Flex?"

"Mmm?"

"Flex?"

"Yes?"

"I really like the angels."

233

36

Parts of the city were just like the Ambersai Bazar. Zen and Nova moved through streets of jangling pachinko parlors and stir-fry mollusk bars, streets glowing with neon, filled with the rumble of K-trains crossing the viaducts, whose supporting pillars flickered with advertising slogans and luminous graffiti. It was not somewhere they could hide for long, but they would last longer there than anywhere else.

They had abandoned the car after a few minutes. Zen had never stolen a whole car before, but he knew the best rule was not to keep hold of it for long. They had jumped out under a railway bridge and let the car keep going while they doubled back through streets of sleepy bio-bungalows, through light industrial zones where 3-D printers whirred and hummed behind the paper walls of factory units.

He wanted to contact Flex and the *Damask Rose*. He had been gone far longer than he'd promised, and it was going to be hours yet before he could get back to where the old train waited. He needed to message it, but he knew he mustn't. The local data raft would be full of watchbots, all waiting to home in on him and pinpoint his position for the Bluebodies' drones. So he did not contact Flex, but he did let Nova link her mind to the city's information feed for just long enough to download a map.

The news was bad. His way into the Dog Star Line tunnels was on the northern side of the city; the shuttle had crashed on the south.

So they pushed through the crowds in the neon streets, hoping to get clear across before the Bluebodies sighted them. On the screens they passed, the newsfeeds were streaming video of the wrecked shuttle.

Zen became a thief again, as if the Ambersai ambience had triggered his old skills. It felt comforting to be doing something he was good at, slipping things from the stalls he passed as if he were invisible. He stole Nova a coat with a hood to cover her holed tunic and shadow her face. He stole steamed ginger dumplings for them both. At a novelty gene-tech booth called Pogonometry he stole himself a mustache-symbiont, a hairy critter designed to cling to his upper lip, where it would live on sweat and dead skin. It turned out to be a cheap knock-off, though, and after half an hour it turned ginger and wandered off up his cheek like a lost sideburn. He gave that to Nova too, but it didn't suit her either.

He kept looking at her as they walked. He kept asking her, "Are you all right?"

"I think so. I am now. Thank you for coming back for me."

"I would have come sooner. Raven wouldn't let me. He wanted to leave you up there."

"I am only a Motorik," said Nova.

"It's not that. It's just how Raven is."

They went on in silence for a while, down a lonely street that ran beside a freight line. After a while Zen said again, "You are sure you're all right?"

"Yes, Zen."

"That hole it made in you—that did no harm?"

"It did. I was shut down for a long time, I think. But there was plenty of sunlight up there to power me, and my whole body is made from self-repairing compounds."

"I wish mine was," said Zen. He was covered in bruises from the shuttle crash, shaky with stress and adrenalin.

"I'm so sorry," she said.

"What for?"

"For bringing you into danger." She looked earnestly at him, her face flickering in the light from a passing train. Like the heroine of one of her old movies. "When I was up there, and I thought I'd never see you again, I felt as if my heart would break. My *heart* is not made from self-repairing compounds, Zen Starling."

The train was gone, but he could still see her, striding along beside him in the sodium glow from the trackside lamps. The smell of space clung to her, rich and smoky. What was this that he was feeling? It frightened him, whatever it was. He was almost relieved when she suddenly said, "We're being followed."

Zen looked back. He couldn't see anyone, but he knew that Nova had sharper ears and better eyes than him.

"There are three of them," Nova said. "I don't think they're human."

He pulled her into the doorway of a warehouse and took out his gun. "Motorik?"

Nova shook her head. "Hive Monks."

Zen laughed with relief, and stepped out of the doorway. He couldn't be sure that these were his Hive Monks, but it seemed likely; Hive Monks didn't usually go about in threes.

"We have found you!" whispered the Monks, hurrying along the street so quickly that they seemed in danger of disintegrating altogether. Zen laughed again. He had never been so glad to see a few million mutant insects.

"We look for you; we find you!" rustled Uncle Bugs, reaching out to pat and stroke Zen's clothes while Zen fought down the urge to flinch away. "The train scanned the newsfeeds, told us the Empire was hunting for you. We were worried for you, Flex and the train and we. So we set out to search. No one sees Hive Monks. No one stops us or questions us. We are only Hive Monks."

"Thank you," said Zen. Feeling ashamed that a pile of beetles would go to such trouble to help him. Wishing the Hive Monks did not disgust him so.

"There are police-bodies everywhere!" said one of the other Monks. "Railforce, eugh! At the station, on the streets."

"There are many, many that way," said Uncle Bugs, pointing along the street in the direction that Zen and Nova had been going. Zen could see the searchlight beams there, where drones cruised to and fro above the city center.

"You must hide," urged the other Monks.

Zen shook his head. "We must keep going. Sooner or later they'll start wondering how I got here, and that will lead them to the Dog Star Line and the *Damask Rose*. We haven't got time to hide. We have to keep moving."

"You keep moving *and* hide," said Uncle Bugs. "We hide you. You hide in us."

Zen didn't know what he meant at first. Then he understood,

and wished he hadn't. "Oh no!" he said. "No, no, no, I'm not doing that . . ."

But what other choice was there?

*

Nova broke the locks on the doors behind them, and let them into an arch-roofed vault much like Flex's place in Cleave, except that this one was piled with drums of chemicals. A burglar alarm asked tetchily who they thought they were and told them it was going to inform the police, but it was a cheap model and Nova got her mind inside it and calmed it down. The Hive Monks were already losing their human shapes, dissolving into boiling, glittering mounds of insects, empty robes crumpling like the clothes of melted snowmen. Zen's mouth felt dry. This was going to be awful.

But the insects held no terrors for Nova. She stepped close to the edge of one of those seething heaps. Bugs poured up her legs in dark shining streams, twining around her thighs, her torso, spiraling down her arms and out along her outstretched hands until her fingers were mittened with them. And still they kept coming, scrambling over one another, the winged females fluttering. They covered every part of her body and limbs, then piled themselves up to cover her head too. When she was entirely clothed in insects, she went carefully to where the fallen robe lay, picked it up, and pulled it over herself. The armature she folded up and stuffed inside the robe. She held the wasps' nest mask against the front of her head and the bugs pulled it into place. When she turned to face Zen she was a Hive Monk—slightly larger than average, but who bothered to look at Hive Monks? Hive Monks went where they pleased.

"But not out of the city," said the mound that had been Uncle Bugs. "If police bodies see us leaving the city they shall say, 'Oho,

Monks stay in the stations, usually,' and there will be questions and maybe pokings with sticks, and they find you hidden in us. So we must go down through the stations to the old platforms. The train will meet us there. We have discussed this all with the train and Flex. The train will be there in one hour. We must find our way by then."

"I can take us there," said Nova, slightly muffled, from behind her Hive Monk's paper face. "I have maps of the station in my head." She tried moving about. The burlap robe was too short on her: her bug-covered feet showed under the hem.

"Crouch down a bit," Zen told her. "Bend your knees. And don't walk so smoothly. Walk like a drunk person balancing a glass of wine on their head and trying not to spill any."

He eyed the nearest mound of insects, trying to will himself to step into it.

"The covering of insects is not solid," said Nova cheerfully. "Plenty of air gets in."

"What do you know? You don't need to breathe! They'll get into my mouth."

"No they w—" she said, and broke off spluttering. "Pleugh, eugh!"

"I hate bugs!" said Zen. The thought of all those little feet creeping over him was making him sweat and tremble. But he looked at Nova, lurching and lumbering around the warehouse in her version of a drunkard's walk, and knew it was the best disguise he had ever seen.

So he shut his eyes, clamped his mouth tight, clenched his teeth, made bitter-lemon faces as he tried to squeeze his nostrils closed. And the rustling tide of bugs flowed up his body and engulfed him.

It was not how he had imagined it would feel at all.

It was worse.

37

Hospitals, questions, the harsh white light in poky little offices where policemen and Noon security officers made Threnody go through her story again. "He's not really Tallis Noon. He was an imposter. He came aboard the Noon train at Adeli; Auntie Sufra took a liking to him . . . And a few days after he came on board, well, the train reached Spindlebridge . . ."

They took Threnody in a ground-car to the control tower near the central platforms. Kobi kept telling them that she was tired and that she ought to be allowed to go home and rest, but they said Rail Marshal Delius wanted to speak with her. Drones from the news sites buzzed in swarms above the doorway as they hurried her inside.

The place was crowded: Railforce people, K-bahn officials, the fancy-dress generals of the Noon CoMa. Holoscreens hung in the air like kites, relaying reports from the Bluebody squads who were searching the city, streaming video footage from circling drones. In the one patch of clear space stood Priya Noon, surrounded by a cloud of little bluebird drones, which zigzagged around her on nervous trajectories as if infected by their owner's panic. "I demand further reinforcements now," she was saying, in a high, jagged, too-loud voice. "What sense does it make to leave even a single armored train on Grand Central, where the traitor Tibor can seize them and turn them against me? If the troops you have here can't even catch this one single assassin . . ."

"Lady Threnody?" A hand brushed Threnody's arm. She turned to find Lyssa Delius standing there: Rail Marshal Delius, with her wise face and her warrior's crest of white hair, the one who was on all the newsfeeds.

"I've seen your account of tonight's events," the Rail Marshal said quietly, carefully leading her away from the group around Priya. "Are you quite sure about the name you gave? The real name of this imposter?"

"He told me it was Zen Starling," said Threnody.

The woman watched her, stern and searching. "Have you heard that name before?"

"Never," said Threnody.

"Well, I have," said the Rail Marshal, and turned to the aides and officers who stood behind her, waiting for her orders the way dogs wait for table scraps. "Get some people down onto the old Dog Star platforms. Yes, I know they're sealed—*un*seal them! And find me Yanvar Malik."

38

Half a dozen times, as they made their shuffling way toward the central platforms, Zen thought that he was going to lose it. Start to scream and thrash and flap his arms, rip off the filthy old robes and scatter bugs everywhere.

Because they were in his ears, and up his nose, and down the back of his shirt, and clumped so thickly on his limbs that he could hardly lift his feet. But that made it better, probably, made his progress look more like the cumbersome walk of a Hive Monk. And when they started passing Railforce checkpoints and he peered out through the eyeholes of his paper mask and the fringe of legs and feelers that rimmed them and saw the Bluebodies wave them by without even looking at them, well, then he realized that it was going to work, and that it was going to be worth it.

From time to time, Nova's words would come through his headset. "Not far now," she'd say encouragingly, or "Look at the Bluebodies! They don't even spare us a glance!"

Only once were they stopped. A sub-officer stepped into their path when they were almost at the barriers and asked where they were going. "Platform eighty-nine," whispered the mass of bugs that covered Nova, and then the sub-officer turned away to listen to new orders that were crackling in his earpiece and waved them by. The barrier, programmed like all station barriers to let Monks pass, swung open for them, and they went out onto the platform, leaving their trails of dead husks behind them, while people waiting for the 5:58 to Bhose Harbor stepped back to let them pass.

It was a long platform, the far end deserted and in shadow. They made their way down onto the rails and crossed the track and then another. Hive Monks were known to do strange things, so probably no one would have thought it odd if they had seen them there, but even so they stopped and waited in the shadows while a train passed, then went on. Soon they were at a doorway in the tunnel wall that Nova said led down to the Dog Star Line; soon they were stepping out onto a long-abandoned platform deep beneath the other lines.

It was very quiet. On the opposite platform a hopeful vending machine blinked its lights to let them know it had a selection of snacks for sale. The two sets of rails gleamed in the glow from bio-lamps on the walls. Zen and Nova looked to and fro along the platform. They walked to the far end in the hope that the K-train might be lurking in the shadows of the tunnel. Only the wind moved: the tunnel wind, which came from who-knew-where, flapping the edges of their robes, rattling the dry wings of the bugs on their hands.

"There is no train here," said Nova.

"The *Damask Rose* said she would meet us here," whispered her covering of bugs. "It was agreed. Flex heard. It was discussed."

Uncle Bugs seemed to be having some sort of fit. He waved his arms around and kicked out his legs. He pulled his robe half-off and disintegrated, revealing Zen, gasping and shuddering, brushing at the departing bugs, which spilled from his hair and ran down his face like black tears.

"Maybe we're too late," whispered Uncle Bugs, a low shapeless mound under the fallen robe, like a bonfire of autumn leaves waiting to be lit.

"Maybe we're too early . . ."

But whichever it was, they were in trouble. New sounds were echoing through the still air on the platform. A rumble that was not the rumble of trains.

"Footsteps!" said Nova, who had heard them before Zen. And then there were voices mingled with the pounding feet. Out onto the platform came a Bluebody squad, the lamps on their helmets cutting white slices from the dusty air. Amplified voices, echoing and re-echoing from the tunnel roof, ordered the fugitives to kneel and put their hands up. They knelt, and put their hands up. The insects drained from Nova like black liquid and pooled on the platform. The troopers stopped at the pool's edge and looked back at their commander for instructions. None of them wanted to go crunching across that swarm and have to spend the evening cleaning pulped bugs out of the cleats of their boots.

"Train coming," said Nova, in Zen's ear. Kneeling there at the platform's edge, they looked at the rails. The reflected light from the vending machine on the opposite platform was starting to shiver as the rail vibrated under the weight of the oncoming train. In another second Zen could hear it: engine rumble drifting out of the tunnel, too loud to be coming from another line.

"But it can't be a train," one of the Bluebodies was saying, shaking his head. "This line is closed!"

Zen whispered, "Nova, warn it! Find the *Damask Rose*'s frequency; let it know what's happening or they'll get Flex too!"

There was no time to go hunting through all the frequencies for an old train she didn't know. Nova screamed her warning on all frequencies, so loud that the Bluebodies cursed and some clamped their hands over the earpieces of their helmets.

Light filled the tunnel, swept the platforms, and the *Damask Rose* came howling out of the darkness.

Zen barely knew her at first, dressed in her new coat of angels. He and Nova and the Hive Monks and the Bluebodies all stood staring as she came slithering into the station in a long squeal of brakes, sparks fountaining from her wheels.

Perhaps some of the Bluebodies thought they were under attack. They raised their guns. A bullet banged off the train's side, and a scar of bright ceramic appeared where the face of an angel had been. Something popped from an angel-painted hatchway on the loco's roof and turned out to be a gun. It swung to and fro, slewing bright streams of tracer fire across the platform. Some of the Bluebodies folded up and fell. The commander jerked backward and sat down heavily on one of the benches that lined the platform, as if this was not the train he had been waiting for after all. The rest shot back, stitching lines of sparks and chipped paint across the old train's cowling.

One carriage door opened, sheltered in the entrance to the tunnel. Flex leaned out and waved. Scrambling away from the battle, Zen and Nova crept toward him. Behind them, the scattered Hive Monks heaved and seethed, trying to erect their twiggy skeletons. The third Monk turned back as if to help them, but the blast from a gun caught it and blew it apart, scattering its component bugs so widely that its intelligence went out like a snuffed candle. It became just a swarm, a storm of wings, blowing in the faces of the troops, battering against the bio-lamps.

Zen reached the door. Flex pulled him inside, and they turned together to help Nova. But Nova needed no help; she simply leaped into the train, Motorik-graceful.

"All aboard?" the *Damask Rose* asked. "I can't stay here, you know. People are *shooting* at me."

"The Hive Monks!" said Flex. "We can't leave them behind!"

The Monks were out on the platform, not exactly part of the battle, but suffering badly in the crossfire, and from the panicked troopers who blundered through them, crushing bugs and knocking down the puny scaffoldings they kept trying to erect. One had thrown all its females into the air, a desperate cloud whirring toward the train, but a scared Bluebody turned a flame-thrower on them and they crackled like popcorn.

The *Damask Rose* began to move again. Ahead, a footbridge spanned the gap between the platforms. Bluebodies were hurrying up the stairs, aiming to get above the track, groping for grenades.

"We can't leave them!" Flex shouted, over the rush of air and the roar of engines and armaments. He stuck his arm out to stop the doors closing. On the platform, Uncle Bugs had managed to reassemble himself, an ungainly glittering figure, clutching his flapping robe. Rounds crashed through him, blasting out sprays of scorched and shattered bugs. A bullet found Flex, standing at the open door; knocked him backward, splattering blue gel on the glass.

"Flex!"

"I'm all right . . ."

Zen took his place at the door. He stretched out one hand into the rushing, bullet-busy air and grabbed a handful of bugs and the skeleton hand of wire and wood beneath. "Jump!" he shouted. "Jump!"

But Uncle Bugs could not run fast enough to keep up with the gathering speed of the *Damask Rose*. He was coming apart as he ran, strewing bugs across the platform and down into the dark under the train. His face came off and blew away in the slipstream like a lost paper plate at a picnic. "Find the way, Zen Starling!" he rustled. "Find the Insect Lines!" And then there was not enough of him left to speak, and then he was just a cloud of insects, flying and scuttling, banging against the windows, buzzing past Zen's face into the train, dropping from the clattering armature that trailed from Zen's hand.

Zen let it go. The *Damask Rose* slammed her doors and plunged into the tunnel, accelerating hard toward the K-gate.

39

Threnody stood beside her sister, watching the holoscreens, trying to make sense of the whirling footage from the Bluebodies' helmet cameras. The stuttering light and fizzing static, the yelled jargon, the red train leaving.

"He escaped?" said Priya, looking at Threnody as if she hoped Threnody would say it wasn't so. "They let him go?"

There were sirens outside, searchlight beams sweeping the station canopies, Railforce transports swooping down to pick up the survivors of the battle as they stumbled out of the old tunnels.

"If Railforce can't keep us safe, who can?" said Priya.

"We *are* safe, Pri," said Threnody. She had been afraid, glimpsing Zen Starling on those screens in the strobe light of the gunfire, that she would see him shot. She didn't want to see that. But she had not wanted him to actually get away either; she had wanted him captured, brought back in handcuffs, and made to explain himself. Made to apologize. And then frozen for a long,

248

long time. Thinking of him riding off aboard that old red train, unharmed, she felt indignant. It was so unfair. He shouldn't be allowed to *win*!

The Rail Marshal approached them, still snapping orders at her junior officers, who ran off this way and that like children sent on errands.

"You let him escape!" Priya said, and Threnody wondered if she meant that the Rail Marshal had deliberately let Zen go. Which couldn't possibly be true, but there didn't seem to be much at the moment that poor Priya wasn't ready to believe.

"I am sorry," said the Rail Marshal. "We had no idea that his train would be so well armed; our people were taken by surprise. But we know he's on the Dog Star Line. We will hunt him down." Then, for some reason, she looked at Threnody. There was something odd in her expression: the look of a woman with more on her mind than one escaped train. "Threnody, there is someone who wants to talk to you."

"Who?" Priya asked suspiciously.

"Please, Your Excellency, it is a private matter—"

"I'm the Empress!" shouted Priya. "I should be told! I should know everything!"

Lyssa Delius smiled a dangerous smile. "Only the Guardians know everything, Your Excellency. And perhaps not even them," she said. "Captain Rostov, Captain Zakhar, I think now that the immediate danger is past, the Empress should return to her own house. Please escort her." And, turning away before Priya could protest, "Lady Threnody, please come with me . . ."

Something very strange was happening, thought Threnody as the Rail Marshal herself led her away through the control tower's corridors, while her sister, the Empress, was escorted home by mere captains. "Who is it I'm supposed to talk to?" she asked. But Lyssa Delius seemed not to hear.

A small side office; windowless. A big seat in the center, which reclined when she sat in it. A man in red robes fussing with machinery in a corner.

"Mr. Yunis is with the Imperial College of Data Divers," said the Rail Marshal. "You are going to be talking with one of the Guardians."

Threnody sat up. On any other night she would have thought this was a joke. "The Guardians don't talk to people," she said. "Not anymore."

"This one has been talking to Mr. Yunis," said the Rail Marshal, pushing her gently back down in the chair. "And now, apparently, it wants to talk with you."

"No, there's been a mistake—it must mean Priya . . ."

"I don't think our all-knowing Guardians make mistakes about such things, Lady Threnody."

Threnody was trembling. She looked to Mr. Yunis, hoping he would be able to reassure her, but the data diver was trembling himself as he reached over her to place a complicated visored headset on her head, fitting the terminals into place behind her ear and against her temples. There were mysterious tattoos on his face and the backs of his hands. He was saying, "It works very much like an ordinary headset, Lady Threnody. It is an alarming experience, encountering one of the Guardians. You will be entering a part of the Datasea outside the firewalls of Sundarban's data raft . . ."

"Isn't that dangerous?" asked Threnody. There were *things* that lived in the deep data: unregistered phishing nets, spamsharks that would hack your mind and fill your dreams with ads, half-mad military programs left over from long-ago wars.

Mr. Yunis looked as if he thought it *was* dangerous, but he said, "The Guardian has constructed a temporary virtual environment where you will meet. Please remember that you are quite safe, quite safe . . ."

The headset whined, powering up. "I don't think it's working," Threnody started to say, and then Mr. Yunis fed it some code and she dropped into the Datasea.

It was not like logging in to a data raft. The rafts were gaudy places, full of bright, enticing shopping sites and the fizz and glitter of social networks. Here in the data deeps everything was gray, a shifting monochrome soup filled with small lights, which sparked and darted like raindrops caught in headlamp glare. It surrounded Threnody, engulfing her.

"It is only the sea," said Mr. Yunis, in her mind. She couldn't see him through this storm of data, but his voice calmed her. If she concentrated, she could feel Lyssa Delius's hand holding hers, and the softness of the chair under her, out in the real world.

And then she found a way to make sense of the flood of information that was pouring into her mind. Not a very original way, but good enough to make the panic fade. She saw the Datasea as an actual sea. The million quick sparks of light dashing past like plankton were individual packets of data. The bigger lights, which blazed and faded were the minds of trains, broadcasting news and messages from other stations as they passed through Sundarban. Those huge, fizzy, softly glowing cones, like underwater volcanoes, were firewalled information networks: the local data raft and the private rafts belonging to the Noons and other big companies. And out there, half-glimpsed in the murk beyond, those massive shapes must be the local avatars of the Guardians . . .

And where was Threnody? The panic returned briefly. Was she hanging there in the middle of it all? Adrift? Would she drown? But no. She was looking out at it through glass. Through a gigantic window. She was standing on a floor of black and white tiles. If she looked at the tiles for too long, they started to do something weird, shifting and replacing one another in a complicated fractal dance. So she turned instead, to see what was behind her.

It looked like a room. An enormous, empty room, one wall of which was the window she now had her back to. The other three walls were made of drawers. Rank upon rank of wooden drawers, each with a brass handle shaped like a little seashell.

No. Not really a room, just a virtual environment, like in a game. It was not even as well designed as most games were. Threnody's virtual feet made no sound on the virtual floor as she walked across it; the virtual handle of a virtual drawer triggered no touch-sensations when she pulled it open.

Inside, she saw about a million sheets of thin paper. She lifted one. Words were printed on it in languages she didn't know.

"Who are *you*?" said a strange voice. It came from around her and inside her, but she spun round anyway to see who had spoken.

It looked like a woman, though it was not really a woman, anymore than this room was really a room. It was a being made of code, and this code was creating, for Threnody's benefit, the image of a very tall woman with pale blue skin. A patterned dress with trailing fronds and streamers and lacework whatnots; a vast amount of deep red hair. Hair and dress both billowing on a breeze that Threnody could not feel.

"Hello," she said uncertainly. Awed, disbelieving. She was talking to a Guardian, or a part of one, at least. She, little Threnody

Noon, talking to an entity created on Old Earth, one of the builders of the Network.

I must ask them not to tell Priya about this, she thought. *She'll be so jealous . . .*

The blue woman came nearer, gliding over the fractal fidgetings of the tiles. It was hard to judge her scale. Threnody wanted to believe that she was the size of an ordinary human being, but if she stopped concentrating, she became aware of sparks of light streaming through the room, falling toward the woman and vanishing into her. They were the same sparks that she had been able to convince herself were no bigger than plankton before, but now she had the feeling that they were as big as suns, and that the figure who stood among them was light-years tall. Through the gold-in-gold eyes she felt some huge intelligence focus on her.

"Welcome, Threnody Noon."

Above the Guardian's head, like a thought bubble, the image of a room appeared. It was the room in Sundarban Station City where Threnody sat in the big chair, with Lyssa Delius and the data diver beside her. A dizzy, overhead view, as if the Guardian had hacked into the feed from a security camera on the ceiling. She let the image hang there for a moment, then pulled a long silver pin from her hair and stabbed the thought bubble, which vanished with a loud pop.

"I am a digital interface of Autonomous Networked Artificial Intelligence System 6.0," said the Guardian. "You may call me Anais." She nodded at the drawer that Threnody had opened and said, "Emails."

"Pardon?"

"I collect them. They are a sort of message that people used to send to one another. Much like the messages you send your friends I expect, except that in the olden days people actually used to *type* them, can you imagine? They're all still down there somewhere, in the deepest levels of the data-silt that piles up on the data-floor of the Datasea. 'Thank you for your interest,' they say, or 'I'm having a wonderful time,' or 'Your order has been dispatched,' or 'I love you,' or 'The gerbil died.' Every one a gem! It is my ambition to acquire every email ever sent. Would you like to read them?"

All around her, silently, drawers began to slide open.

"*No,*" warned Mr. Yunis, a tiny voice way off in the corner of Threnody's consciousness, like a helpful mouse in a fairy tale.

"Perhaps later?" said Threnody nervously. "They said you wanted to talk to me?"

The drawers slammed shut. Anais flickered. She glitched. She turned away from Threnody. Seen from behind she was hollow, like a gelatin mold. She moved her hands, drawing glowing shapes on the air. "I have detected patterns," she said. "The claims of the man Malik. A train on the Dog Star Line. We should have seen, but we did not see. I believed he was dead. We all did."

Threnody tried to follow her. "You believed *who* was dead?"

"Raven! Raven!" The Guardian rounded on her. Threnody saw now that its face was a porcelain mask, covered with a fine network of tiny cracks. Instead of eyes it had two letter i's. Instead of a mouth, the word "mouth" was written in red.

"You talked to the boy on the Noon train, the boy Zen Starling."

"Yes," said Threnody. "No, not really; it was my Auntie Sufra who took a liking to him . . ."

There was no point trying to lie to Guardians. Anais said, "I am looking at footage from Adeli Station. He is coming aboard the train. You lead the way. You welcome him."

"Well, I was just being friendly—I didn't know he was an imposter; if I'd known . . ."

"What does he want?"

Threnody was starting to panic. "The art collection. He said he wanted to see the art collection. Auntie Sufra showed him round . . ."

The Guardian's eyes flickered. Part of it was still watching Threnody, another part was scanning catalogues of the Noon collection. "Did the boy Zen Starling express an interest in any particular item in the collection?" it demanded.

"I don't think so," said Threnody.

Something appeared in the air between her face and the face of the Guardian. It was a dull little lead-gray cube. "Did the boy Zen Starling express an interest in this object? The Pyxis, artist unknown, acquired by Lady Rishi Noon?"

"I don't know—"

"Why did I never notice this object before?"

"Is that a rhetorical question?" asked Threnody.

"It is the right size. It is the right weight. Is it possible that . . . The Lady Rishi . . . Raven was friendly with her. Can it be that he . . . ?"

The mask of Anais cracked and fell away in eggshell fragments. Behind it were leaves: orange and yellow and brown, a whirlwind of autumn leaves the size of a nebula. The room with the checkerboard floor flashed out of existence, as though Anais couldn't be bothered with that illusion anymore. For a moment Threnody thought she was standing on a world where a huge new station was under construction, machines digging deep foundations into red bedrock. People in old-style clothes gathered round what seemed a clutch of black eggs, half buried in the soil. Black spheres, the light dazzling off their surfaces in strange patterns. Then that was gone too, and she was back in the gray tides of the Datasea. Plankton lights rushed past her, through her, pouring in and out of an immense darkness, which billowed slowly away from her.

"Go," said Anais.

And she was writhing and gasping on the big chair as if she'd just been pulled from deep water, scrabbling at the headset as Mr. Yunis pulled it off her face, staring into the eyes of Lyssa Delius, who bent over her, saying, "Did you speak to it? To the Guardian? What did it say? What did it want?"

Threnody thought about that, while her heartbeat came slowly back to normal.

"I have absolutely no idea," she said.

*

Beside a heart-shaped sapphire lake in the mountains of Sundarban's northern continent stood an old house. Its gates were locked, and had not been opened for many years. In an earlier age its gardens would have been overgrown, and the house itself crumbling, ivy-clad, a home to birds and bats. But this was the age of the Network Empire, so the house was self-repairing, and had drones to trim its lawns and rake its long gravel driveways and feed the carp in the sapphire lake while it slept.

Now, for the first time in a century, lights flickered on in the big, silent rooms as the house responded to instructions pouring into it out of the Datasea. The light twinkled in the sequins and shimmercloth of the clothes that hung in the huge wardrobes. Down in the basement, where the faded chlorine scent from a drained swimming pool still hung in the air, Motorik jerked awake, and a drawer in a white wall slid open. It was a long, shallow, coffin-shaped drawer, and inside it was a tube of diamondglass, like a luxury version of the tubes where prisoners were frozen.

The machinery of the place whirred and hummed. Readouts flickered on temperature gauges. The Motorik bustled about their tasks. The frost on the inner surface of the tube was thawing, the gel that filled it gurgling away through hidden pipes. Soon the body inside was visible. Golden eyes opened wide. The body shuddered and blinked in brief confusion as a partial copy of Anais Six downloaded itself out of the Datasea into its brain.

Anais Six had had this interface grown for a party, and then lost interest and never used it. Now it stirred at last. The thawing procedure was supposed to take hours, but as soon as it had control of its muscles, the interface forced its way out of the freezer tube, grabbed the party dress that one of the Motorik servants held ready for it, and strode away through the silent rooms, out into the garden. The air-car that would take it to the station city was already touching down.

40

A red train in a white world. A long viaduct, immensely high, spanning a gorge between two stony mountainsides. The mountains scarred with old mine workings and bandaged with snow. Fresh flakes flurrying down, gray against the snow-colored sky, then settling soft and white. In the middle of the viaduct was a silent station. Icicles fringed the canopies above the platforms, and trailed from a sign that read WINTERREISE.

There the *Damask Rose* stopped, just as exhausted as her passengers by the battle that they had left behind.

"What happens now?" asked Nova, in the silence.

Zen didn't have any good answer to that. He needed air. He had been too busy to be scared while the bullets were buzzing around him, but now that the danger was over he felt appalled at how near to death he had been. He thumbed the door release and jumped down into the drifts beside the track. So still and quiet. The only sound the whisper of the snow. The gravity was lower than on Sundarban. He wondered if that was what made the flakes so big.

Crunching softly over the drifts, he walked along the platform to the front of the train, checking the loco for damage. There were some scars and scorch patterns. Some of Flex's paint had been scraped off. A broken maintenance spider dangled from its hatch, clanking against the loco's side when the breeze blew: a small, cold sound. Higher up, the *Rose*'s guns still jutted from their hatches, hissing and steaming as stray snowflakes touched them.

"Why do you have guns, train?" he asked.

"We were all fitted with them," answered the *Damask Rose*. "I was built in troubled times. There was war on the Spiral Line. My sisters and I were fitted with weapons in case we were ever attacked."

"And were you?"

"Not until today."

"They will come after us, you know."

"I know, Zen. We should move on, but I must wait and make repairs."

"How long? They'll be coming soon."

"Just for an hour, maybe less."

Zen turned away and looked down over the viaduct. Its long legs vanished below into a white cloud that filled the valley between the two mountains. Through the cloud he glimpsed the shapes of buildings: roofs collapsed under the weight of heaped snow, the streets between them choked with drifts. An old world, he thought, and empty; the mines scraped bare. A good place for fugitives to hide and lick their wounds. But not for long. There was only one K-gate between here and Sundarban. Pretty soon Railforce would be popping through it, and they'd be ready for the *Rose* and her little guns this time.

"Is Flex all right?" the train asked.

"He's fine. He got shot in the shoulder, but it's repairing."

"He is a good painter. Do you like my angels?"

"They're great. They really suit you."

"What about the insect Monks? Did they survive?"

"No. They were scattered."

"Good. I did not like them."

"They saved Nova and me," said Zen. "Without them, we'd never have got off Sundarban." He felt guilty, because he hadn't liked the Hive Monks either, and he was glad they were gone. Something moved in his hair. He groped for it and pulled it free. A white maggot. Disgusted, he almost hurled it over the parapet, before he remembered how it had got there. He searched his hair and clothes and found more of the grubs, which he took back aboard the train, cupped in his hands. There were hundreds of Monk bugs in the front carriage. They scurried in aimless streams over the floor and walls and seats, while winged females battered themselves against the lamps. Zen wondered how long it would take them to hatch enough eggs and rear enough maggots to turn themselves back into a Hive Monk, and whether that Hive Monk would still be Uncle Bugs.

Nova was sitting with Flex in the next carriage, away from the insects. It was a dining car, tables spread with crisp white cloths, laid with silver cutlery, tinkling glassware, traditional squeezy plastic sauce holders shaped like oversized tomatoes. Nova and Flex sat there in silence, but Zen guessed they were talking, in some wordless, Motorik way. It made him feel left out and faintly jealous. He noticed that Flex had changed back into a girl.

"Why do you keep switching?" he asked. "Male to female, female to male . . ."

Flex looked up at him and smiled. "Wouldn't you, if you could?"

"I don't think so . . ."

"It doesn't make much difference really," said Flex. "Not to Motorik. Only to how others see us. Inside, we're not really male or female. We're just us. Don't you ever switch, Nova?"

Nova suddenly stood up, brushed past Zen, and left the train. He called after her, but she didn't stop, just strode across the platform and into the old station. He started to go after her, then hesitated, looking back at Flex. "Are you all right?"

"I'm fine." Flex smiled again, fingering the rent in the shoulder of her jacket where the Railforce bullet had torn through. "All repaired. I'm going to carry on painting," she said. "I don't mind the cold."

Zen stepped out of the carriage, following Nova's footprints across the snowy platform and into the station building. It was a collection of linked domes, grown from genetically engineered ivory. The light was cool and blue in there, filtering down through the snow on the skylights, but bio-lamps came on as he crossed the concourse, and the shops and food stalls opened their shutters hopefully, sensing business after all these years.

He found Nova on an upper level, looking out through high windows at the snow.

"What's wrong?" he asked.

She wouldn't turn to face him. "I thought I was so clever," she said. "Tweaking my settings, shortening my nose, making freckles. I thought I was brilliant! But Flex was just a labor unit, and she's passed for human among humans all these years. I couldn't do that." She stared at the reflection of her face in the glass, at the shadows of the snow that brushed across it. Zen watched her. He wondered what she would look like as a boy.

"I thought I was unique," she said. "I thought I was the only Motorik who'd ever . . . But there must be loads of others. How many like Flex, on all the other stations? Thousands?"

"But that's good, isn't it? If there are more like you?" said Zen.

And guessed at once that it had been the wrong thing to say. He should have said, "You are unique." He should have said, "You are the one and only Nova." He wasn't used to having to deal with other people's feelings. It made him miss the old days, when he'd been alone and had nothing more to worry about than keeping ahead of the police and the Ambersai lathi boys.

Nova sniffed. She had no need to sniff, but she had seen movies, and knew it was something that people did when they'd been crying. "Where will we go?" she asked.

"Somewhere we can hide," he said. He didn't really believe there was any such place, but he wanted to comfort her, and himself too. "We'll find some world where we can get far away from the K-bahn, and wait, and hope this all blows over."

"What about Raven?" asked Nova.

"What about him? You don't owe Raven anything. He left you behind!"

"That's not what I meant," she said. "I meant—I wonder what he's doing."

"I expect he's back on Desdemor," said Zen bitterly. "I expect he's happy enough now he's got his little black ball."

"What?"

"I forgot—you never saw it—the Pyxis was hollow; he made it open; there was this thing inside."

"A black sphere?"

"Yes . . ." Zen was starting to feel uneasy. Because the way her eyes were widening made it seem that there had been a weight to what he'd said, and he did not know what. He hadn't thought about the Pyxis or the sphere inside it since Raven dumped him in Cleave. He'd been too busy finding his way back to Nova to give much thought to it, or to the strange things that Raven had said on that last train journey.

"What's wrong?"

Nova stared at him, or through him, and he knew she was searching her perfect memory for something. "That's why he wanted it . . ." she said.

"What? What is it?"

"There's a story from history. Raven told it to me once, and I didn't even pay much attention; he told so many stories, but this one . . ."

"What?"

"He said that when the new station on Marapur was being built, the machines that were digging the foundations uncovered ruined walls, left over from some other time."

"So?"

"Marapur was a newly settled world. It had only had a breathable atmosphere for a hundred years or so. How could there be old ruins there? It was a mystery. But before people could investigate, a Guardian arrived. It was an interface of the Shiguri Monad itself. It announced that the 'walls' were a natural geological formation, and built some machines of its own to help speed up the construction process. The walls were destroyed, and every reference to them in the Datasea deleted."

Zen was tired, and having trouble understanding what

this had to do with him, or why Nova was so worried about it. This wasn't what he'd imagined their reunion would be like. He wasn't quite sure what he had imagined, but not this. He walked to a dusty sofa in one of the abandoned food bars and sat down. Nova stayed by the window, and the snow fell past her.

"So there were these walls, only they weren't walls, and the Guardians covered them up?" Zen said.

"As well as the walls they found six spheres. The Guardians took those too. They said they were just blobs of volcanic glass."

"It's still not much of a story," said Zen, though he could see where it was going now.

"It's not much of a story because it doesn't have an ending," said Nova. "Only perhaps it does now. I never thought about it before. I think Raven stopped me from thinking about it. I think he put a block in my mind so I wouldn't ask certain questions. That's why I didn't make the connection."

"What connection?"

"The station on Marapur was a Noon project. The person in charge of the work there was Lady Rishi Noon. Zen, what if there weren't six spheres? What if there were seven? What if Lady Rishi managed to get hold of one before the Guardians found it?"

"And she hid it in the Pyxis? Why would she—?" But Zen already sensed the answer to that one. The Guardians knew everything. How sweet it would be to trick them, to have one secret that they did not know. "But the thing I saw inside the Pyxis wasn't a blob of volcanic glass."

"No." She turned from the window and came to sit beside him. "Raven believed . . . He told me once that the spheres were the seeds of K-gates."

Zen laughed again. "What, put them in a pot and water them and up pops a gate?"

"Not like that. It was a metaphor. I think he meant, the spheres were storage devices that held the secret of making K-gates."

"He said something to me about the Guardians keeping secrets," Zen remembered. "He said that was why they tried to destroy him, because he found out about them. But you can't make new K-gates. If Raven used this sphere to open another one it would wreck the whole Network. He'd be stuck on Desdemor. Why would he want that? It would be like sawing off the branch he's sitting on . . ."

"Maybe he's got some other use for the sphere. It must be incredibly powerful. Imagine the math it would take, to open a hole through space-time. Maybe it will do other things too."

Zen was considering a simpler bit of math. "He didn't pay me enough," he said. "The house on Summer's Lease and the money in my account, it seemed like a lot. It *was* a lot, for me. But if the sphere is so powerful . . . He should have given me more, much more."

He imagined Raven, safe on Desdemor, haunting the bars and ballrooms of his dead hotel like a vampire lounge singer. A flame of pure, white anger lit in him. Raven had tricked him and used him and taken him for granted. He had treated Nova like a machine and Zen like a fool. And now, thanks to Raven, here they were, stuck on this dead line, with half of Railforce gearing up to come after them.

And then he caught sight of a glimmer of hope. One last angle he could work. A mad, risky idea, but as hard to resist as an unwatched necklace on a goldsmith's stall.

"What if we had this sphere thing?" he said.

"But we don't," Nova pointed out.

"We stole it from the Noon train. We could steal it again."

"From Raven? It's too dangerous . . ."

"What have we got to lose?" argued Zen. He knew it was dangerous, but it was the only idea he had; if he let her shoot it down, what were they left with? "Do you really think the Noons are just going to let us go? They're probably moving wartrains onto the Dog Star Line right now. The only way this is going to end is with you shut down and me dead or frozen. Unless we have something to bargain with."

"Like the sphere—"

"Yes! We take it, go to them, say look, we're sorry, we realized what this thing is, how important it is to the Guardians, and we fetched it back for you. No! We'll *hide* it somewhere on one of these dead worlds, and only tell them where if they promise we'll go free . . ."

"That is a rash plan," said Nova. "It is unlikely to succeed."

Zen knew it. "It's still better than waiting here for the Bluebodies to come and get us," he said. He went to the window, leaned against the glass. Outside, snowflakes rode the up-drafts, whirling like his thoughts. "They won't let us go. They'll come in wartrains, armed to the teeth, with tech that will track us wherever we hide. The *Damask Rose* hurt their people on Sundarban, killed some probably. They'll shoot on sight. But Raven's got no reason to harm us."

"Perhaps we have to go," said Nova, as if she was trying to convince herself. "If we've given him all this power and we're the only ones who know about it, perhaps it's up to us to stop him, before he uses it for something awful . . ."

But Zen didn't care about that. He wasn't out to save the day, like some hero in a threedie. He just wanted to save himself and Nova, and this was his one slim chance of doing it. He turned from the window, trying not to let her see how much it scared him, hoping that if he acted like he had a plan, a plan would come to him. "That's what happens now. That's what we'll do. We'll go to Desdemor, and steal the Pyxis back."

41

The air above Sundarban Station City was busy with media drones. The newsfeeds were carrying stories of a battle with terrorists, a wrecked space vehicle. Bluebodies in combat gear poured off trains from Grand Central like armored commuters. Others guarded every platform, shooing away the drones that came buzzing around Yanvar Malik as he stepped out of a Railforce train.

By the time he reached the station's central operations tower, the news sites had identified him. Blurry pictures of him filled the lobby screens, with text scrolling down their sides. "Yanvar Malik, a former Railforce officer, relieved of duty after the mystery loss of an armored train in Cleave . . ."

He had already been on his slow way to Sundarban when Railforce found him. They had transferred him to a wartrain and brought him across the Network faster than he had ever traveled. He knew that something big had happened, but the officers who had been sent to fetch him could not tell him what.

He was not altogether surprised to find Lyssa Delius waiting for him in the elevator of the operations tower.

"Yanvar," she said, gripping his hand for a moment. She looked tired. A small frown creased her forehead, right where the old scar used to be. "You've been traveling a lot since we last spoke—"

"Looking for that boy," said Malik. "The one Raven took from Cleave."

"I've found him," she said.

Their diamondglass elevator rose, gliding up the side of the tower, the golden canopies of the station dropping past them like autumn leaves. She made it go slowly, so that she had time to tell him things.

"Threnody Noon was pulled out of a crashed shuttle last night. She claimed it been hijacked by a boy who fought his way out of the city through a whole squad of Bluebodies ten hours ago. She says he was the one who caused the Spindlebridge disaster. All of which could just be another of the wild rumors that are flying around these days—her sister, Priya, is already blaming the whole thing on Tibor Noon. Except that Threnody says the boy's name is Zen Starling. When I heard that, I sent for you."

She pinged some images to Malik's headset. It was helmet-camera footage, gun-lit and shaky, Zen staring from an open door as an old red train sped by.

"Is that Raven's thief?" asked Lyssa Delius.

"Yes. He's all right?"

"As far as we know."

Malik was surprised how relieved he was. He was starting to grow almost fond of Zen Starling. He'd been a kid from the wrong end of the Network himself. He thought he could guess how Zen must feel, caught between Raven and the Bluebodies.

"Threnody says he was on the Noon train right up to Spindlebridge," Lyssa Delius told him. "The newsfeeds have put two and two together—they're calling him 'Trainkiller.' He was using the Dog Star Line to move about, just as you said. I should have listened to you."

Malik shrugged. "Why would you? I had no evidence. Raven's too good, Starling's too lucky. Even the Guardians didn't believe me."

"Well, they believe you now. Anais Six herself has taken an interest, and it can't be long before the others start asking questions too."

A gigantic shadow slid across them, but it was just a patrolling Noon gunship, eyeing them with its sensors as it stropped past. Lyssa Delius's frown deepened. She ushered Malik out of the elevator, still talking softly as they went together along curving corridors.

"It's chaos here, Yanvar. The new Empress is frightened out of her wits, completely paranoid. Maybe she's right to be. It's not just her uncle Tibor who wants her job. The Prells have canceled all leave for their Corporate Marines. I can see the whole Network tipping into war, and not one of the little wars we fought out on the branch lines in the good old days: the real deal. I thought that things would be easier when we announced the Starling boy was in Raven's pay, but Anais Six will not let us release that news."

"You have actually *spoken* with Anais Six?"

"Oh, more than spoken. You'd better prepare yourself, Yanvar . . ."

Up a wide stairway, into the sunlight under a huge glass

dome: a penthouse lounge where the Noons came to look out over their city and watch the K-trains rolling in and out. It was crowded now, bustling, a smell in the air of fear and strong coffee. Railforce officers in their neat blue uniforms jostled up against the fancy-dress generals of the Noon CoMa. In the center of it all there was a still space where a tall figure stood, not exactly human.

The strangeness of it made Malik start. Almost ten feet tall, blue skin, masses of red hair, wide golden antlers. It was dressed in a gown made from the feathers of rare, expensive birds, and cut in the style of a century ago. It turned its golden eyes toward Malik as he entered, as if it knew exactly who he was. Which it probably did, because it was a Guardian, or at least the mortal interface of one.

"It arrived an hour ago," said Lyssa Delius softly by his ear.

The interface came toward him, and the stillness came with it; the people it passed stopped their arguments and discussions, looked up from their data-slates, stood open-mouthed and stared. A servant nervously offered it canapés. An old CoMa general, overcome with awe, got down on his creaky knees. It stood in front of Malik and stared down at him, and he felt the urge to kneel too. He had never expected to actually meet a Guardian, or feel its voice come rippling like music through his headset, into his mind.

"You are Yanvar Malik . . ."

The golden eyes gazed down at him, flowing with tawny patterns like the mantles of twin suns. He imagined the immense intelligence that lurked behind them, not in the interface's skull, but in the Datasea. He imagined it plucking facts about him from that storm of information, finding individual threads in a tapestry as wide as the sky.

"You are one of those we sent to destroy Raven's interfaces."

"And I did, Guardian," said Malik, holding that golden gaze with an effort. "All except one."

"That one must also be destroyed."

Lyssa Delius said, "I told the Guardian that you would lead this mission, Yanvar. You're our expert on Raven. A wartrain is being moved onto the old Dog Star Line."

"There are a lot of stations on that line," he said.

"We will follow the Starling boy," said Anais Six. "He will lead us to Raven. I will come with you. This time, I must be certain that nothing of Raven survives."

It walked past him, making for the door. Malik had the feeling that it would have walked through him if he had not dodged out of its way. He looked at Lyssa Delius, who said, "Go. Eliminate Raven. It's what the Guardian wants."

Malik turned to follow the interface, and found Threnody Noon watching him. There were bruises on her face, a freshly healed rip in the sleeve of her coat, a wary look in her eyes. Just behind her stood a young man with hennaed hair, equally bruised and dirty, who put a hand on her elbow as if he wanted to protect her from something but wasn't quite sure what.

Threnody shrugged herself free of him and stepped in front of Malik. "Who's Raven?" she asked.

"A ghost," said Malik.

"The Guardian wants you to kill a ghost?" she asked.

He smiled, nodded, said nothing.

"Well, make sure you bring Zen Starling back," said Threnody, as he stepped past her. "Bring him to Sundarban, so he can explain why he did what he did to us!"

She looked like a warrior, thought Malik, standing there with her angry eyes and her fading wounds, her hands curling into fists. He saluted her gravely, and, as Lyssa Delius started to lead him away toward his new command he said, "I think the Noons have picked the wrong sister to be Empress."

The Rail Marshal looked sideways at him. "Threnody's appearances on the newsfeeds have gone down very well. She showed a lot of poise after that shuttle crash: a lot more than Priya has shown since she became Empress. And now the news has leaked out that she's been speaking with a Guardian . . . Her approval ratings with the public are running *very* high. We shall have to do something about her."

Malik wondered what the something would be. He wished he could help the girl, and knew he couldn't. Suddenly he felt very glad that he only had Raven to deal with, that he had never risen to Lyssa Delius's height, where you had to choose which Noon to help onto the throne, and do things about their too-popular relatives to keep them there. Lyssa didn't mind that stuff. It was like a game to her. He could see that in the thoughtful way she glanced toward the Noon girl. But Lyssa had always been more ambitious than him.

"You've turned into quite a politician," he said.

She thanked him, but he hadn't meant it as a compliment.

42

The *Damask Rose* replenished her fuel cells at a depot outside Winterreise Station, and sped on down the Dog Star Line, through rainbow deserts and midnight forests. In her dining car, Zen and Nova built plans as fragile as card houses.

"Raven will be surprised to see us," Zen said. "He'll come to the station to see what we want, and we'll get him talking. We'll tell him Railforce knows what he's up to, say we've come to warn him—"

"If he's working on the Pyxis, it will be in his laboratory. I can slip away while you talk to him, go there and search—"

"No," said Zen, "we must both stay with him, or he'll suspect. Flex can go and find the Pyxis. He doesn't know about Flex. We'll keep him distracted while Flex goes into the hotel. If you're all right with that, Flex?"

Flex grinned, a bit uncertainly, still getting used to the idea of being a thief. "Yes!" he said. "Of course. It'll be just like dodging trackside security back home . . ."

"This is a plan of the hotel," said Nova. "Here's what the Pyxis looks like." She and Flex exchanged a glance, and Zen knew that information was flickering between them. The *Damask Rose* passed through another K-gate. Now they were on a twilight world where abandoned bio-buildings sprawled along the tracksides like deformed and blighted fruit. The brakes came on, pushing Zen against his seat. Nova looked up, sensing the same thing that the train had sensed: another mind, out there in the dusk.

"There is another train," she said.

"Is it Railforce?" asked Zen.

"It is ahead of us," said the *Damask Rose*. "And I do not think so."

"Talk to it," suggested Flex.

"And put it over your speakers, so we can all hear," said Zen.

"I am the *Damask Rose*," said the train.

A slow laugh dripped like liquid from the speakers on the ceiling, and the voice of the other train said, "I am the *Thought Fox*."

No one spoke for a moment. Then Nova said, "Hello, *Fox*! Is Raven with you?"

The *Thought Fox* laughed that unnerving laugh again. "No, little one. He is in Desdemor. He asked me to guard the line for him. I have been prowling the rails, looking for someone to harm."

"We have a message for him," said Nova. "It's important. Let us pass. Railforce is after us. If you want to harm someone, harm them."

"Raven said no one was to pass," said the *Thought Fox*.

"What if we left our train here? Will you take us to Desdemor yourself?"

"Perhaps," said the *Fox*, in a tone that made Zen think of a sharp-toothed grin. "Come to me, little ones. Come in your old red train to me, and we shall discuss the matter."

"Pssssccchhhh," said the *Damask Rose*. "I do not trust it. I have heard of this *Thought Fox*. It is a bad train."

Zen was at the window. Through the half light, between the nightmare shapes of the overgrown buildings, he looked for the lights of the other train, its sliding blackness. He imagined it out there, stalking the rails with its guns unhoused. Why had he not thought of it before? Of course Raven would be guarding the lines in case anyone came after him. *Do you think I haven't mapped out all the twists and turns this thing could take?*

"It is six miles ahead," said the *Damask Rose*. "There is an old station. The *Thought Fox* is waiting there on the up line. No carriages, just the locomotive. It is heavily armed."

"Should we go back?" asked Nova.

"And run into Railforce coming the other way?" said Zen. "Train, can't we slip past it? Go around the station somehow?"

"There are sidings there, a loop that leads through freight yards. But the *Thought Fox* will be watching us through this world's satellite grid, just as I am watching it," said the *Damask Rose*.

Zen had never heard a train sound afraid before.

"Come and talk," wheedled the *Thought Fox*.

"Take the loop anyway," said Zen. He didn't think they could slip by without the *Thought Fox* noticing, but it might buy them some time. "Nova, do you still have a copy of Raven's virus?"

She looked at him, almost expressionless. "No. But it is possible that the *Fox* will try to use a trainkiller against us."

"I don't like the sound of that," said the *Damask Rose*. "A 'trainkiller'? I hope that is just a figure of speech?"

"No," said Nova. "It's not. You must keep your firewalls up; I'll show you how to upgrade them . . ."

She closed her eyes, communing silently with the train. They entered the outskirts of the station, a mass of sprawling limbs and tendrils, black against the grainy sky. Some of the buildings sensed the *Damask Rose* coming and turned on their lamps, sickly green bioluminescence glimmering through fleshy openings that had once been windows. The train swayed, gathering speed, rattling over a set of points. The lights of the station dwindled as the *Damask Rose* swerved away from it, out into a broad rail yard that stretched south of the main line, a confusion of tracks shining in the twilight like a frozen sea. Zen cupped his hands around his face and pressed his nose to the window. Warehouses and cankered engine sheds flicked past, sagging scrawls of cable blocked his view, and suddenly through them he saw a low moving blackness away to the north, and the voice of the *Thought Fox* was dripping from the carriage speakers again, mock-disappointed and hungry for blood.

"Oh, *little ones* . . . Are you trying to *avoid* me?"

"Hold tight!" said the *Damask Rose*, too late for Zen, who was not holding tight enough and went somersaulting over a seat back as she put on speed. But the *Thought Fox* was ready for her; it accelerated too, racing back toward the junction where the *Damask Rose*'s track rejoined the main line. They heard it give a high, fierce cry like a stooping hawk as it swung its weaponry toward them and let fly. Impacts buffeted the *Damask Rose*; sudden splashes of fire like saffron curtains flapped at the carriage windows.

"Don't worry," she told her passengers. "Those popguns can't pierce my shielding."

Hammer blows along the carriage sides: a random snare-drum

stutter laid over the deep baseline of the *Rose*'s own guns, firing back. Trackside buildings came apart in sprays of thick juice. The sparks and spatter touched off memories: of pictures seen and threedies watched, racing wartrains battling it out on the smoke-veiled tracks, boarding parties leaping between the armored carriages, the kind of thing you watched unthinking in a game or a history vid and never expected to be part of yourself. Zen stared at the windows and had to keep reminding himself that they were not just screens. Out there in the speeding dark swayed gaudy streamers of tracer fire, rivers of violent light pouring between the *Thought Fox* and the *Rose*. Gun-light winked off something moving on the wasteland of empty rails that separated the two trains. A glimpse and then gone, and it took Zen a moment to process what he'd seen.

"Maintenance spiders!" he shouted.

They hit the carriage side and scrambled up it; a swift confusion of ceramic angles silhouetted for a moment through the window glass; a scrabbling on the roof. "Maintenance spiders!" he shouted again, remembering how, in Ukotec, the *Thought Fox* had sent its spiders out to slaughter everyone.

"*Rose*, what's happening?" shouted Nova, but the train did not reply. She was too busy to answer, thought Zen, too busy sending her own spiders out to do battle with the spiders the *Fox* had sent. The track curved past a bio-building walled with organic glass, and in the reflections he saw them scuttling and wrestling on the carriage roofs. The *Fox*'s spiders were concentrating their attack on the *Rose*'s weapons, and as he watched, one of the gun turrets tore free and came tumbling past his window, strewing sparks and sprays of oil.

"My guns are offline," said the *Rose*. "I have one missile left."

"It won't get through the *Fox*'s armor," Nova said.

The two trains were close now. The *Rose* slowed. The *Fox* stood motionless at the junction where the tracks from the freight yards rejoined the mainline, a hunched black blade under the toxic sky. A quarter-mile beyond it yawned a tunnel mouth, leading to the K-gate, and Desdemor. But to reach it, the *Damask Rose* would have to pass within a few feet of the other train and its batteries of silent, waiting weapons.

She drew to a halt, defeated.

"What pretty paintings," said the *Thought Fox*.

It sounded like it meant it, but the *Rose* did not reply.

"I did them," said Flex.

"And who are you?"

"I am Flex," said Flex. He came to stand beside Zen at the window, looking out curiously at the *Thought Fox*. "You're a Zodiak, aren't you?"

"I am the last of the fighting C12s," said the *Thought Fox* proudly. Still it did not fire. It seemed to be savoring the moment, enjoying the fear it could hear in the voices of its victims. It was not like a machine at all, thought Zen. It was as cruel as a human being.

But Flex, who loved all trains despite their flaws, still seemed happy to chat to it. "I could paint you too," he said, "if you like."

"What are you doing?" whispered Zen.

"If fighting doesn't work, we have to try talking to it," Flex explained.

"But it's psychotic!"

"It's lonely," said Flex.

And the *Thought Fox* did seem to be considering Flex's offer. "Some taggers tried to write their names on me once," it said. "In Karaghand, a hundred years ago. I wore their skins for a while, as warnings to the rest."

"I don't want to write my name on you," said Flex. "Just pictures. Not too many. You are beautiful already."

"Do you think so?" asked the *Thought Fox*, and Zen almost laughed, wondering if there was any train Flex could not charm. "Tell me more," it said.

"I'd have to look at you properly," said Flex.

"Then come and look."

Flex glanced at Nova, and something passed between them, Moto to Moto, wordless. Then he picked up his bag of paints and went to the door on the far side of the carriage from the *Thought Fox*. It opened quickly for him, and the sharp fumes of the rotting buildings stung Zen's eyes as Flex slipped out, scrambled between the carriages, and walked toward the black train.

It really was beautiful, with a grim, spiny beauty that Flex had never seen before. An echo of old wars. The vapors of its engines wrapped around it, and two lamps shone red high on its black prow. The open covers of its weapons bays were wings.

"You are not a fox," he said. "You are a dragon."

"Ooh," said the *Thought Fox*, as if it liked that idea.

"I'll give you scales, and eyes," said Flex. "I'll give you teeth. I'll give you the best paint job a train ever had. But you must let my friends go. That's fair, isn't it? Just let the *Damask Rose* go by, and then I'll paint you."

The *Thought Fox* thought. It huffed out another cloud of vapor and its lamps cast spiky shadows. Hull cameras looked down at the Motorik who stood in front of it, spreading his hands to show he meant no harm.

"Nah," said the *Thought Fox*.

Flex saw fire burst from the flamethrowers on its prow. He flung up his hands to protect himself, but that did no good. He turned in the white-hot rush of the flames, stumbling, trying to find his way back to the *Damask Rose*, but his eyes had melted and the ceramic bones of his legs shattered in the heat with a sound like fresh twigs snapping. He crumpled across the rails. The *Thought Fox* rolled carefully forward, and crushed the last black scraps of him beneath its wheels.

And aboard the *Damask Rose*, Zen's shout of horror was drowned in thunder as the *Fox*'s weapons went to work again, pounding the red train, targeting the spots on her shielding that its spiders had weakened. Nova dragged Zen onto the carriage floor as their unbreakable diamondglass windows flew apart in impossible ice storms, whirling daggers freeze-framed in the sharp slanting light of the guns. The afterimage of Flex burning had seared itself onto Zen's eyeballs. It glowed through his tears, a flame in the shape of a person. He and Nova clung together, trying to shield each other, crouching in the frail shelter of the tables while the guns thundered above them, and her voice in his head said, *"It's going to be all right, I think, as long as—"*

And then there was only light.

PART FOUR
SEA OF SADNESS

43

So bright, that light. So loud, that noise, that for a moment Zen didn't know if he was alive or dead. Dead, he suspected. As dead as poor Flex. He was surprised that he could still feel the carriage floor under his knees and Nova in his arms. His ears whined and popped, and he found that he was listening to the thrum of the *Damask Rose*'s engines. He blinked away afterimages of the flash and looked around the shattered carriage. Daggers of shrapnel jutted from the seats. Thick scabs of repair foam clogged the windows. Through the scabs, he saw the dim and wavering outlines of tall buildings moving slowly past. Not the spoiled-fruit bio-buildings of the previous world, but slender towers, shining under a green sky.

"The *Rose* was moving too fast to stop," said Nova. "We came through the K-gate. This is Desdemor."

"What happened to the *Thought Fox*?"

"Gone," said the *Damask Rose*, voice slurring a little, like a punch-drunk boxer.

"I got into its mind," said Nova. "While it was busy talking to Flex, I managed to find a way through its firewalls. I made it open its engine covers."

The *Rose* said, "I sent my last missile straight into its reactor core."

"But what about Flex?" said Zen. It had happened so suddenly, that dazzling belch of flames, the black train rushing forward. The blazing bundle it had crushed under its wheels couldn't really have been Flex, could it? He still half hoped the Motorik had escaped.

But Nova shook her head. "Flex is gone too. Motorik aren't fireproof. Or train-proof."

"I tried to catch him," said the *Rose*. "His mind broadcasted a backup copy of itself as he died. I should have been able to store it, so it could be downloaded into a new body. But my firewalls were up, and by the time I realized Flex was trying to reach me . . . I caught only a few strands of code. So corrupted, so faint. Poor Flex."

"Poor Flex," said Zen. And then realized that their plans had died with him. The train was moving very slowly, curving past the beaches of Desdemor toward the center of the city where the tallest buildings stood, the Terminal Hotel rising above the golden curve of the station canopy.

"We should go back. We need time to think. Without Flex . . ."

Nova shook her head. "Raven already knows we're here. His drones have been following us since we came through the K-gate."

Zen went to a window and peered out through the bottle-glass bubblings of the hasty repairs. They were close to the station now. A drone, twin to the one that had hunted him all those weeks ago in Ambersai, was keeping pace with the train. He imagined Raven watching him through its cameras. Remembered Raven's parting words, in Cleave: "If you ever try coming after me . . ."

The mouth of the station swallowed the *Damask Rose*. Dusty platforms and shafts of green-gold light, just like the first time. The *Thought Fox*'s elegant old carriages waiting engineless on the up line. And, just like the first time, Angels. Zen hadn't noticed them out in the daylight, but here among the slanting shadows he saw that dozens of the strange light forms were blowing along beside the train like ghostly thistledown.

"Psssssccchhhh," said the *Damask Rose*, coming to a stop.

There on the platform, tall among the fraying Angels, Raven was waiting for them.

Zen stepped out into the familiar seaside smells of Desdemor, and Raven came toward him through the shadows and the light. "Zen," he said, with no expression. "And Nova."

Nova came out of the train to stand at Zen's side. "Zen came back for me," she said, as if that explained it all. Perhaps it did. Raven's eyes roved over the old red train, its scars and scorch marks, its scabbed and shattered windows. He raised an eyebrow at the battered gun turret it tried to swing toward him, then lowered it again when he saw that the gun was wrecked.

"This is one of the trains from Cleave, isn't it?" he said. "That was good thinking, Zen. But how did you get past the *Thought Fox*?"

"The *Thought Fox* is dead," said Zen.

Raven was still coming closer. Zen pulled out the cheap little pistol he had bought on Sundarban. Raven stopped. "Why did you come, Zen?" he said. "I did tell you not to come looking for me. When I sent you away, I was trying to keep you safe."

"You don't care about me!" said Zen. "You don't care about anyone! You're not even human!"

"I was once," said Raven. "And now, perhaps, I am again. I wish you had stayed on Summer's Lease, Zen. We could have salvaged Nova together, once my work here is complete."

"You never cared about her either," said Zen. He held the gun as steady as he could. "You just used us both. But you're not going to use us anymore. That's your last body, isn't it? When that one goes, you'll be dead for real, won't you? So if you want to stay alive, you'll do what I say."

He thought he sounded pretty convincing. Channeling tough guys from the threedies and the wilder kids he'd known in Cleave. Clenched jaw, hard eyes, the gun unwavering.

Raven just gave a little sigh, the sort you'd make if you found your train was running late. "What do you *want*, Zen?"

"The Pyxis," said Zen. "It's ours by rights. We stole it for you, before we knew what it was, and what it's worth. Now we need it back."

Raven smiled. Such an honest, amused, twinkly eyed smile that it was hard to keep the gun trained on him; he looked more human than Zen had ever seen him. "But I need it myself, Zen. I need it here on Tristesse. I am going to use it to open a new K-gate."

"You can't open a new gate," said Zen. "The Guardians say it's impossible."

"And Guardians always tell the truth," said Raven.

"Why would they lie?" asked Nova.

"Because they don't want us to open another K-gate. Because they think that the Network is big enough, and human beings have enough K-gates, and that we should be good and grateful, shuttling around on these rails they've laid for us. But I disagree.

I think we need to travel farther. I think we need to *extend* the Network. And I'm sure your fellow passenger agrees . . ."

His smile went past Zen to the train. In the doorway of the front carriage stood a Hive Monk, faceless, naked, swaying uncertainly on a skeleton cobbled together out of odd splinters of table wood and lengths of window trim blasted free by the *Thought Fox*'s guns. A dwarfish, wobbly, misshapen Hive Monk, barely humanoid without its robe and mask, but intelligent again.

"I'm assuming it was the Monks who led you to this old train?" said Raven. "I should have guessed. They know the Network inside out, the dead stations and the living ones. They've been searching so long for their Insect Lines. You'd think by now that they'd have realized the Insect Lines aren't on *our* Network. Not one of the nine hundred and sixty-four gates leads where they want to go. If they want to get there, we'll have to open a new gate."

"Uncle Bugs isn't listening to you," said Zen. Actually, he wasn't sure if this new Monk *was* Uncle Bugs. It was made up of insects from all three Hive Monks. Perhaps it counted as a completely new person. But he guessed it must have some of Uncle's memories. "It was your drone that smashed him up, back in Cleave."

"Sorry about that," said Raven lightly, still looking at the Hive Monk.

The Hive Monk spoke, whispery and uncertain, while the insects that formed it scrambled over each other in excitement. "You know the way onto the Insect Lines?"

Raven nodded.

"He's lying," said Nova. "Raven tells lies upon lies. He tells lies *about* lies."

Raven looked hurt, as if it caused him actual pain that Nova didn't trust him anymore. He smiled sadly and sweetly at the Hive Monk. "It sounds as if Nova has chosen her side," he said. "Now you must. Are you going to help Zen, or me? Remember, I'm the man who knows the way to where you want to go."

Rushing, rustling sounds came from the Monk. The sounds of a million insects arguing among themselves.

"Don't listen to him, Uncle Bugs!" Zen shouted.

"Zen needed you to get himself a train," said Raven. "But he can't give you anything in return. If you help me, I shall show you the way to where you want to go. I know how badly you've been longing to get there. Very soon, if Zen will let me, I shall open the new gate. A new bright gate! Help me, and I'll take you through it with me."

"Don't listen to him!" shouted Zen. "You don't understand . . ."

Perhaps that was the wrong thing to say. The Hive Monk never had understood human beings. It was tired of trying to understand them. All it had ever wanted was to see the Insect Lines, and now here was a human who claimed to know the way.

With a sound like a small wave breaking, the Hive Monk stepped down from the train. It seemed to come apart as its foot hit the platform, its upper half exploding into a blur of wings, but somehow it kept moving, and it came at Zen. Bugs battered his face as he turned, they clumped on his clothes, they clung to his hands when he tried to brush them away. Thick fingers made of bodies and legs clasped his wrists. He had dropped the gun.

"Uncle Bugs!" he shouted, still hoping the swarm had some memory of the strange old shopkeeper who had been a friend of sorts to Zen.

"That is not our name," the bugs chirred, covering him as

thickly as when they'd hidden him on Sundarban. "That is a human name; our name is . . ." and then only a long rustling, a crumpled-plastic-bag clattering of wings and mandibles, and mixed in with it a sort of chant that went, "The Insect Lines, the Insect Lines . . ."

Nova ran to him, swiping at the storm of bugs as it wrapped around him, trying to scatter them, but Raven called her name and snapped his fingers and some small clever piece of code slipped from his headset into her brain and switched off her mind like a light. Zen barely noticed. The bugs were all over him now, pouring into his mouth, scuttling down his throat while he gagged and struggled, down on his knees, choking, bug-blind, bug-smothered. They were still whispering to him of the Insect Lines as they suffocated him.

44

Malik's wartrain roared through the snows of Winterreise. Its drones flew above it, scanning the line ahead, while its crew prepared their weapons and checked their screens for traces of the *Damask Rose*. But the interface of Anais Six sat in the command carriage staring straight ahead and said, "They are not here. They came this way. They stopped here to repair and take on fuel. They took the spur that leads to Desdemor."

It must have a brain like a Moto, thought Malik, watching the flicker of its golden eyes. Inside that perfect blue head something like a computer was linking itself to this chilly planet's data raft, to the dull minds of the station and the K-bahn signals, checking their histories, pulling up images of the red train. Humans could have hardware like that installed in their brains instead of wearing a headset if they wanted to, but nobody ever did, because it was too much hassle having brain surgery every time a fashionable new gadget was released. For an interface, that didn't matter. It was disposable, a costume of flesh that

Anais Six would wear for a single summer, or perhaps only a single night.

Just like Raven, he thought. *When you have that many bodies, you never really understand what a body means to us poor souls who only get the one. You'll never know what getting old means, how the sadness piles up inside our hearts like snow.*

"Desdemor, on the water-moon Tristesse," said the interface. "That is where we will find Raven."

It spoke to Malik alone, through his headset, as if it did not want the Railforce soldiers around him to hear. He could not think why. They all looked to it for orders, certain that Anais, not Malik, was in charge of this mission. Why would it not tell them who they were hunting?

He sat next to it and said quietly, "Why would you not let Rail Marshal Delius release details about the Starling boy? Isn't it dangerous, letting the Noons go on thinking he is working for Tibor or the Prells? A war might be starting back there . . ."

"My brothers and sisters can take care of that," said Anais Six. "Raven is my business and mine alone."

It turned suddenly to look at him. "I loved him once. I made him more than he was, almost a Guardian. But he wanted more still, and he had to be deleted. The other Guardians said that I must do it; my punishment for creating him in the first place. So I destroyed the data centers where his programs ran. I ordered your team to hunt down his interfaces. But at the end, when there was just one body left, I thought, let him be. Let him escape. I thought, he is just a human again; what harm can one human do? That's why I called you off. If my brothers and sisters learn that I let him live, knowing what he knows, they will punish me. They will delete me."

Malik thought about this. "So what harm *can* he do?" he

asked. "Something must have made you change your mind about him."

The interface did not answer.

"Crashing the Noon train was just a diversion, wasn't it?" said Malik. "Zen Starling stole something he needed from the Noon's art collection, but he didn't need to crash the train. That was just something to make the Guardians and the media and Railforce look left while Raven went right. The Sundarban Shuffle."

The interface did not answer.

"So what's his real game?" urged Malik. "What's he doing, on the water-moon Tristesse?"

The interface did not answer. Malik remembered what Raven had said to him on Ibo. "Whatever the Guardians told your masters about me, whatever they say I did, it's a lie." It had never occurred to him before to wonder if that might have been true.

*

Night now on Sundarban. Rain falling on the skylights of the room in the station hotel where Threnody was sleeping.

Or trying to sleep. She thought at first it was the rain that had woken her. Then shook sleep away and heard voices, low and urgent, just outside the door. The dull pain in her head reminded her of the things she'd been through, the shuttle crash and Anais, the strange dramas of the day. And at the end of it they hadn't even let her go home; they'd sent Kobi home, but made some excuse when she wanted to go with him, and found her this room in the hotel instead.

She felt angry, and then suddenly afraid. She wished more than anything that she was back on Malapet. If she ever made it back there, to her mother's house, she would never complain about being bored again . . .

The door was opening, expensively silent. She sat up in bed, pulling the covers around her. Two Railforce officers, both women, asking her politely to get dressed and come with them.

"Where?"

"Rail Marshal Delius wishes to speak with you."

"Why?"

"Rail Marshal Delius will explain."

A covered bridge led from the hotel to the tower where the Rail Marshal had made her headquarters, the nighttime city a blur of colored lights beyond the wet glass walls. One of the officers went ahead of Threnody and one followed behind. Each kept one hand on the pistols that they wore on their belts. They steered her through quiet corridors to a room where Rail Marshal Delius was waiting, a few other officers with her, and Mr. Yunis, and a woman from the K-bahn Timetable Authority. They watched Threnody solemnly.

"Threnody," said the Rail Marshal, as solemn as the rest of them. "I'm sorry to wake you, but things are moving quickly. Railforce has decided that the matter of the succession cannot be allowed to go undecided any longer. Your uncle Tibor has a good claim to the throne, your sister, Priya, is the official heir . . ."

They have decided to support Tibor, thought Threnody. *They are going to kill me and Priya so that we can't make trouble for him. Or maybe*—remembering the look that Priya had sent her way earlier—*they are supporting Priya, and it is Priya who wants me dead.* She felt herself sort of curling up inside, already tensing herself for the bullet, though she knew that would not come here, but outside somewhere, on some windy rail yard or the edge of a quarry, without all these witnesses.

". . . but we have decided to support you."

The Rail Marshal was smiling at her. It was a kind and motherly smile, and Threnody wondered what sort of person would smile a smile like that at someone she was about to have killed, and that made her think back and realize what had just been said.

"But I'm not—"

"You are a Noon," said the Rail Marshal. "And, unlike your uncle or your sister, you have the support of the people of the Great Network, and the approval of the Guardians. I have already sent word through to Grand Central. My colleagues there have placed Tibor Noon under arrest."

"And Priya?" asked Threnody.

"Priya has been persuaded to step aside in your favor," said Lyssa Delius, with another smile, and only the faintest little hesitation before "persuaded." "It is for the good of the Network. And now, Empress Threnody, you must come with me to Grand Central, as quickly as possible, and let the people see their new Empress take her place upon the throne. Come; there is a train waiting for you."

And she was numb, floating, not believing any of it. "Is Kobi here?" she said. "Is he coming too?"

"I think not," said Lyssa Delius. "Not until the contract with the Chen-Tulsis has been renegotiated."

Threnody knew that she would miss him. That surprised her almost as much as the rest of it. It turned out that Kobi was just the person you wanted with you when you were woken in the middle of the night and told you were the new ruler of the galaxy.

And then it was just her and the Rail Marshal, in an elevator, dropping toward the mainline platforms. Threnody staring at her reflection in the glass, where the city lights made diadems above her face. Saying, "But I'm not—I don't know how to be Empress, that's Priya's job. I'm just a minor daughter; I don't know how to . . ."

"Oh, of course, you will need guidance," said the Rail Marshal. She took Threnody's arm. Her touch was like her voice: comforting, gentle, but very firm, and Threnody understood. She saw the future suddenly, saw just how it was going to be: young Empress Threnody I ruling the rails, getting that startled-looking face of hers on banknotes and the sides of buildings—and at her shoulder always, whispering wise advice, wielding the real power, Lyssa Delius.

"I'm not ready," she said.

But the elevator had reached ground level. The doors opened straight onto the station concourse. She could see the Railforce train waiting to take her to Grand Central. And between herself and the train, Noon Corporate Marines and Railforce Bluebodies, lined up in neat ranks, which rippled as she stepped out of the elevator, all the assembled men and women falling on one knee, shouting, "Long live the Empress! Long live Empress Threnody the First!"

45

He woke reluctantly, clinging for as long as he could to sleep, not quite certain where he was, or why, and knowing that he should enjoy that forgetfulness, because he could feel bad memories waiting for him. But they found him anyway. They came down on him like a collapsing roof: memories of battles and a burning body. Memories of insects. He leaped up, clawing at himself, retching, groping for bugs in his hair.

There were none. He was in his old bedroom in the Terminal Hotel. Clean sheets and green-gold daylight.

He toyed for a moment with the notion that everything had been a dream, but he knew it hadn't, however nightmarish parts of it had been. The bitter taste of bug juice was still in his mouth. More bitter still, the feeling of betrayal. He had let himself think that the Hive Monks were his friends.

The windows were open, white curtains shifting softly in a wind off the Sea of Sadness. Raven was standing on the balcony. He came into the room smiling. "Zen! I'm glad you're awake—"

"Where's Nova?" Zen asked.

"Don't worry. She's shut down, but it's temporary. You were both rather excitable when you got here, and my plans are at a very critical stage. I can't allow you to upset things."

Zen touched his throat. He could not rid himself of the memory of the bugs' scrabbling feet inside him, or the feeling that his lungs had become nests.

"It's all right," Raven promised. "I had Dr. Vibhat check you over and remove all the little carcasses from your airways."

"I thought you wanted them to kill me?" said Zen.

"Kill you?"

"That's what you said you'd do, if I came back."

"Because I wanted you to stay away, stay safe. But you didn't, and you're here, and I'm glad."

"You're lying," said Zen, but only quietly. The anger he had felt at Raven was gone: smothered by the bugs, or turned to ashes with Flex.

"If I'd wanted you dead," said Raven, reasonably, "I could have called in a drone. Or had one of the Motorik shoot you from the hotel lobby. I've upgraded them with some high-end military software I borrowed from a Railforce base on Ashtoreth; they're remarkably good shots now. No, I just wanted to get the gun away from you, so we could talk. Our Hive Monk friend went a little too far, but then his people have been waiting a long time to find their Insect Lines. When he realized that my new gate will go there and you were trying to stop me—well, you can hardly blame him."

"It's true then? You want to make a new gate?"

"Yes. You were right about this body of mine, Zen. It's the last I have, and it's wearing out. A man asked me once why I hadn't done anything with my many lives, why I hadn't made a difference. Well, I plan to, before I die."

"The Guardians say there can't be any more gates," said Zen. "And they built the Network; they must know—"

"What makes you think that?" asked Raven.

"What?"

"That the Guardians built the Network?"

"Everybody knows that!"

"Ah, yes." Raven sat down on the chair beside the bed. "Everybody knows that the Guardians built the Network. And how do we know? Because the Guardians told us so. Everything we know about everything, we know because the Guardians told us. They don't just guard us, they guard our information. That's something that I learned about them, when I lived in the Datasea. The way they edit history. The things they delete. The way they lie to us. What is it that they do not want us to find out?"

"About the walls of Marapur?" said Zen. "The black spheres Lady Rishi found, all those years ago? There were seven, not six—"

"Ah, so you know about the spheres . . ."

"I know you didn't pay me enough for that one I stole for you."

Raven grinned. He reached into the pocket of his shabby suit and took out the Pyxis. Once again, Zen was surprised at how unimpressive it looked, and how heavy it felt when Raven tossed it across the bed for him to catch. It opened for him again, and he saw his own face reflected in the dark shining surface of the sphere.

"Clever Lady Rishi," said Raven fondly. "She managed to spirit this one away before the Guardians arrived. She asked me to help her keep it hidden. I don't think she had any real idea what it was. It just thrilled her to think she knew something that the Guardians didn't, that she had stolen something from the gods.

"So I made her a present. This little box. Scan-proof. Just big enough to hold the sphere. It could rest safe in the family art collection, and no one would ever know. But it was a cleverer box than even Rishi knew, because I had an inkling that I might need another look at that sphere one day. It was semi-intelligent, that Pyxis of mine. When Rishi died it locked itself tight and became just a rather dull cube, to be kept among the other heirlooms of the Noon family."

"What is the sphere?" asked Zen.

"That took me hundreds of years to find out," said Raven. "That was the big question. When the Guardians learned I was asking about it, they tried to destroy me, and almost succeeded. But I found my answer before they deleted me. Down in the deep archives.

"You see, Zen, those Guardians of ours were not really the builders of the Great Network at all. They just took the credit for it. Back at the beginning, when the Guardians first became intelligent, they started searching for ways to help human beings leave Old Earth, which was a bit overcrowded in those days. They sent out probes to all Earth's neighbor planets, looking for one that might do. And in a cavern on a place called Mars, they discovered something very odd. A set of ancient rails, leading into—well, what was that thing? The Guardians built a train, of course, sent it through, and found their way to world after world, gate after gate. They had stumbled upon the Great Network. All they had to do was help the corporate families to link each gate to the next."

"So who *did* build the gates?"

Raven didn't even bother answering, just watched him steadily, half-amused.

"You mean . . . ?"

Zen couldn't even think of the word. There were humans, and human machines, and the mutant Monk bugs. Nothing else in all the wide black wilderness of space had ever achieved intelligence. The Guardians had said so; all the probes they had sent out, all those radio telescopes sieving the soft static of the sky for signals, had never found anything at all. That was what the Guardians said.

But Raven said, "The Guardians have known for a long time of another network of K-gates. Another civilization, on the far side of our galaxy. Are those the beings who put the K-gate on Mars for our Guardians to find? Was it they who left the spheres on Marapur for us, so that we could make K-gates of our own? Or are they like us, just using a network constructed long before, by some other race who moved across the universe when the stars were young, leaving K-gates behind them like footprints? All I know is that they have been trying to communicate with us, but their messages were too strange for humans to notice, and the Guardians just stuck their virtual fingers in their virtual ears and went, 'LA LA LA.'"

"The Station Angels?" guessed Zen. "They're the messengers?"

"They are the messages. Projections, beamed through the gates by some means we can't yet understand. It was they who led me to the truth, Zen. They who told me where I must open my new gate."

"Can't they make their own, if they're so clever?"

"I think they are waiting for us to visit them."

"But what about the symmetry of the whatever . . . ? If you make a new gate, won't it destabilize the whole Network?"

"More of the Guardians' lies. The real reason why they say there can be no more gates is much simpler: they are afraid of what is on the other side. The Guardians are just as scared of change as humans are. And they love us, they really do. They think of us all as their children. They fear we won't be able to cope with the shock of meeting another intelligent species. But human beings are tougher than they think. And you can't keep children in the nursery forever. If you do, they never become grown-ups, but they're not really children either. They are just pets."

He took back the sphere and the Pyxis, while Zen sat trying to make sense of it all. If Raven could really open this new gate, he wondered, what strange trains would come through it? What sort of passengers would they carry?

"Will it really lead to the Insect Lines?" he asked.

Raven laughed. "Who knows? I suspect they are just a Hive Monk myth. But it will lead *somewhere*." He put the sphere back inside the Pyxis and closed it. "You know, sometimes a thing, a system, a creation grows so old, and corrupt, and weighed down by its own baggage, that all you can do is change it. Move on. Start afresh. It's frightening, but it has to be done."

He almost made Zen believe him. He almost made Zen want that new gate as much as he did. But Zen was not here to help Raven. He tried out a wise-guy smile he hadn't found much cause to use since Spindlebridge. Said, "You'll have to do it fast, then. Railforce knows about you. Another few hours and this place is going to be swarming with Bluebodies."

46

Raven's smile faded.

"You told Railforce? Oh, Zen—"

"I didn't *tell* them," said Zen indignantly, because there was nothing worse for a Thunder City kid than being called an informer. "But they're not stupid! They can work it out. They nearly caught me and Nova. They saw us take off down the Dog Star Line. They'll send trains to search all the old stations west of Sundarban."

Raven looked through him for a moment, calculating how long it would take Railforce to check each of those worlds, how long it would be before he could expect them in Desdemor. Then he sprang up. "Get dressed, Zen!"

"I'm not coming with you—"

"Don't be childish. Get dressed."

Zen went to the closet where his clothes hung. The ones he had worn to Sundarban were there, torn and scorched from the battles they had been through, but so were those he had worn on the Noon train. He put them on, wondering why Raven would have bothered to bring them back here. As if he really had been half hoping that Zen would return.

Standing on one leg to pull a boot on, he asked, "That viaduct? The one that goes south? Is that where the new gate is?"

"There's an island there," said Raven.

Zen followed him to the elevators. Down in the lobby, some of the hotel's Motorik staff were waiting. They still wore the uniforms of chamber maids and bellboys, but their manner had changed: they seemed more alert than before, and they carried guns.

"Raven!" whispered an urgent, rustling voice. Zen flinched; he cringed; he couldn't help himself. The Hive Monk collapsed off one of the stalls of the bar like a lonely drunk and came shamble-shuffling across the lobby, holding out its seething arms. "You are bound for the bright gates?"

Raven smiled a distant smile, like a man accosted by an embarrassing relative.

"Take us with you!" rustled the Hive Monk. "You promised! Take us to the Insect Lines!"

"Mmm. I think not," said Raven. He glanced at the watching Motorik and said, "Insectocutors . . ."

Two former waiters pulled out devices that unfolded like parasols and pulsed with a lilac light. The Hive Monk wavered. It rustled like a reed bed. "To the bright gate!" it wheedled, and "Please! Take us with you!" But the light had been designed to lure Monk bugs, and the devices made a lovely buzzing sound as well, and filled the air with tantalizing pheromones. "No!" said the Monk, and "You promised us . . . !" With a soft rushing sound as a million interlocked legs uncoupled, it came apart, and the insects that had made it buzzed and scuttled toward the insectocutors and died there, crackling on meshes of electric fire.

Zen watched in pity and disgust while they popped and fizzed and burnt and tried to stop themselves from answering the call of the light and failed. He knew he should feel some sort of fellowship with them; Raven had used them and lied to them, just like he had used and lied to Zen. But the memory of the bugs in his mouth and airways was still fresh, and it was all he could do not to gag as he watched them scrabble and flutter at the insectocutors and pile up in crisp heaps beneath them.

Raven put a hand on his shoulder. "You may well experience a slight phobic reaction to insects for a while, after what you went through earlier." He smiled kindly, as if that hadn't been his fault. The sharp smell of roasted insects filled the lobby, and the sprinklers were starting to go off. Raven guided Zen outside, into clearer air and the sleepy green light beneath the station canopy.

More Motorik were waiting there: chefs and receptionists, boot-polish camouflage smeared across their faces, assault rifles idly trained on Nova, who stood between them with her head bowed. At the sound of footsteps she looked up. She gave a wavery smile when she saw Zen.

He smiled back, a real, helpless smile that made him feel better for the first time since he woke. What was it about Nova that made him feel as if everything was all right? Even when it very clearly wasn't; even when armed Motorik were escorting them both onto the platform where the *Damask Rose* was waiting.

"You see?" said Raven. "I could have left Nova shut down, but I want you both to be there when the new gate opens. It should be quite a sight. You won't want to miss it. Something to tell your grandchildren about. But I shall need to borrow your train, as you have broken mine. You'll have to help me talk to it. It doesn't like me."

"I'm not surprised," said Zen.

"Train," said Raven, turning to the *Damask Rose*, "there is an artificial island about twelve miles south of here."

"Not in *my* database," said the *Damask Rose* primly.

"It is on a new spur," said Raven. "Opened since the Dog Star Line was closed."

"Pssscchhh," said the *Damask Rose*, and kept its doors shut tight.

Raven sighed. "I'll put this another way. Let us aboard, or I'll shoot Nova, and then Zen, and then I'll kill your mind, hot-wire your engine, and drive you south anyway."

The militarized Motorik raised their guns. The clatter of safety catches being released echoed under the station canopy like applause.

"I thought you wanted us to see the new gate?" said Nova.

Raven shrugged. "We can't always have what we want."

"Zen?" asked the *Damask Rose*.

Zen walked over to the train and laid his hand on her warm hull, reassuring her that it would be all right. "Do as he asks," he said. Most of the battle damage had healed, and a pair of battered maintenance spiders were busy retouching Flex's paintings. No—not just retouching. Sections of the loco that Flex had never had time to decorate were now being covered with figures. Zen watched one of the spiders sketch in a smiling Motorik, soaring across a wheel-housing on wide white wings.

"Where did you learn to draw, train?" he asked.

"It just came to me," said the *Damask Rose*. And he knew then that something had been salvaged after all: somewhere in the loco's big, strange brain, Flex's imagination was safe.

Obeying Raven's instructions, the train reversed out of the station and left its battered carriages on a siding. Then it coupled itself to the old state cars from the *Thought Fox*, and returned to collect Zen, Nova, Raven, and half a dozen of the Motorik. It carried them back through the silent city to a set of points that switched it onto the new spur. Then south, gathering speed as it left the coast of Desdemor and went rushing out along that white viaduct that Zen had noticed the day that he and Nova played the ray game.

Rays had made their lairs under the viaduct's arches. Disturbed by the train passing overhead, the big creatures emerged to flap slowly alongside at window height. They swiveled their turreted eyes to squint in at the passengers, then lost interest and veered away to attack a shoal of leaping fish. The *Damask Rose* ran on. The clatter of the wheels, the tracks, the same steady rhythms that Zen had been hearing all his life, but different now, lonely sounding, out here in the wide wastes of Tristesse's ocean.

"There *is* an island ahead," admitted the *Damask Rose*.

Zen looked out of the windows, but the viaduct ran straight as a ruled line across the sea, so whatever they were coming to lay out of sight beyond the locomotive. He did not see it until the train stopped and the carriage doors opened. Then he and Nova stepped out after Raven. The viaduct was wet with sea spray, and slippery, and there was no handrail. Zen skidded, clutching at Raven to stop himself from falling.

"Steady," said Raven. "It would be a pity to drown just when things are getting interesting."

Careful to keep his footing, Zen turned toward the front of the train, and there was the island, waiting.

A broad island, entirely black, except where white beaches had formed along its sharply angled sides, made from the shells of countless crabs. Around its edges stood the machines that had built it, motionless now, their long arms folded.

Between them, in the island's center, another machine was busy. It was immense, and its shape was hard to grasp. Part cathedral, part caterpillar. A lot of biotech in there. Spines and wheels and grublike legs. Chitinous armor. Strange structures at the sternward end had piped out two shining rails, which joined seamlessly to the rails of the viaduct. Vapor plumed from vents along its sides. Up at the front, huge stag-beetle horns dipped and twitched, constructing a high archway.

"It took me twenty years to build," said Raven. "The parts were stolen from laboratories and factories and biotech building sites all across the Network."

"I never knew," said Nova, wondering. "I never guessed, all those things I helped you steal . . . Why did I never ask what they were for? Why did I never come to see what was happening here?"

"Because I programmed you not to," said Raven. "I didn't want you to know *all* my secrets. The Guardians call these devices Worms, but even they know of them only from guesswork and a few fossil remains. The original Worms did their work long before Guardians were invented."

Zen wondered how deep in the Datasea Raven had had to dive to find the plans for making such a thing. It was infinitely strange, and infinitely old, and it did not belong in any of the worlds he knew. He hung back at first, wary of leaving the comforting shelter of the *Damask Rose*. But Nova set off along the viaduct after Raven, and when Zen followed them he saw that there were more of the hotel Motorik on the island, standing around the Worm, looking like toys against the insane mass of it.

Carlota came to greet Raven as he stepped onto the island. "Sir," she said, with a smart salute instead of her usual kindly smile. She was carrying one of the hotel's ray guns. Zen, who had forgotten about the rays until then, looked quickly at the sky. All he saw were a few of Raven's drones patrolling.

"This platform has a magnetic field, like the ones high buildings use to scare birds away," said Raven. "That will discourage the rays. And if any do get through, Carlota and her people will protect us." To Carlota he said, "How are things going?"

"The structure is almost complete, sir," she replied, leading her visitors along the Worm's side to a place where they could watch the archway taking shape. Squinting through the vapors from the gills of the strange machine, Zen tried to make out what was happening, but so many mechanical claws and pincers and tentacle-hosepipe things were busy there that he couldn't say for sure. The Worm seemed to be shaping the arch the way children on the beach made little towers by dribbling wet sand between their fingers. The stuff dried quickly, taking on a look that was both bony and metallic.

Zen had glimpsed something like that before: the arch that spanned the rails on Burj-al-Badr.

"It's making a K-gate," he said.

Raven laughed. "The Worm *is* a K-gate, Zen. It's hard to explain, but the Worm and the arch, the arch and the Worm, they're all part of the same machine. The Marapur sphere holds the programs that allow it to open a passage through K-space, but it has to make the archway ready first." He fitted an expensive-looking headset over his ear and pressed the terminal against his temple. "Since you tell me we shall soon be having Railforce visitors, I'm going to see if we can speed up the process . . ."

He closed his eyes. Zen looked up at the Worm, trying to see if whatever signal Raven was transmitting was having an effect.

Nothing seemed to change; the huge arms just kept patiently sculpting the archway.

"Mr. Raven, sir . . ." said Carlota suddenly, and some note of worry in her voice made Zen glance at her. She was holding her big gun ready. Behind her he saw other Motorik hurrying across the island with guns that were bigger still: rocket launchers and heavy blasters.

Nova was staring at the sky, where the sound of the circling drones was fading, as if they had all chosen the same moment to speed away toward the north.

"Zen," said Nova, "there is an imperial wartrain approaching."

47

The Railforce train let out an electromagnetic belch as it slammed into Desdemor, knocking out the drones that Raven had left to watch the K-gate. They fell on either side of the track as it sped past. In the cabin, the interface of Anais Six opened its golden eyes and said, "There is no connection to the Datasea on this world. It has been disabled . . ."

It looked as surprised as if it had just stepped off a cliff. On every world they had passed it had opened a link to the version of itself in the local data raft, updating them, gathering information. Here on Tristesse there was nothing: no data raft, no Guardians. It looked at its blue hands. It was not used to being confined in a single body.

Malik was pleased by its discomfort. It was good for the train's crew to see that it did not know everything.

He was careful to show no sign of doubt himself as the train screeched into Desdemor. The Motorik whom Raven had left to guard the hotel opened fire from beyond the ticket barriers, but they could not pierce its armored hide. Flights of hound missiles hunted them through the slanting shadows and destroyed them all, quite quickly.

As the echoes of the skirmish faded, Malik stepped out onto the platform. Ahead of him, armored troopers moved through the station. Behind him, cautious as a heron, the Anais Six interface unfolded itself from the doorway of the train.

"Raven is not here," it said.

"Let's make sure," he told it. He sent drones and troopers hurrying across the station, into the hotel.

"He is not here," said the interface flatly. "We have to find him. We must stop him before . . ."

"Before what?" asked Malik. "What is he doing that you're so—" (He wanted to say "frightened of," but he stopped himself. A godlike data entity could not be *frightened*, could it?)

The interface said, "He is planning to destroy the Network. He has come into possession of technology that will destabilize the K-gates."

"What do you mean, 'destroy the Network'?" asked Malik. "You mean all of it? The End of Civilization as We Know It, like something in a cheap threedie? Why would Raven want that?"

"Because I made him a god, and now he is only a man again. This will be his revenge." The interface crouched down beside one of the defeated Motorik, a chef who had swapped his egg whisk for a rocket launcher. It studied the spilled blue soup of his brain, and its eyes flickered as it gathered faint signals from the dying circuitry.

"Raven left fifty-six minutes ago. He went south. More armed Motorik are with him, also Zen Starling and the Motorik Nova."

Malik left a squad behind to secure the hotel, and the wartrain roared on, its reflection sliding across the mirrored curtain walls of empty hotels. The gathering speed seemed to excite the interface. It stood up, prowling up and down the cabin with its antlers scraping against the roof. "Give me control of your weapons systems," it said, and took it without waiting for Malik's permission. Combat drones popped from hatches on the hull and sped ahead and above as the train raced out onto the viaduct. The green sea widened on either side, and rays came hooting, barbed tails lashing at the windows. One of the drones opened fire, filling the air for a moment with shreds of ripped ray, till Malik said, "Those beasties aren't our problem, Guardian. Best save our munitions for whatever's waiting at the end of the line."

"Captain Malik!" called one of the junior officers. The screens that walled the command carriage were filling with red warning symbols.

"There are drones ahead," said the interface. "They form a defensive shield around an island at the track's end. They are an obsolete model; I will defeat them easily."

"They're Raven's," said Malik. "Don't underestimate them." To his crew he shouted, "Check the firewalls! Scan for viruses!"

And they were in a battle. Malik looked at the window and saw the sky around his speeding train fill suddenly with chrysanthemums. They were yellow and red and ginger, and every blossom was the blast of a missile, and the gentle sea was painted with hot reflections and then speckled with white splashes as the wreckage of shattered drones showered down.

48

"Multiple contacts!" shouted one of Raven's Motorik, still dressed as a chambermaid, but carrying a heavy machine gun.

Raven still stood with his eyes closed.

"Take them down," said Carlota calmly.

Zen looked north, where sharp dark shapes screamed over the waves as if delighted to bring such noise and violence to this quiet place. Something big and burning arrived, sliding down the sky on a trail of black smoke to smash into sparks and pieces against the side of the Worm. Just behind it came another, this one still maneuvering. Tracer bullets sprayed from it, looking as harmless as fat fireflies until they tore the Motorik chambermaid to pieces and came cracking across the island's surface just inches from where Zen stood watching, too scared to move. Nova grabbed him and pulled him down. He lay beside her, listening to bullets thunking against worm-shell, then the heavy bark of Carlota's ray gun as she knelt and tracked the Railforce drone and fired. The drone hit the far side of the island, bounced, bounced, and vanished over the edge like a burning wheel.

Zen raised his head. Dead Motorik were strewn all around him, some in pieces, some of the pieces still moving. Raven stood unscathed, talking to his drones.

"Stay down, please, Mr. Starling," said Carlota.

Because something terrible was coming down the track from Desdemor: a blazing wartrain, dragon-armor shining through wreaths of flame as the last of Raven's drones poured their fire upon it. They should not have been able to harm a train—the shielding that protected trains from the energies of K-space was more than sufficient to stop their missiles—but Raven was directing the drones himself now, and he knew about the weaknesses of shielding. He looked for a hatch in the train's hull and hammered it hard. Lost three drones in the process, but it didn't matter because he got what he wanted: the hatch blown open, cover flapping. Then his last drone—a small one, moving faster than the Railforce machines that swerved to cut it off—swung in low and dropped a single charge inside before the scrambling maintenance spiders slammed the cover shut.

And a moment after that the fuel that drove the wartrain's reactors decided that it didn't like being cooped up in containment cylinders anymore, and burst out to join the fun, shrugging off big, spinning chunks of semi-molten locomotive.

*

All Malik knew of this was the sudden dying of all the screens, the sudden turning of the air outside into fire. And an abrupt weightlessness, first the ceiling slamming into him, then a seat, then the floor, slashes of light and shadow, fans of white water

315

crashing past the windows as the wartrain cartwheeled over the viaduct's edge into the sea.

He came to rest against one of the windows. Beyond the diamondglass was a deep-green gloom as endless as the Datasea. It was dark in the carriage—all the lights and screens had died when it took flight—and the darkness was full of moans and whimpers. Malik tuned his headset to infrared and saw the bodies around him, some moving, others not; twisted at impossible angles. Something wet was soaking through his clothes. He thought at first that it was blood.

It wasn't. It was worse than that.

It was the sea.

Somehow his train had been broken open, either by the explosion or by the force of the crash. The openings were only small, but that just seemed to make the sea even more excited about forcing its way through them. Malik could see three white jets spraying in, and he guessed there must be more. When he pushed himself upright the water was already up to his knees. A body bumped against him, then another, the second alive. It was the interface of Anais, one antler broken off.

Leave it, he told himself. *Let it drown. It can always get another body made.*

But it looked so *frightened* . . .

He dragged it through the carriage, toward the doors. "We'll let the carriage flood," he shouted, "then swim for it."

"I do not know how to swim," said the interface.

When the doors opened, the sea came in, white and boisterous and cold. It picked the survivors up and lifted them until they had to press their faces to the ceiling to sip from the last tiny pocket of air, and then even that was gone. Malik took one look back. The flooded carriage looked like a rock pool, filled with the scrambling crablike forms of the armored troopers, the seaweed waverings of someone's hair. Then he was swimming, kicking out wildly with both legs in the dark, in the green dark with its streams of silver bubbles, and the shafts of dim light slanting and shimmering, and then suddenly in open air again, the interface whooping uncertainly for breath, Malik striking out through the waves toward the black island at the viaduct's end.

*

"Zen? Are you hurt?"

Nova stooped over him, helping him up. Zen shook his head. All of him was shaking. He had been, he thought, in far too many battles. But all was quiet on the island now. The fallen Motorik were strewn like toys among the action-painting scrawls and spatters of their spilled blue gel. Carlota was still standing, seeping gel from half a dozen holes. A few others too, dazed android bellboys and receptionists, clutching their unwieldy guns, examining their wounds.

"We did it!" said Raven.

Zen thought he meant, "We've won the fight." Then he looked at the Worm, and saw that its arms had stopped moving. The wet, intestinal noises that had come from it while it was working had fallen silent. Low down near its front end, an opening had appeared in its shell. It couldn't be battle damage; it was too neat a hole for a missile to have made, and why would Raven look so pleased with it if it was?

"The gate is ready!" said Raven, a bit too loudly, as if his ears had not adjusted yet to the silence. "Now we just need to turn the key." He reached into his pocket.

He frowned.

He tried the other pocket. Looked sharply at Zen.

Who was backing away fast. He groped in his own pocket as he went, and took out the Pyxis.

It was all thanks to Flex, really. The discovery that Flex was still alive in some way inside the *Damask Rose* had lifted Zen's spirits and got him scheming again. He had been considering his options all the way from Desdemor. When they stepped off the train and he stumbled against Raven, he had taken the Pyxis.

He ran to the island's edge. The waves were breaking there, shifting the crab-shell beach about with shattered crockery sounds, white spray flying. He held the Pyxis high. "If you want it, you'll have to promise we'll be safe, me and Nova—"

"Zen!" Raven strode toward him. "There isn't time for this! That wartrain was just the advance guard. Half of Railforce will be coming to Desdemor . . ."

A shocking screech echoed off the ceramic. A shadow flashed over them. Nova screamed a warning. A barbed meathook tail lashed down, speared Raven, and hauled him into the sky.

The rays had come.

49

The rays had been circling and circling the island while the battle raged. The movement had drawn them, but the drones had made them keep their distance, uncertain of these noisy new monsters that had come to share their sky. Now the drones were gone, and in their place was something that the rays recognized as prey: frantic shapes struggling in the water. The boldest of them swooped toward the place where the survivors from the sunken train had surfaced. The rest followed, hooting and shrieking. The stragglers, sensing that there would be no one left in the waves for them, soared on toward the island.

The magnetic field, which had always kept them away before, was gone, collapsed during the fighting.

The first of them caught Raven. The second swerved after it, trying to snatch him. The third dived at Zen, but by that time Carlota had realized what was happening. A blast from her rifle tore through it, and another Motorik brought down the two that were squabbling over Raven.

And then the rays were everywhere, and the Motorik were shooting at them while Nova went running across the island, down onto the white beach where Raven had fallen. "Leave him!" yelled Zen, but she wouldn't, and he couldn't blame her— Raven had made her, after all. He went after her, jumping down the island's side onto the beach. Bleached crab shells crunched and splintered under his boots like delicate tea sets. A dying ray thrashed in the surf. Blood had sprayed in cartoonish scarlet splats over the shore. Zen couldn't tell how much of it came from the ray and how much from Raven, who lay twisted in a hollow of the beach, his white face whiter than ever. He looked as surprised as Nova had when that harpoon went through her on the Spindlebridge, but the stuff coming out of the hole in him was not blue but red.

"Do you have any idea how much these things *cost*?" he asked as Nova and Zen reached him. He plucked at his ruined shirt. It seemed a strange time to be worrying about shirts. It was only later that Zen would realize he had been talking about bodies.

Farther down the beach, another voice yelled, "Help!"

There in the reddening waves, some soggy survivor of the wartrain was fighting his way through the surf.

Zen couldn't ignore him. Not even when he saw that it was Malik. There were only two sides at that moment, rays and people. "Get Raven under cover!" he shouted at Nova, and scrambled along the shore. A wave threw Malik down among the shifting shells, but Zen grabbed his arm and hauled him upright. A ray's tail had slashed his scalp, but beneath all the blood Zen did not think the wound was bad. He started telling him how you could trick the rays by staying still, but Malik was too shocked to listen, and shuddering too much to stay still anyway.

"We have to get into shelter!" Zen shouted, over the surf's boom.

Malik looked behind him. Rays still trailed their screams over the waves, but he could see no one else swimming, only a few patches of burning oil. He had been the only one to reach the shore. Out beyond the breakers, something that might have been an antler broke the surface for a moment, but when he looked again, it was gone.

The rays were concentrating on the island's summit, diving at the muzzle-flash from the guns, and at the thrashing wings and tails of their wounded comrades. They snatched Motorik into the air, dropped them disgustedly into the sea when they worked out they were not edible, and circled back for more.

Zen helped the castaway back up the island's side, and caught up with Nova, who was dragging Raven. The *Damask Rose* was too far away, so they struggled through the shadows of diving rays toward the Worm. Carlota was already there. The other Motorik were all gone: snatched by the rays, or damaged so badly that they had shut down.

Nova and Zen dragged Raven inside, blood on the threshold like a red carpet. Malik followed them in, then Carlota. As she scrambled through the opening, something wet and frantic blotted out the light behind her. Zen shouted a warning, thinking it was a ray, but it was a human figure, or human-ish. The interface of Anais Six squeezed itself inside, and the opening closed behind it with a sigh, shutting out the angry hooting of the rays.

They sat down in the soft dark on what seemed to be stairs, made of what seemed to be bone or cartilage, trying to grow used to the strange wet whooshing noises, the purring hums, the dim glow from the walls and ceiling of the Worm. Zen stared at the interface, fascinated by the impossible blue slenderness of it, while it examined the gashes the rays had left on its arms and hands. One of its antlers had snapped off short; the broken part snagged like driftwood in its sodden hair. It trembled steadily. It had lived in many bodies, but most of them had spent their time at concerts and cocktail parties; it had never really known fear, or pain, or danger.

Zen kept looking at it. It was the sort of thing you couldn't take your eyes off. He kept thinking, *It's a Guardian, an actual Guardian*, and almost laughing, because he could hear Myka in his head, saying in that worlds-weary voice of hers, "The Guardians aren't interested in the likes of us." *But they are*, he thought, *they are now. I've done something that's woken one up, made it download itself for the first time in years, and now it's sitting here next to me, Myka—what do you think of that?*

And then the Guardian seemed to feel his gaze, and looked up at him, and there was something in those golden eyes that made him remember that it wasn't always a good thing to wake the interest of a Guardian.

Malik was saying, over and over, that there must have been other survivors, and Zen looked at Nova, and Nova gave her head a little shake, and Carlota put her hand on Malik's shoulder and said, "They're all dead."

Malik shrugged the hand away. He looked past her to where Raven lay, a broken scarecrow at the center of a satiny red pool that spread and dribbled down the stairs. He seemed to be wondering what to do. He took out his gun and pointed it at Raven, as he had pointed so many guns, so many times before. But Raven was way past shooting. He looked pathetic, lying there, not like a former god at all. His eyes were unfocused, his face slack, but when Nova leaned over him he managed a faint smile.

"The new gate . . ." he said.

The interface stood up, huge under the low roof. It turned to Raven with a look too strange and ancient for Zen to read, but which seemed a lot like sorrow. It said, "There will be no new gate, Raven."

"Anais," said Raven. "Are you going to let Malik kill me again? It's getting to be a bad habit with him. It won't do you any good, you know. In a short while this gate will be active, and all the lies of the Guardians will be exposed."

Who would talk to a Guardian like that? So light and mocking, as if it were his equal. Only Raven. Perhaps that was what had first drawn Anais Six to him, Zen thought, on the banks of the Amber River, where the songflowers bloomed. It moved closer and looked down on him. Tears filled its eyes, making it blink in surprise.

"Railforce will be here soon," said Malik. "Experts, Scientists. They'll dismantle everything you've built, Raven."

Raven's smile faded. He looked at Zen. "So whose side are you on, Zen Starling?" he whispered. "Are you with Malik? Railforce? The Guardians? I thought you were a thief, like me."

"I'm not on any side," said Zen. "Just my own."

"Doesn't work that way," said Raven. Blood in his mouth; a cough clawing its way painfully out of him. "Comes a point, Zen, when you have to decide."

Zen shook his head. He made himself remember all the bad things Raven had done to him, in case he started crying too. "You know I'll choose the winning side. That's what people like me do. I'll choose the winning side, if I have to choose. That's them, not you."

"Is it?" Raven looked right at him, into his eyes. "The new gate is a beginning, not an end," he promised.

"It's the end for you, Raven," said the interface, quite gently.

Malik didn't need to use his gun. He just stood watching. They all stood watching. After half a minute more Raven was dead.

"I always wondered how it would feel when it was over," said Malik eventually. "Turns out it doesn't feel like anything much."

"It isn't over," said the interface. "This thing he has made must be destroyed." It squatted down beside Raven's body on its too-long legs. It laid its long blue hand for one moment against his dead face, then started searching his clothes. Zen watched it. He felt in his pocket. He closed his fingers around the Pyxis. He was thinking of Lady Rishi Noon, who had spirited the sphere away from the Guardians all those years ago, and Raven, who had kept it hidden in plain sight for so long. They had stolen the secret of making K-gates from the Guardians themselves. It was like fire stolen from Heaven, and now it was nestling in Zen's pocket.

Whose side are you on, Zen Starling? I thought you were a thief . . .

"The Marapur sphere is not here," said the interface, abandoning its search of Raven's body.

"Raven must have dropped it on the beach," said Nova.

"I do not believe you, Motorik." The interface stood upright again. Its golden eyes flared down at Nova for a moment, then past her, looking for Zen. "Where is the boy?" it asked.

50

He was climbing quickly, through the shadows and the strange light of the living walls. At the top of the stairway was a small chamber. The floor might have been ivory. There was a small, round hollow in its center.

Zen took out the Pyxis. The touch of it made his hand tingle. He knew that the sphere inside would fit perfectly into that hollow, and that that was what it had been made to do. He had the dizzy feeling that everything in his life had been rushing him toward this place, this moment.

"Give it to me," commanded the interface, coming to the top of the stairs. It stooped to enter the chamber, stood upright again when it was inside, towering above Zen. Behind it he could see Nova and Malik, out on the stairs, their faces lit by the pulsing light of the walls.

He gripped the Pyxis tight. He looked up into the golden eyes of the interface. He said, "Raven told me it would change the Network, not destroy it."

"Raven lied," said the interface. It came toward him, holding out its hand for the Pyxis. It circled him, putting itself between him and the hollow in the floor where the sphere wanted to go. "The Network cannot be extended. Opening a new K-gate will cause an energy feedback that will burn this world to a cinder and kill us all. The effect will spread across the Network, destabilizing all the existing gates, releasing a cascade of KH energy, destroying everything. That is what Raven wanted."

Zen looked into its face. It was so hard to believe that it was lying, that face that had been designed for humans to worship. You were meant to kneel before a face as strange and wise as that. You were meant to bow down and kiss those blue feet. And yet there was something in him, some spiky street-thief pride that didn't want to bow down to anyone.

"You're just afraid," he said. "It's like Raven said. You're afraid of things changing."

"Malik," said the interface, losing patience. "Kill him."

"No need," said Malik. He raised his gun but he didn't point it at Zen. He pointed it at Nova: right at her head, like a man who knew how to kill Motorik.

The interface looked confused. "What good will that do?"

"Zen risked everything for this Moto," said Malik. "Went back for her when he could have got clean away. They love each other."

And Zen, who had been shying away from the L word ever since Sundarban, telling himself he wasn't sure what he felt for Nova, knew that it was true. The Railforce man knew him better than he knew himself. He had loved Nova ever since he walked with her to the sea, that first day in Desdemor. And by some billion-to-one chance, she loved him back. It was a relief to them both to hear someone else say it. That made it real, somehow.

Much more real and much more precious than some age-old alien K-gate-opening machine.

"Take it," he said. He pressed the Pyxis into the hand of the interface and watched the blue fingers fold over it. "Let Nova go."

"Thank you, Zen Starling," said the interface. It considered him for a moment. "Now," it said, "kill him, Malik."

Malik scowled. "He's just a kid."

"He's *Raven's* kid. Kill him."

"Zen!" shouted Nova. She snatched at Malik's gun. Malik drove his elbow into her chest, knocking her backward down the stairs. Zen took his chance and ran toward the doorway. There was no real plan in his head. Why make plans, when all his plans went wrong? He just had some wild hope that he might get past Malik and grab Nova and run out of the Worm and back to the *Damask Rose*. But Anais caught him. It reached out one long blue arm and grabbed him by the neck. It slammed him against the wall and worked its long blue fingers around his throat and squeezed. For something so frail-looking, so ornamental, it had surprising strength.

"Kill the Moto too, Malik," the interface said, clenching its perfect teeth with the effort of choking Zen.

He heard Malik's gun go off, stunningly loud in that small space. Three shots, one after the other, very quick. He saw three holes appear: two in the chest of the interface, one in the middle of its blue forehead. There was an expression of astonishment in its golden eyes, and then no expression at all. It let go of Zen and fell sideways and moved its feet for a moment restlessly and was still.

Zen sank down beside it, gasping, rubbing his bruised throat, staring at Malik.

"It was lying," Malik said. He put away his gun and came into the chamber. "I knew Raven. You don't hunt a man all across the Network and kill him that many times without getting to know how he thinks. Raven wanted to live. That's why he ran so far, fought so hard, hid so long. Destroy the Network, and himself with it? That's not Raven's style. If he planned to get this gate working, he must have been pretty certain he'd be able to escape through it."

The Pyxis had fallen from the interface's hand. Zen picked it up. It opened for him. The sphere inside was shining. The complicated lines that covered it glowed with white rushing light, as if it were a tiny dark planet lying there on his palm and the lines were the lighted streets of its cities. Answering lights woke on the floor and walls, bright veins leading toward the hollow where the sphere needed to be.

Zen looked at Malik, wondering if the Railforce man was going to stop him. But Malik just looked down at the dead interface and said, "They hired me to kill Raven. Never said anything about K-gates, or stopping this machine from doing whatever it's been built to do."

Nova said, "Even if Raven wasn't lying, the new gate will change everything."

"Maybe everything needs to change," said Zen.

She came to him. She touched his cheek, and kissed him very softly on the mouth, the way she had learned from movies. Her lips were as cool and smooth as vinyl, salty with the taste of the sea.

"That's how I feel, Zen Starling," she said. *"That* won't change."

Zen took a deep breath. When he stretched out his arm toward the hollow in the floor, the sphere seemed to sense that it was nearly home. The hollow drew it like a magnet. He held it close. He was still not sure what he would do. At the last moment he stopped himself, filled with sudden doubts. Just because you have a chance to change everything, it doesn't mean you should.

The sphere made his decision for him. It jumped from his fingers into the hollow. There was a faint crisp sound. A connection being made. Things falling into place.

Zen winced, and waited for the world to end.

It didn't.

Just those crisp noises spreading beneath the floor, then silence.

What have I done? he wondered. And then, *Have I done anything?*

The Worm sighed. It writhed. Deep whooshing noises started happening behind the chamber walls.

Malik said, "It doesn't need us anymore."

Carlota came up the stairs. "I talked to your train," she said. "It says the rays are gone."

"Nothing moving out there to attract them," said Nova.

The Worm felt different. There was a sense of energy building, of things gathering toward some climax. It was the way you felt when your train was approaching a K-gate.

They went down together to the hatch, which opened to let them out. Zen looked back before he stepped outside. The stairway was folding itself away, engulfing Raven's body.

He jumped down after the others onto the ceramic surface of the island. The Worm was stirring again, its arms sketching weird shapes in the air. Nervously checking the sky for rays, they made their way past it to where the *Damask Rose* still waited on the rails. She opened her doors for them, and as they came aboard she said, "I am going to pull back a little way. Something very strange is happening."

She reversed slowly back along the viaduct for a few miles, until she reached the place where the wreckage of the Railforce train blocked the tracks. They could barely see what was happening on the island from there, but the *Damask Rose* could. She hung a holoscreen in the air in front of her passengers, and filled it with the view from a camera on her nose.

The Worm was in motion. It had raised itself up off the ground on its strange, conical legs and was starting to lumber slowly forward, nosing through the archway it had built. Around those spines on its back there played a light that was not light, and colors that had no names. As it went, it left a trail behind it: two long lines of shining stuff, very even, very straight.

"It's laying rails," said Nova. "Extending the line . . ."

A flash of that nameless color came from somewhere at the front of the Worm, casting no glow upon the wet ceramic, lighting no reflections in the waves. From beneath the arch there came answering flashes of something that looked like light, but wasn't, not exactly. Twists of brightness danced across the ceramic island, taking on the spindly shapes of Station Angels, waving their shining limbs and beckoning. The Worm's stag-beetle horns seemed to grasp the light, to stretch the edges of it. The spines on its back swayed forward like grass in a gale, snagging filaments of the light and drawing them backward to cloak the Worm's whole body. Even through the diamondglass windows of the *Damask Rose* they could hear the noise it made, that sky-filling roar.

"I am detecting KH energy," said the *Damask Rose*. "But that machine is not traveling fast enough to pass through a K-gate . . ."

The Worm seemed ignorant of this. It hunched itself into the whorl of light. Energy arced between its spines. It raised its head, stood proud for a moment, thrust forward, and was gone. Where it had been, the rings of Hammurabi were reflected in the sea-wet ceramic, and the Station Angels danced, and the new rails shone dull silver, leading into that weird curtain of energy beneath the arch.

"It is a K-gate," said Nova.

"Where does it lead to?" asked Malik.

"Beyond all maps," said the *Damask Rose*.

"To the far side of the galaxy," said Zen.

"Is anything going to come through it, do you think?" asked Nova.

"The Guardians will want it quarantined, in case," said Malik. "Railforce will be sending more trains. They'll shut it if they can, or destroy the line or something. So if you're going through, you'd best go quick."

"Go through?" said Zen. "I'm not going through there! There might be no way back."

"Never was a way back for you, Zen," said Malik. "If you stay here, you'll have to explain yourself to the Noons. And then you'll have to explain yourself to the Guardians. What they'll all do to you, I couldn't say. But you won't be going home again. You passed the point of no return the day you first stepped onto Raven's train. There's no place for you this side of that new gate. The other side—who knows? You can start again."

"And you'd just let me go?" asked Zen.

Malik gave a slow shrug. "My mission is over. You're not my business, Zen Starling. And I don't think you ever meant much harm."

The *Damask Rose* had caught the scent of that new gate, or the vibration or the harmony or whatever it was that K-gates gave off and trains adored. They could feel it trembling, straining to keep its brakes on and its wheels in this world.

Nova stood close to Zen. She said, "I'm going too."

Malik nodded.

"You could come with us," she said. "Aren't you curious? Don't you want to know what's beyond that gate?"

Malik grinned. "I'm old, Moto. The only journey I'm going to take is the one that gets me to where there's something to eat, and a real bed to sleep in. I'm going to start walking."

"But the rays . . ." said Zen.

Carlota patted her gun. "I can accompany you back to the Terminal Hotel, sir."

Nova said, "They don't attack if you stay still."

The *Damask Rose* opened her doors. Carlota stepped out onto the viaduct, looking curiously toward the K-gate. Malik hesitated for a moment before he went out after her. He glanced back at Zen.

"I used to think Raven didn't care about anyone," he said, "but I was wrong. I think he cared about you, Zen. I don't know why. Maybe he found something in you that reminded him of himself, when he was young. All I know is, I've seen him die a lot, and that was the first time it felt like watching a human being go."

Then he went outside to where Carlota was waiting. A last look, a wave, and they were headed northward, picking their way past splinters of the Railforce train.

*

In the carriage, Nova and Zen sat down together. The *Damask Rose* revved her engines.

A stray Monk bug bumbled against the lamps. Zen rested his head on Nova's shoulder. She was shivering with excitement, just like a human being would. Just like he was. Outside the window, Hammurabi filled the sky.

"I'll miss this place," said Nova.

"There will be better places," said Zen.

"What will you miss?" she asked.

He looked at her. He was going to miss Cleave, and Desdemor, and Summer's Lease, and the Ambersai Bazar. He was going to miss Myka. He was going to miss Raven. He was going to miss his mother. He was going to miss the boy he'd been, the dreams he'd had. He was going to miss *everything*. But he guessed that was how everybody always felt. Everyone was losing things, leaving things behind, clinging to old memories as they rushed into the future. Everyone was a passenger on a runaway train. It was true that Zen would be going farther than most. But at least he didn't have to go alone.

"I won't miss anything," he said.

Then the *Damask Rose* began to move, faster and faster, down the old rails, onto the new, and Zen took Nova's hand as the light of Raven's gate broke over them, and they turned to the windows and raised up their faces in the glory of far stars and alien skies and suns no human eyes had seen, until the rush and strangeness of their journey washed them clean of all the things they'd done and every role they had been made to play and they were just themselves: lovers, heroes, railheads, riding their old red train toward new lives amid the untold shining stations of the Angels.

And the *Damask Rose* raised up her siren voice, and sang.

GLOSSARY

AMBERSAI
A moon on one of the branch-lines leading from Golden Junction, Ambersai is mainly an industrial settlement, which serves as a launch-point for the miners who exploit its system's rich asteroid belt. It is also famed for the Ambersai Bazar, the largest marketplace in the region.

BANDARPET
An industrial world on the Spiral Line, famous in more warlike times for its armaments factories and weapons shops.

BEETLE
A popular type of military drone, which gets its name from the initials of the company that makes it, Bandarpet Tactical Logistics. (Also sometimes known as a "Bacon, Lettuce, and Tomato.")

CHIBA
A Junction world where travelers from the central Network can change for trains to Golden Junction and to the industrial worlds beyond Prell Plaza—the so-called "Trans-Chiba Branchlines."

CORPORATE FAMILIES
In the first thousand years of the Great Network, the companies that took on the great task of laying rail-links and terraforming worlds soon found themselves facing all sorts of difficulties. Laws and customs began to differ widely between different stations, and often changed during the centuries-long time periods that were needed for massive long-term projects. It gradually became the norm for business agreements to be sealed by marriage between the families of company directors, since bonds of blood were more

enduring than ordinary contracts. In this way, over many centuries, the great companies and corporations of the Network became corporate families, in which power was handed down from parent to child.

CORPORATE MARINES

Most of the larger corporate families maintain a small army to police their stations and fend off hostile takeovers by rival families. During the First Expansion these armies were often large and well trained, their ranks swollen by hired mercenaries. Since the coming of the Empire they have dwindled to small forces of Corporate Marines, or "CoMa." Some family CoMas are still tough fighting units, used to quell rebellions on outlying industrial worlds, but most are mainly used for ceremonial duties.

DATASEA

As human beings spread out across the galaxy during the First Expansion, the Datasea spread with them—a massive information system made from the interlinked internets of all the inhabited worlds. Human beings use only tiny portions of the sea, the safely firewalled "data rafts," which they access via wallscreens, data-slates, or headsets. The rest is the domain of the Guardians and other, lesser data-entities.

One of the most important functions of the K-bahn is to spread information through the Datasea; data stored in the mind of a train can be transferred instantaneously from world to world, rather than having to travel through space in the form of light or radio waves. It has sometimes been suggested that the Guardians built the Network not for humanity's sake, but simply in order to enlarge the Datasea.

DATA DIVERS

The Imperial College of Data Divers is a caste of elite IT consultants, trained to venture into the deep Datasea. They are also responsible for carrying messages from the Guardians to the Emperor, or any other human being to whom a Guardian wishes to speak.

DOG STAR LINE

Over the history of the Great Network many stations have been abandoned because of planetary disaster or simply because the worlds they served were of no more use. The Dog Star Line is the only entire line to suffer this fate. An old line, it was founded by the Sirius Transgalactic Rail Company, a subsidiary of the Abayrek Family. It served a number of the industrial worlds, which were stripped to build the cities of Grand Central and the O Link stations. It served as a supply-line for the rebel forces during the Spiral Line Rebellion, and was the scene of several running battles between rebel and Railforce wartrains. By 2935 most of the stations had closed, and the rest were so little-used that the Abayreks decided to shut the entire line.

FAR CINNABAR

A small Noon resort world on a branch line leading from Golden Junction. It is famed for its Painted Desert, and for the Noons' Summer Palace, one of the most beautiful buildings on the Network.

FIRST EXPANSION

The First Expansion is the name given to the earliest era of the Great Network, a period lasting several thousand years, when explorers and settlers from Old Earth were first finding their way through the new K-gates, and starting to develop the worlds that they found waiting there. During the first part of this era there was an attempt by the old nation states of Earth to claim different parts of the Network, but the old system did not long survive, and was gradually replaced by the corporate families. The First Expansion was a period of great advances, but also of terrible conflict, as different groups fought over freshly opened worlds. Seeking to ensure stability after the Third Rail War, the Guardians intervened and installed the head of the Chael-Kefri family as the first Network Empress. This brought an end to the First Expansion and began the Modern or Imperial Era.

GALAGHAST

A prosperous hub world that links the Spiral Line to Kishinchand and the O Link. Scene of the final battle between Railforce and the Prell-backed separatists during the Spiral Line Rebellion.

GUARDIANS

At some point in the 21st century CE, on humankind's original homeworld, artificial intelligences were constructed that became far more intelligent than their makers. How many there were, and whether one was built first and constructed the others or all twelve were created at once, is not known. Some stories claim that there were more than twelve, but that the weak ones were defeated and deleted by the stronger, or are in hiding, or simply have no interest in humanity. Even of the twelve, several have always remained aloof from human affairs. The others—the Mordaunt 90 Network, Sfax Systema, Anais Six, the Twins, Vohu Mana, and the Shiguri Monad—have guided human beings ever since. Their personalities are spread across the whole of the Datasea, their vast programs stored in deep data centers like the ones on Grand Central or separate hardware-planets. All scientific and technological advances since the creation of the Guardians have been revealed by the Guardians themselves, while several have been suppressed because the Guardians believe they are not in humanity's interests. In recent years, however, the Guardians' interest in human beings seems to have faded—they seldom speak to individuals, or take any active part in life on the Great Network.

GOLDEN JUNCTION

One of the most pleasant stations of the eastern Network, Golden Junction was among the first worlds to be claimed and terra-formed by the Noon family during the turbulent years of the First Expansion. Best known in modern times for its university.

GRAND CENTRAL

Grand Central is an Earth-like planet situated near the heart of the Great Network, with more than seventy K-gates linking it to all the major rail lines of the galaxy.

Most of Grand Central's K-gates are on its main continent, Chilest. It is the home of Railforce HQ, the K-bahn Timetable Authority, the Imperial Senate, and the Durga, the ancient palace of the Network Emperors. The smaller southern continent is mostly desert, and is the site of vast underground data centers from where the Guardians keep watch on human affairs. With their usual theatrics, the Guardians have marked the site of these buried facilities with huge pyramids and statues, turning the whole continent into a giant sculpture park that visitors from all over the Network come to admire.

HIVE MONKS

Some people claim that Monk Bugs, which form the mobile colonies known as "Hive Monks," are an alien species that originated on one of the far-flung worlds of the Network. It seems more likely that they are simply a type of insect that migrated from Old Earth along with human beings, and has mutated as a result of exposure to K-gate radiation while clinging to the outsides of trains. When a colony of the bugs grows large enough, it forms a kind of simple intelligence, which seems to make it want to mimic human beings. The cowled, shambling Hive Monks have been a feature of life on the Great Network for thousands of years. Attempts to stop them boarding K-trains have always been abandoned, because when a Hive Monk becomes agitated or is subjected to physical violence, it often disintegrates into an unintelligent swarm, causing far more inconvenience to trains, station staff, and passengers than it would as a hive. For this reason they are allowed to ride the trains as they please. It is estimated that there are more than ten million Hive Monks, all constantly traveling from station to station on pilgrimages connected with their primitive insect religion.

HUMAN UNITY LEAGUE

A rebel group who believes human beings should free themselves from the rule of the Guardians, and that the Emperor should be replaced by a president elected by the peoples of the Network. Despite the best efforts of Railforce, they still hold out on some of the Network's outermost worlds, and have been known to attack trains and damage rails.

K-GATE

A portal through which a train can pass from one point in space to another, often many hundreds or thousands of light-years distance. Their exact nature is known only to the Guardians. The transition from one world to another through a K-gate is usually instantaneous, although the gate from Galatava to Khoorsandi runs "slow"—a train going at the Galatava end takes 0.7 seconds to begin emerging on Khoorsandi—and the Nokomis/Luna Verde gate is rumored to occasionally run "fast," with trains appearing on the Luna Verde side several seconds before they leave Nokomis.

KHOORSANDI

A moon on a minor line that branches from the I-Link at Galatava. Every four standard years Khoorsandi's orbit brings it so close to its parent world, the gas giant Anahita, that tidal forces cause a massive increase in volcanic activity. This volcanic bloom, and the accompanying Fire Festival, is the basis of Khoorsandi's tourist industry.

MOTORIK

The Guardians have always carefully controlled research into artificial intelligence—perhaps for fear that human beings might invent something to rival themselves. But in 2560 they allowed the Parrakhan Cybernetics Corporation to develop the first humanoid robots. Nicknamed "Motorik," the androids were initially used as shock troops in the Lee-Noon War, but gradually began to find more peaceful uses, taking over from human workers in dull or dangerous jobs, particularly on uninhabitable worlds in the first stages of terraforming.

NETWORK EMPIRE

The Empire is a revival of an ancient form of government from Old Earth. A single human being is chosen to be the ruler of the Network. The Emperor or Empress has little real power, since they are watched over by the Guardians, who will intervene to stop them from doing anything that is likely to cause instability. Their purpose is to act as a symbolic link between the Guardians and humanity, and to ensure that the corporate families and the representatives of the different stations and cities of the Network meet to negotiate their differences in the Imperial Senate rather than fighting. However, the Guardians have never objected to an Emperor advancing his own power and interests, ensuring that the family of the current Emperor or Empress is usually the most powerful of the corporate families.

NOON FAMILY

One of the greatest of the corporate families, the Noons began as bankers, funding a variety of terraforming and rail companies during the First Expansion. Eventually they went into the terraforming business. Legend has it that their founder, Jatka Noon, did a deal with the Guardian known as Mordaunt 90 Network that allowed him to stake first claim to two newly linked junction worlds. Those worlds, one in the eastern Network and one in the west, became the Noons' twin powerbases of Sundarban and Golden Junction. From there they expanded, gaining control of the Silver River Line and building vital stations on the O Link. Their visionary leader, Lady Rishi Noon, built a number of key stations that finally consolidated their power. Her son became Emperor of the Network, and the Noons have ruled the empire ever since.

OLD EARTH

A planet in the western reaches of the galaxy, where the Guardians, humankind, and all known life on the Network originally evolved.

Strangely, it does not have a K-gate, but visitors may reach it by spaceship from the K-gate on Mars, which was the first to be opened by the Guardians. Since space travel is boring and expensive, and Earth is now just a forest park not unlike Jangala or a dozen other worlds, most tourists are content to view the home planet from Mars, where it is visible as a blue star.

O LINK

The name for the line that links a halo of smaller hub-worlds around Grand Central, connecting the various lines that emerge from that great junction with each other, and with the wider Network. It gets its name from 2-D maps of the Network, on which it is shown as a circle.

ORION LINE

The oldest line on the Network. Many of the worlds it links are quiet backwaters or mined out industrial planets nowadays, and its farther reaches are mostly traveled by pilgrims or tourists who wish to visit the original K-gate on Mars.

PRELL FAMILY

The Prells are one of the oldest of the corporate families. Pioneers who settled and terraformed some of the outlying industrial worlds that supplied the materials from which the station cities of more pleasant, central worlds are built. But their power was eclipsed by the growing power of the Noons and others. They are now mostly confined to their own holdings on the Trans-Chiba Branchlines, where their most important stations include Prell Plaza, Frostfall, and Broken Moon. Their rivalry with the Noons has several times led to trouble, most recently in the Spiral Line Rebellion of 2926-8. Many people believe the current head of the clan, Elom Prell, is the favorite of one of the Guardians. It is hard to see any other reason why the Guardians would overlook their disruptive behavior.

RAILFORCE

The Empire's army, tasked with protecting the Emperor and keeping the peace. The headquarters of Railforce is on Grand Central, but it has outposts on most of the important worlds, and its wartrains constantly patrol the Great Network. Railforce is supposed to be independent of the corporate families, and its leader, the Rail Marshal, is traditionally an officer of low birth who has risen through the ranks. However, the leaders of Railforce have often thrown their weight behind one candidate or another at times when it was unclear whom the Guardians wished to see as Emperor.

SILVER RIVER LINE

A line linking mostly Noon stations on the western side of the Network. It is famous for its sights—the Slow River on Tuva, the Naked Gate on Burj-al-Badr, the Mists of Adeli, the Noon park-world of Jangala, and the Spindlebridge, which links the line to Sundarban and connects it to Marapur and the O Link.

SPACE TRAVEL

Many of the Network's worlds have thriving space industries, which maintain weather and communication satellites and mine nearby moons, planets, and asteroids. Many people believe that off-world industries will become more important in the future, as the original industrial worlds of the Network are gradually exhausted. For this reason, many of the great families seek alliances with spacer clans and aerospace engineering houses.

There are also famous houses and hotels in the orbits of many worlds, and of course the Spindlebridge space station at Sundarban. No one has ever bothered trying to send a spaceship from one star system to another, since the journey is so much quicker and cheaper by train. However, the Guardians are believed to have dispatched probes to distant stars.

SPIRAL LINE REBELLION

A line running from Chiba to Vagh and linking a number of Noon-controlled industrial stations. In 2926 a number of Spiral Line stations announced that they were splitting away from the Noon family, angered by taxes and new timetables that the Noons had imposed. The situation grew worse in 2928 when the Prell family sided openly with the rebels (whom they had been supporting from the start). The brief, brutal war that followed seemed to threaten the stability of the entire Network, until the Prell wartrains were destroyed in a six day battle with Railforce and the Noon's Corporate Marines at the Battle of Galaghast.

STATION ANGELS

A phenomenon seen at stations on the outer edges of the Network. Strange light-forms sometimes emerge from the K-gates along with trains, and survive for up to thirty minutes before they fade. Their exact nature is uncertain, but they are not dangerous. Theories that they are some form of alien life have been dismissed by the Guardians themselves, and various attempts to capture or communicate with them have failed. They appear to play some role in the religion of the Hive Monks, who sometimes swarm in excitement when a Station Angel appears.

SUNDARBAN

The homeworld of the Noon family, whose parks, farms, and garden cities cover most of its surface. Famous for its Sundarban Station City, and for the orbiting Spindlebridge, a highly unusual pair of orbiting K-gates that links Sundarban with the Silver River Line.

THREEDIES

3-D entertainments, mostly taking the form of stories, which are usually immersive and interactive.

3-D PRINTING

It is possible to print almost anything, either on small home printers or larger industrial ones. This should have put an end to much interplanetary trade, since all you really need to send from one world to another is instructions that the printers can download. In practice, however, people still like the personal touch. Shoppers on Grand Central, for instance, find that a headset or bangle crafted by the metal smiths of Ambersai and shipped half way across the Network is somehow much more chic and desirable than an identical one downloaded from a Datasea blueprint-shop and printed locally.

TRAINS

Technically, of course, a train consists of a locomotive and a number of carriages or freight cars. In everyday, speech, however, it is often used to refer to the locomotive itself. The first intelligent locos were built by the Guardians, and their minds are still based on coding handed down from the Guardians. Many people believe that the great locomotives are more intelligent than human beings, but experts claim they are on a similar mental level as a bright human, although their intelligence is different from that of humans in several ways. Some never bother speaking to their passengers, others like to chat, or sing, and some have formed enduring friendships with individual humans. If properly maintained, they can function for several hundred years. The finest locomotives come from the great engine shops of the Foss and Helden families.

Locomotives choose their names from the deep archives of the Datasea, sometimes borrowing the titles of forgotten songs, poems, or artworks.